FRESCO NIGHTS

Romantic Suspense Among the Ruins

Book 1

Deborah L. Cannon

FRESCO NIGHTS SAGA

Fresco Nights

Pompeii at Dusk

Midnight in Palmyra

Baghdad before Dawn

To Barbara Kyle

Editor, Mentor, Friend

CHAPTER

1

There was no point in waiting. Arianna Chase was in conference. Her secretary informed me in various nasal intonations that I'd have to make an appointment. She dropped her gaze back to her computer and left me twiddling my thumbs. I was about to interrupt her again when a tall muscular man in the reception area caught my eye. He had close-clipped, light brown hair against an attractive, angular face. He wore a tight t-shirt over a broad chest, with a massive T emblazoned on it. Ordinarily, I would have ignored him but, well, just look at him. What was such a hunk of man meat doing in Arianna's waiting room? Our eyes touched briefly as I turned to leave. His expression had an unexpected warmth. Was I imagining it? In the next moment, it vanished. And a kind of sneer replaced it. I pulled away first.

I fussed with my hair, was about to exit when I noticed him remove a cigarette pack from the folded sleeve on his shoulder. A smoker. Didn't he know there was no smoking in this building? He lowered his gaze, dislodged a cigarette and tapped it on his palm. What was *that* about anyway? His eyes slid up and caught me staring.

"*Salut.* Can I help you with something?" he asked. I

swear there was a hint of amusement in the question.

"You can't smoke in here," I said.

"Wasn't planning to." The voice that came out of him was deep and rumbling, and slightly accented. Montreal maybe? Surely, he was not born here in Toronto. There was nothing CN Tower about him, except maybe his height.

"Was there something else?" he asked.

I was a sucker for a French accent. *His* was knee-buckling sexy. It made me forget that I was supposed to make an appointment to see Arianna.

I realized I was still staring at him and the suppressed amusement on his face was growing more obvious. I scrambled for something to say and came up with a pretty lame line. "If you're waiting for Dr. Chase she's in a meeting."

He gave me a barely perceptible nod, then a look like: *I know what you're thinking, and that secretary is thinking likewise.* I had the gall to glance over at her and saw that she was indeed mentally drooling over him, before she swiftly cast down her eyes.

Conceited bum. Honestly. I was not thinking anything of the sort. This time I definitely intended to leave. When I swung about to do so, the papers I had meant for Arianna to sign flew out of my hands and onto the floor. I dropped to my knees to retrieve them, banging my head on the secretary's desk when I rose.

I clutched my skull, mortified, halfway to my feet. I wanted to curse from the pain.

"You okay?" he asked, squatting to help me up.

"I'm fine," I muttered, gathering the papers from out of his extended hand. "Gotta go, I'm late."

After that bit of amateur theater I deserved to tumble down the rabbit hole.

I escaped the director's office. I rode the elevator back to the art department, annoyed with the stranger in the tight t-shirt, but even more annoyed with myself.

I sat down in my office, a cubicle partitioned off from

the main studio. I was supposed to illustrate Roman artifacts but instead I doodled incredible biceps. *His. Geez.* I grabbed my hair. What was wrong with me?

Disgusted with my thoughts, I rubbed the sore spot on the crown of my head. I forced a smile when one of my illustrators poked her face into my office. "I'm headed for lunch, Lucy."

"Fine," I said and slapped the sketchpad facedown with my hand, embarrassed that she might have seen. I ripped out the page and crumpled it into the garbage after she had gone. *Concentrate.* Some head illustrator *I* was. Nothing was coming out.

On my drafting table was a row of flat, intricately designed pieces from a broken fresco painting. The images on these fragments were unique, but strange. Odd little cupids, riding—what—sea serpents? And along the outer rim were curly grape vines with leaves on. Lord help me, but I could not draw one more cutsie cherub—not even to save my life. I sighed and put the frescoes aside to try later.

I took the elevator downstairs to see if there was anything easier to sketch. Shaun, my sister's husband, was curator of Classical collections. He was selecting objects for a special exhibition, and was supposed to be in the basement inspecting the latest shipment.

It was cool down here. This part of the museum was the original concrete and stone, and held onto the cold like a refrigerator. The upper floors and exhibition galleries were extensively renovated in glass, hardwood and marble. My eyes had to adjust because it was dimly lit and even a bit spooky. A confusing array of corridors with doors opening to storage spaces and labs formed a maze. Normally it was bustling. At the moment it was quiet.

A ways down the hall one of the doors stood ajar. Beyond the opening it was dark. Doors in the basement were *always* locked. I ducked in, puzzled, and switched on the light. This was a large storage unit stacked from floor to ceiling with valuable historic objects on sliding shelves, and no one around. I spent ten minutes searching the place before I returned to the entrance. Should I lock it? Maybe Shaun had left it open. I went to the wall to switch off the light. As I returned to the exit someone went past. I jumped, caught a whiff of tobacco.

No visitors were allowed down here. Not without a pass. I thrust my head out to view down the hall. This man was clearly a stranger. He was huge for one thing and his casual attire... The whiff of tobacco had reset my memory. Oh no. It wasn't...? Could it...? I swear I turned fifty shades redder.

The figure shrank as it reached the end of the corridor where the elevators met. He turned and saw me watching. He was too far away for me to make out facial features, but his powerful build, yeah, that I recognized. What was he doing down here? I hesitated, raised a hand for him to wait.

Did I trust myself near him again? I worried that he would see it all over my face. I shut the door of the storage room, heard the lock click, and went to meet him.

The clumsiness I had shown earlier made me shy. "Hey. Can I help you? This area is for employees only."

"*Salut.* I know." His brows narrowed in recognition. "*Hé.* I know you."

The French was threatening to make me lose control. I hung my head theatrically. "I'm the klutz from Arianna Chase's office. Thanks for helping me off the floor by the way. And I apologize for my rudeness. I should have thanked you then. And of course, you knew you weren't supposed to smoke indoors. I'm sorry I said anything."

If he were a dog he would have cocked his head. "I do not recall you being rude."

That was because most of it happened after the fact.

A small glint of humor appeared in his eyes.

Something about him made me—what—stupid? If I remained here any longer my legs would refuse to walk.

I smiled and turned, keenly aware of his observing eyes and his fine physique, and forced myself to speed away.

Why hadn't I asked him what he was doing in the

basement? I was halfway down the corridor by now. It was too late. If I turned and ran back, I'd make my feelings too obvious. Maybe it was too late for that as well. I'd already made my thoughts pretty obvious. I risked a backwards glance but he was gone.

I continued to the lab.

Only rows of dusty countertops in here, buried under cardboard cartons and wooden crates—and a stuffy, perpetual smell of old things. It was the perfect perfume to send all thoughts of him out the window. *Get a grip, girl.* I was behaving like an idiot. My only excuse was that I was experiencing a dry spell. No dates, for God knows how long. I couldn't even remember. The man wasn't interested.

I glanced at my smartphone. Already 2:05 PM. Where were all the technicians? Late lunch? I hadn't eaten yet. Shaun must be around here somewhere. He never left the museum for lunch. His office door showed a gap, but no sign of movement. No one at the back shelves either.

Time was pressing; an angry grumble came from my stomach. I was supposed to meet my sister for lunch.

Something caught my eye.

On one of the counters a cardboard box was open. Beside it were some pieces of Roman silver laid out on foam board: a knife and spoon, both with a delicate motif barely visible beneath a green-black tarnish. The motif was a cluster of grapes. Must be part of a dinner setting. I looked up and saw a spill on the other side of the counter.

A carton had broken through from the bottom and expelled its packing material all over the counter and onto the floor. Scattered Styrofoam and bunches of crumpled newsprint and stripped packing tape rolled into balls. This must have happened after the artifacts were removed, and the delicate pieces of silver relocated to a safe spot.

The new shipment of artifacts was half unpacked. Most of the crates were still sealed. Whoever had been opening them was careless. Or else in a frantic hurry. Clear bubble wrap and white Styrofoam peanuts were everywhere.

I bent to pick up a few of the strays, only to attract electrostatic fragments to myself. I had no time for this. I plucked at the Styrofoam impatiently, and then looked to the wall where some jumpsuits and lab coats hung. I shrugged on a pair of coveralls to protect my clothes.

I needed a broom, found one leaning against the wall, and returned to the scene of the crime. Most of the pesky things were cooperating and gathering into a pile where I could shovel them up and into the empty boxes.

I was concentrating so hard I slipped backwards. I had missed hearing Shaun return and landed in his arms. But when I found myself in the masculine embrace I realized it wasn't him. I had crashed butt first into some stranger's groin. I turned to apologize.

No, it wasn't the French hunk.

Although it might as well have been.

"Sorry. I didn't see you there," I mumbled awkwardly. "Um… did I hurt you?"

Dumb question. I could not possibly have hurt him. He was six feet four inches tall and built like a quarterback. This I learned after he tipped me upright and straightened to his full height. I struggled to control my fluster. What was with the museum today? It was crawling with gorgeous guys.

I scrambled to regain my cool. You would think I had never seen a man before. "Are you looking for the curator?"

He waved a yellow post-it note at me. "Yes, Shaun Templeton. I think. This scribble isn't clear. Is that what it says? I was told I could find him here."

I checked out the spelling when the note stopped moving. "He stepped out for a bit," I informed him.

"Obviously." He glanced at my janitor's uniform. I decided to ignore the presumption. "You can't have been doing your job long. You're kind of clumsy. Until I saw what you were wearing, I thought for sure you were him—or her? These days you can't be too sure. Men's and women's names seem to be interchangeable."

"Mine's not," I said.

"Neither is mine. I'm—"

"I know who you are—Mr. Trevanian." Yes, I had recognized him. He and his wife Arianna Chase, who just happened to be the director of my museum, were getting a divorce. Their photos were plastered all over the news media. "I was looking for him myself."

His brows rose in a slightly crooked arch.

"I work here," I explained.

"I can see that." He was giving my custodian outfit the once over. He kicked at some Styrofoam on the floor. "Ever think you might be in the wrong profession? You missed some bits here—"

"I am *not* the janitor!" My fingers were curling into fists. Now, I was definitely ticked off!

"You're not?"

Even if I was, he had no right to look down his nose at me. I found myself stripping out of the coveralls right there—in front of him—to reveal myself in loose blouse and skinny jeans. I was really beginning to dislike him. Who the hell did he think he was?

"That's better."

A look of approval came into his eyes. A look I recognized. *Oh no mister.* No way was I going to fall for his charms. Handsome or not.

I stalked over to the wall and hung up the uniform. Then I returned to retrieve the broom.

"So, if you're not the janitor, what do you do here?"

As if it was any of his business. I leaned the broom against the wall. "I'm the museum's head artist."

He repeated the title with the emphasis on the first word. "*Head* artist…. I see."

"What do you see, Mr. Trevanian?"

His face sharpened. He looked surprised at my tone. I suppose no one had ever spoken to him like that in his life.

"I only meant I'm pleased that you're an artist."

And why would that be? I was about to voice my question aloud when a large shadow appeared in the doorway. It was the man from the corridor. His eyebrows arced in recognition; I nearly fell backwards. They were together? He was also the hunk I saw in Arianna Chase's waiting room. Who could forget that secret smirk in his eyes? Despite my best efforts my face reddened. A kind of unspoken interaction between employee and boss passed between them. So that was who he was, one of Trevanian's minions.

My fantasies turned to dishwater. These two men were out of my league. They jetsetted around the world on Lear jets and mega yachts, and had connections with politicians, celebrities and royalty. Trevanian hired bodyguards to protect himself from thugs in the antiquities trade. It was dangerous in politically unstable countries like the Middle East. People shot first and asked questions later. And from what the media leaked, Trevanian dabbled in this twilight world. Was the gossip true? That his acquisition of artifacts and the people he hired were iffy?

The newcomer stepped towards us. I avoided his eyes. I observed once more the shirt with the big T embossed on it. Why were these two allowed to wander around unescorted in the museum's prohibited zones? Then I noticed that both had visitor tags clipped to their collars.

I wanted to accuse them of wrongdoing, except.... Exactly what were they doing wrong? An overabundance of testosterone seemed to thicken the air. My own hormones were doing somersaults. My heart was beating too fast. Where was Shaun?

He came just as I was about to give in to the adrenalin shooting through my veins.

"Oh, Dr. Trevanian. You found your way down. I went upstairs to look for you." Shaun extended a hand and apologized for his absence.

Trevanian firmly returned his grip. "Arianna gave me a visitor's pass."

"I'm Shaun Templeton, Curator of Classical collections. Hope you weren't waiting too long?"

"Not at all. Call me Luke. And this is my associate, Norman Depardieu."

Depardieu looked up from where he'd been studying the Roman spoon cradled in foam-board. He extended his hand. When he spoke the accent was almost gone. He sounded more like an American. "Actually, I'm his head of security."

Was that a nice way of saying 'bodyguard'? Well, that could explain the sharp attention to detail. Especially as it pertained to Shaun's recently unpacked Roman relics. Why was he so interested in those artifacts anyway? They certainly weren't the most striking objects in this room. I frowned at him and his mouth twitched at me. So this was the famed watchdog, the billionaire's bodyguard. Rumor was that Luke Trevanian never went anywhere without him. But why the big T emblazoned on his shirt? Was Trevanian bragging to the world that he owned this man?

Then I realized what it meant to be a billionaire—especially a billionaire archaeologist. Luke Trevanian handled valuable objects all the time. Not only did he need personal protection, he also needed guards to escort his precious finds.

He was a real-life Indiana Jones who financed his own digs. He only needed to obtain permission from the relevant authorities, and he could buy their cooperation. After all, since so much of the world's treasures still waited to be unearthed, the powers-that-be always capitulated if a project put their city on the map. A headline attracted tourists and investors—and that meant bucks. *Big* bucks. And who, in his right mind, turned down anybody willing to finance a project out of his own pocket?

"My sister-in-law and museum illustrator, Lucy Racine," Shaun said.

"Ms. Racine." Trevanian nodded, breaking into my private thoughts.

"Just call me Lucy."

Shaun frowned at me as though I'd misspoken.

"Lucy," Trevanian acquiesced. I swear he was tasting

the name. He did not return the courtesy and insist I call him 'Luke.'

Well, I had better epithets for him. Like *snob*.

"I'll get straight to the point. Arianna was civil enough to direct me your way. She said you might be able to help me."

"Of course," Shaun said.

This bit of info sent my mind speculating. Arianna Chase, our museum director and Luke Trevanian's soon-to-be ex-wife, *sent* him to Shaun? Here was a juicy bit of gossip my sister would gobble up. So maybe their split-up was rumor? Colleen's nosiness was beginning to rub off on me.

So, tell us, Mr. Trevanian, what are *you doing here in Shaun's lab. And what the hell was your gorilla of a bodyguard doing snooping about? And yes, what do you—the notorious, world-travelling adventurer—want that we have?*

Fortunately, none of that came out of my mouth.

"Please excuse the mess in here." Shaun darted a quick glance to the spill on the floor. He seemed unusually nervous. He had an abnormally taut expression like he was trying to control the muscles in his face from twitching. "We're in the middle of unpacking a shipment from Naples. I'm curating a special display of the latest finds from Pompeii."

"That's why I'm here," Trevanian said. "Italy just happens to be one of my interests. My expedition is to Positano."

Despite myself I felt filled to bursting. Positano was a seaside villa that—like Pompeii—was buried when Mount Vesuvius blew in A.D. 79. After the ancient villa was interred the town was rebuilt on top of the ruins. The site had been, and still was, a popular resort for the rich and famous.

"I want to hire some specialists from your team. I plan to hire most of the labor from the local village where we'll be working, but I need a few people who actually understand archaeology."

Shaun nodded. "Arianna gave me a heads-up. I drew up a list of names for you. If you like I can set up interviews."

"No time for interviews. I'll have to trust you on this one."

Trevanian snatched a quick glance at the printout and skimmed names and qualifications. From where I stood I recognized some of them. A chosen few of Shaun's research techs were to be in on this project. How exciting! A twinge of jealousy surged through me. Those selected were about to embark on the most thrilling archaeological expedition of their lives! As I understood it, Luke Trevanian had a massive luxury yacht outfitted with a state-of-the-art archaeology laboratory. With money to burn, no expense was spared. Whatever his team needed he supplied. Dammit, if I hadn't disliked him so much I would have been burning from envy right now.

And then he said my name. "What about Lucy?"

CHAPTER

2

"Excuse me. What did you say?" Shaun asked. Mortified by my unexpected feelings, I was grateful the lighting in the lab was dim. I was frozen with astonishment, and also a sickening sensation of—what—pleasure?

"I said I also need an archaeological illustrator."

Trevanian turned his eyes my way. His expression could be interpreted anywhere from indifference to disdain. "What about Lucy? Is she any good?"

"She's the head of our art department. I'm not sure she can be spared."

They were talking about me as though I wasn't even there.

"I happen to be the best," I cut in defensively.

Then I flushed. Because, honestly, Luke Trevanian had a way of getting under my skin. Ordinarily I would never make such an arrogant pronouncement. I'm sure there were artists more talented, skilled and qualified than me.

"Add her to the list. I need seven technical specialists and the artist. You choose the best ones, and then send me their names. I'll contact each individual with the particulars. But I want Lucy Racine for my illustrator."

I planted my hands on my hips. "Just who do you think

you are?"

"Lucy!" Shaun said.

I was tired of everyone pandering to this egotist. Just because he was rich, and yes, powerful (and kind of gorgeous), didn't mean he could treat people like garbage. "I'm not going," I spat.

Luke Trevanian finally turned to me. He smiled. "If you're the best then you will want to work with the best." He poked a finger into the firm muscle over his ribcage. "That's me."

His eyes rolled away from me, surveyed the entire lab as though he were assessing it for some purpose. Then he shook hands with Shaun and signaled to his bodyguard that they were leaving. No offer was made to shake my hand. The bodyguard gave me a jeering look that unnerved me, and nodded. Crap, was it possible that he knew I had noticed his body? I made a mental note to myself to burn the crumpled sketch of his biceps before I left work.

I growled my frustration under my breath.

"Did you say something, Lucy?" Shaun asked.

"No." I scowled at him as the two visitors left the lab.

"He's promised the museum a large endowment."

"I don't care."

"He's one of our most important donors."

"Not my problem."

"Lucy!" he commanded. "Listen to me."

I turned from the doorway where I had intended to exit and head back to my office. My reason for being here completely fled my mind. "Did you hear the way that egomaniac spoke to me?"

"We need his patronage."

"The *museum* needs his patronage."

"It might mean a matter of keeping our jobs."

"No."

"Yes," he said.

"It's that bad?"

He nodded. "They're talking about downsizing. Some

programs are going to be cut." His eyes took on an intensity that was unusual for him. My sister—his wife—was a spendthrift. Money was always an obstacle and an issue. And now that she was pregnant he was triply concerned. He dreaded her shopping sprees. And how was he ever going to stop her from turning their kid into a designer baby?

"Are you threatening my job, Shaun?"

"I'm trying to save it. And mine too. We don't know what the administration's plans are, but the last time they downsized we lost the art department. They thought it was cheaper to contract out."

I'd had this job for seven years. Started work here as a junior illustrator when I was twenty-three. Now, I was thirty and Shaun was forty-one. He had worked for the museum for sixteen years.

"You weren't working here yet when they cut the art department. It was only reestablished a year before you were hired."

I shook my head, wanted to tear my hair out. Luke Trevanian had an impossible ego. It would be hell working for him. But how could I deny that under my stubborn resistance some part of me was aching to learn what made a man like him tick?

I was also curious as to why he was such a big supporter of his estranged wife's museum. I thought they hated each other.

"I'll think about it," I said, and stalked out the door.

***

The Crystal Lounge restaurant is located inside the newly renovated section of the museum, which just happens to be a unique feat of architecture designed in the shape of a massive crystal. The extension was made possible because of a generous donation by a local millionaire, hence the name of the recent addition: the Michael Lee-Chin Crystal. Some people think it's a fabulous work of art; others describe it as a fiasco of glass and steel. The original stone structure of the museum was erected in the early 20th century, in classical style, and then, in the new millennium, the massive crystal addition was built.

"They say Trevanian is worth thirty-eight billion dollars," Colleen said cheerfully. "Thirty-eight billion. Can you imagine? If I could have one hundredth of that I'd retire."

My sister loved to shop and to eat at upmarket places. That was the reason we were having a late lunch—well, afternoon tea really—at the Crystal Lounge in the Royal Ontario Museum's chic eatery.

"And his greedy wife wants half of it!"

"Well, doesn't she deserve it?" I asked. "After all she had to put up with his pompous arrogance for years."

Colleen went silent for a moment. Her brows gathered in puzzlement. "What makes you think he's pompous...? *Or* arrogant?"

"Those two have been constantly in the media. They are splashed all over the magazines, news programs and the Internet. It's hard not see how he thinks so much of himself," I blustered.

She smiled. "Oh yeah, I forgot. Arianna Chase AKA Mrs. Luke Trevanian is your *boss*."

"Not my boss. She's the director of the museum. I've actually rarely spoken to her."

"But naturally you would side with her."

"Well, wouldn't you?"

She shrugged. "I like to hear all sides of the story. That's why I'm following this one so closely."

"Oh, give me a break, Colleen. You know you couldn't care less who wins this divorce settlement. You just love the gossip. Admit it!" I reached and poked a teasing fingernail into her well-moisturized, suntanned arm.

Her pretty yellow sundress rustled; she jerked away playfully, laughing. "All right, all right. You know me too well. But it's so exciting. The story is happening right before your eyes. You should get to know her. Maybe you'll get a promotion if she likes you."

"Promote me to what? I'm already head of the art department. There's nowhere else to go."

"Oh, I wouldn't say that. You're very good. I'm sure there are lots of opportunities. You only have to know where to look for them."

A couple appeared at the door of the restaurant. Colleen's stylishly coifed head, with its geometric cut and glinting highlights, turned.

"Lucy! Isn't that—?"

My heart skipped three beats. It was indeed. Entering the restaurant right this second was the director of the museum, Arianna Chase—and her soon to be ex-husband, billionaire archaeologist Luke Trevanian.

Dr. Chase was exceedingly well dressed in a navy Chanel suit with a white crepe blouse. She had that sun-kissed, dark blonde hair that made you think of seaside resorts and luxury yachts. Her figure was slim and tall. She was stunningly attractive and made Colleen who was pretty by any definition (albeit pregnant) fade into the wall. And she had an air about her that caused anyone standing in her path to give her a wide berth. What was it about people like this? Without all their money for clothes and hair, makeup and spa treatments, and personal trainers, would they look so good?

And Trevanian. I shrank down, hoping he wouldn't see me. He was tall, with an athletic build, gorgeously muscular, but I had already hinted at that during our earlier encounter. He wore expensive, casual chic shirt and slacks.

He didn't notice me as they strolled in so I took the opportunity to really observe his appearance. What was so great about him other than his billions? His hair was a little on the unruly side, thick, and beach boyish. If I must describe him in two words, I had to admit he was brutally handsome. Against my will my gaze was drawn to the places where his deeply suntanned skin was exposed—like his lean biceps below the Valentino short sleeves, and his throat, especially the V at his crisp shirt collar where a few chest hairs showed between his collarbones... Ugh. What was the matter with me? Was I as smitten as everyone else? I knew better. He was a *jerk*.

"What do you suppose they're doing here?" Colleen asked.

"Same thing as we are." I feigned disinterest, and delicately licked the butter cream icing from my thumb. I noticed that his bodyguard remained at the doorway. I made a supreme effort to guide my eyes away from his impossible physique.

She snorted. That was one thing my dear sister liked to chide me for—eating with my fingers. I wiped my sticky hands with the napkin on my lap, and popped the last of the green tea sponge cake into my mouth. I chewed sensuously, wondering if he was watching.

"You think they're having afternoon tea?" Colleen half twisted in her seat.

"More like a late lunch. Or maybe just coffee."

"But together?"

"Not everyone has a bitter divorce. Some peoples' are quite amicable."

"You have not been following the news, have you, Lucy? They hate each other."

I shrugged. "It's none of our business."

Colleen dropped a half-eaten scone, liberally dolloped with clotted cream and homemade strawberry preserves, onto her china plate. Her gaze stalked the notorious couple to their table by the window. Despite myself my eyes followed, and I regretted it instantly. Trevanian turned his head just a smidgeon. His eyes touched mine and I swear he *winked*.

I looked away instantly to see if Colleen had noticed. She hadn't.

Under a soaring peaked ceiling, in the far pinnacle of the restaurant, windows looked out onto a rooftop garden and revealed the cityscape. A staggered grid of trees bordered the lake-blue skyline, capturing the movement of the wind, and in the foreground bloomed a field of purple chive. It was beside this spectacular view that Arianna Chase and Luke Trevanian sat down.

"Stop staring, Colleen," I ordered.

"I can't help it. I can't believe they're having lunch together."

Holy smokes. It was close to 4:00 PM and the white and chrome restaurant was almost empty. We were just finishing up our meal. It was delicious, of course, and an indulgence for me, someone who was used to ham on rye or a slice of pepperoni pizza for lunch. The server came to return my sister's credit card. It was always her treat because it was she who insisted upon dining in places like this, and it was just too rich for my pocket.

I took one last sip of the exotic African Nectar tea from my china cup. Then I mopped my lips with the white linen napkin and placed it beside the empty Wedgewood that previously held pink peppercorn Madelines—before my sister and I had made short work of them.

I tapped the Styrofoam container holding the remains of my chanterelle and cave-aged Gruyere quiche (I never let anything go to waste) and said, "I have to get back to work."

It was a good thing the museum's director was ignorant of my identity. Else she'd be wondering why she was paying me to have a luxurious tea with my big sister in the middle of a workday.

Nor did I want to draw her attention my way. I needed her to sign off on some expensive equipment for the art department. We were exploring digital graphics and hoping to purchase a 3-D printer to replicate artifacts. I'd had no luck with her office. Because of cutbacks, most discretionary spending had to go through the director's office. I was told that she would have to sign off on this purchase herself.

Colleen knew about my hopes to make the art department a state-of-the art facility. She was also well aware of my frustration with the museum bureaucracy.

"Why don't you go up and ask her?" Colleen urged.

This was not only an outrageous idea for more reasons than I could count, but Luke Trevanian was sitting right there. What would he think of me, groveling in front of his soon-to-be ex?

"Go on," she coaxed. "She's not going anywhere."

"She's having lunch."

"Not yet. They haven't ordered yet."

"But they're going to."

"If you don't ask for what you want, you'll never get it. Didn't you just tell me that you've been hovering around her office all day waiting for a free minute of her time? Go! Be assertive." She kicked me under the table. "Then tell me what Luke Trevanian is *really* like." She giggled.

I could have told her right then. But I carefully avoided any mention of my recent encounter with him. My sister was five years older than me and had bossed me around from the time I could walk. I was so used to her telling me what to do that I had learned a neat trick. I ignored her advice without hurting her feelings, often without her even being aware. But this time her digs had the desired effect. I was miserably self-conscious of my ineffectiveness. And why should I have to acknowledge Luke Trevanian's existence?

I tucked my briefcase between my knees, hoping Colleen had forgotten that I had brought it with me.

"Go," Colleen said.

I shook my head. "Look, I have to get back to work."

I rose. Just as I found my feet I crashed into Arianna Chase who was headed towards the Ladies Room. "Oh... I am so sorry," I said.

She scowled but made no comment. She brushed herself off like she was brushing off a fly.

"Follow her!" Colleen urged.

"No. I am not following her into the bathroom to ask her to sign my requisition form."

And I wasn't. I most definitely wasn't. Colleen must be crazy if she thought that following the director into the bathroom was appropriate. I kissed my sister on the cheek and she air-kissed me back. "Don't be a stranger. This lunch cost me an arm and a leg."

"We could have gone to the deli," I teased.

"No—no, we couldn't."

Of course, we couldn't. Colleen, a high-school teacher, and at the moment on summer vacation, abhorred delicatessens. She and Shaun had a double income, adequate to live comfortably, but which Colleen found barely sufficient. I on the other hand made do on one salary, was currently unattached, and quite happy to be so (or maybe not). I seem to have abysmal taste when it comes to men. So bad in fact that I decided this year to take a break from romance altogether. It was just like the universe to send two hunky muscle men to mock me. All one could do in such situations was mock back.

As it turned out I did have to go and use the bathroom before returning to the art department, but not for the reason my sister wished. I hid in the stall and waited until I was sure the director had left before I came out to wash my hands.

Twenty minutes later, I strolled leisurely down the hall to the elevators.

At the elevator I pushed the UP button.

The doors slid open, and so did my mouth.

I was tempted to wait for the next car, but I wasn't about to let Luke Trevanian get the best of me. Because, yes, he was there. Big as life. Bigger.

CHAPTER

3

"Hello, Lucy," he said.

"Where's your gorilla?" I asked sardonically.

Luke's face broke into a smile. Why did he look tired? I wondered. What was he doing that was wearing him out so? Had he and his wife spit fireballs at each other in the restaurant? He looked like he had stayed awake all night.

"Why are you looking at me like that?" he demanded.

I turned my back to him when I realized I had walked into the elevator without turning around to face the door the way people normally did. "Get lost?" I asked over my shoulder. "Lose your bodyguard on the way?"

"I sent Depardieu on an errand so that I could talk to you alone."

My pulse began to quicken along with my breathing. We could not be any more alone than inside a closed elevator. I went to push the button to my floor but his athletic hand shot out to cover the buttons.

"Do you always get your way, Mr. Trevanian?"

I would not, and could not—like my brother-in-law Shaun—flatter him with the title of 'Dr.' because—well... did he even *have* a PhD?

"Always," he said.

His voice was soft and kinder, and it surprised me, and so I tilted my chin to look back at him. He was smiling gently down at me. Now I was confused.

"Lucy," he said. "Why don't you want to come on my expedition? You'll have all the equipment and support you need. Plus perks. We'll have our home base on my boat. The yacht is outfitted with all the luxuries you could want, including an international chef and a high-class spa."

"What on earth makes you think a spa matters to me?"

"You're a woman, aren't you? All women like to be pampered."

"Do they? And yet all your pampering couldn't keep your wife by your side."

He scowled.

My heartbeats sped up. Oh crap, now what had I done? My mouth could get me in more trouble.

I faced him and said, "I'm sorry, that was uncalled for." *Oh, God, what was I thinking?*

"No. You're right. All of my wealth meant beans to her. She wants money of her own. And power."

I was more careful of what I said this time. "I would think she already has that. She's the director of the Royal Ontario Museum. There has never been a female director at the most prestigious museum in Canada before. I'm sure they pay her well."

He grinned. "Your concept of high finance is sweet. Refreshingly naïve."

What? He was laughing at me. I paused—flustered and frustrated. He was right. My God, he was right. He was a billionaire. I had no concept of what that meant. To someone like me, the director of a museum made a fortune. While I was barely making ends meet, she was pulling in a hefty six figures. But to him...

"All right. Laugh all you want," I said. "You can afford to."

I turned my back on him completely and reached out once more to push the button to my floor.

"I'm still talking," he said. "Turn around and look at me."

Oh how I wanted to roll my eyes at him, but that would require me to *turn around and look at him*. And if that's what he wished I refused to comply. For Pete's sake, since when did I take orders from rude strangers? I huffed, my shoulders stiff, and stared at the closed doors.

Strong hands landed on my shoulders and I was bodily forced to turn. "Hey," I said. "I could have you arrested for that! Don't touch me."

Amusement danced in his sparkling green eyes. He had green eyes. Who has green eyes? Mine were light brown or was that hazel? Who knows, but nothing as special as his. I was mesmerized, fascinated. I was facing him now and his lips were stretched in a deceptively straight line.

"Lucy," he said, letting his arms swing to his sides. "What will it take to convince you to join my team?"

Aggressively, I maintained my stance. Colleen would have been proud of me. If it wasn't for the fact that she was obsessed with the billionaire.

She wanted to see me assertive? No amount of sweet talk was going to change my mind about him. I pressed my lips together to emphasize my stubbornness. Unfortunately, my muteness only seemed to further amuse him.

"I'll give you a raise. How much do you want?"

"Keep your money," I snapped.

Was he ever tall. And now I realized just *how* tall. He towered over me and if he wanted to take me sexually, there was no way I could fight him.

Oh dear, he had read the fleeting thought in my mind.

A blush overcame me and I turned away. I had to get out of this elevator before I revealed any further inappropriate thoughts. No. Correction. Outrageous thoughts.

"Lucy," he repeated.

Why oh why did his speaking my name send shivers up my spine—like ice water, but in a good way. His voice was hoarse, but he made no attempt to touch me again.

"The expedition leaves in three days. Shaun informed me that you are officially on vacation in two. You have three weeks to do, as you will. The museum will spare you. I'll make sure of that. You don't have to worry about them firing you. I'll make certain of that as well."

I turned back to face him. "When did you speak to Shaun concerning my vacation plans?"

The corner of a smartphone poked out of his breast pocket, and he tapped it. "Must have been when you were hurrying down the hall to meet me in the elevator."

"I had no idea you were in the elevator."

"But you were hoping."

"Was not!"

"I felt the sparks fly, same as you when I saw your lithe, lovely figure step out of that janitor's suit. Did anyone ever tell you, you have the body of a ballerina?"

"You're insane."

His hand went to touch my cheek. Instinctively I jerked. I wanted to draw my face away but some irrational sensation of pleasure held me in check. His fingertips landed lightly against my hairline. They were cool and sensitive.

The elevator door suddenly slid opened. It was my floor. Thank *God*. I yanked back from him without speaking a word. He wet his lips and I turned. I stepped out without a backward glance or saying goodbye. Never had I felt so mortified in my life. I was hot and perspiring and threats choked in my throat.

The elevator doors ground together. He had not followed me out. I spun back to look, and caught his expression of mild amusement, as the doors closed and delivered him out of my sight.

Trying to keep the swear words in was debilitating. There were so many epithets I wanted to throw at him. I stormed into the art studio and saw that everyone had gone home. Was it really that late? I stole a peek at my smartphone. It was. I had spent way longer at tea with my sister than I'd intended. It was time I went home, too. I grabbed my purse from my desk drawer, and tied the thin cardigan I had worn this morning overtop my sleeveless blouse around my waist. After locking the door to the studio, I jiggled the lever to be sure. You never knew who might be lurking around. It seemed they gave out visitor passes to any billionaire and his gorilla that wanted one.

By now the elevator car must be well away. I fidgeted, hesitated a moment more before pressing the button.

CHAPTER

4

Office buildings are strange after hours, when everyone has gone home, and the nightshift cleaning staff has yet to arrive. There is a peculiar electronic hum that is pervasive. Whether it comes from the lighting or office machines, in a museum it is so much more pronounced. Maybe it's because you know downstairs are the skeletons of past creatures, rocks and minerals from an unfathomable geologic past, and the everyday objects of ancient civilizations, that could, like the movie (Night at the Museum), spring to life in your imagination.

When the elevator doors ground open, thankfully the unit was empty.

Peace at last.

At the lobby I crossed the polished hardwood floors to the exit, my long brown hair flying out past my shoulders. I may have unnerved myself after my over-stimulating encounter with the billionaire archaeologist. *May have?* That was an understatement. I had most definitely unnerved myself.

Oh, why did he invade my thoughts so often? I shook off the memory of his face and his touch, and hurried to the front entrance.

Through the raindrop beaded glass doors a mob of reporters and other media gathered outside. A sudden shower had dampened the streets and left puddles and leaves on the sidewalks. The rain had stopped, and the crowd milled as though waiting for something to happen. Everyone had smartphones poised, ready to capture a photograph. Had word got around that adventurer playboy Luke Trevanian was at the museum? Nothing, it seemed, not even the threat of further inclement weather would prevent them from a selfie with their hero.

Who could blame them? It wasn't everyday Indiana Jones came to visit.

The clouds swarmed away from the low sun. I had no umbrella, but the sky was clearing. I had my hand on the door handle ready to exit when I detected a distinct grunt from behind me.

A hissing sound of exasperation followed. Luke Trevanian accompanied by his bodyguard stepped up to the glass door.

"Hell," Trevanian said, taking note of the crowd outside. "God help me. Will they not leave me alone?"

I shot a sideways glance at him. *And hello to you, too.*

"What *did* you expect?" I asked. "You're one of the richest men in the country and a famous archaeologist to boot. Not to mention you are married to Arianna Chase."

"*Was* married," he corrected. "The divorce will be finalized as soon as I can get her to agree on a reasonable settlement."

I scoffed. "What were you thinking, Mr. Trevanian? No prenuptial agreement?"

My sarcastic quip was met with silence. Then he said, "I thought we were in love."

Oh why did this man bring out the worst in me? My nature was to be kind, not mean. Was it the lack of love and sex in my life? I was sorry for that remark. Couldn't have been sorrier. But when it came to Luke Trevanian I found it impossible to form the words.

"Is there a back way out of here?" he asked.

Actually there was. It was the route that the cleaning staff used. "Only if you don't mind being mistaken for a janitor," I said.

He laughed. "Touché." He darted a quick glance through the glass doors. The throng was getting thicker. A sea of smartphones bobbed in the air. Waiting to go live, reporters cast aside their dripping umbrellas to take a chance with the weather. They adjusted their clothing and microphones in tune to the jostling of video cameras.

Trevanian addressed his bodyguard. "Norman. Give me ten minutes to get out of here. Then phone the car to pick you up and wait for my call. I'll tell you where to collect me." Then he nodded. "Okay, Lucy. I'm all yours. Show me the way out."

"Are you sure you want to play it this way?" I asked.

He sighed, long and heavily. "Oh, you have no idea."

A little piece of me felt sorry for him. Maybe that's why he looked so tired today. He was trying to get an expedition together and the media refused to cooperate. His imminent divorce was big news, as was his recent bachelor status. "Fine," I said. "But you owe me."

I gestured for him to follow. Our route took us to the back of the museum, down a set of stairs to a service entrance. We walked past the cleaning staff's lockers where several hooks held uniforms.

"Do you have a car?" he inquired of me.

I shook my head. Was this a further jab at my relative poverty? I decided to go high. "I take the subway."

He frowned.

"You're worried people will recognize you on the street and want autographs?" I asked. I hadn't meant to be sarcastic; it just came out that way.

"Autographs are the least of my concerns." His frown instantly transformed into a chuckle. It was a nice sound and I found myself hating him less.

I said, "I was joking."

Did people actually stop him and ask him for autographs? My mouth opened to ask; I clamped it shut. No doubt, they probably did.

He nodded and I gestured for him to follow me. "Well, maybe there's a way we can get past the museum without being seen."

"You got an idea? I'm game."

Fourteen minutes later, we were back at the janitors' lockers. I removed a pair of worn coveralls (more like a jumpsuit) and a cap. I chose one of the largest sizes to accommodate his height. I dangled the ensemble in front of him. "Still game?"

He laughed.

The outfit did nothing to dampen his attractiveness, much to my detriment. He was confusing the hell out of me. He zipped up the front to cover his expensive duds and slapped the cap over his sun-bleached curls. He must have been desperate to avoid the media today because he made no qualms about getting into the custodian's uniform.

The service entrance exited into a large parking lot. I opened the door to a blast of humidity and we slipped out the back, without being seen. Most of the parking spaces were empty and dry. But around the areas where the cars had sat the pavement was dark from the cloudburst. The air was heavy with moisture and felt hot, even oppressive. It was getting late. The sun broke through the clouds and leaned between the rain-streaked buildings and dripping trees surrounding the museum. Shadows reached over the rain-spattered hoods of the remaining cars, and across the puddled concrete. To my far right, golden light danced off the peaks of the wet crystal extension in a dazzling array of sparks.

He could call his limo to pick him up here, but if the media caught sight of it they would follow it to this exact spot and his escape would be foiled.

"Lucy," he said. "Take me to the subway."

"Are you serious?"

A squint, and then a short nod. "I have to get out of here.

I have a headache to beat all headaches and if I don't get out of here I'm afraid of what I'll say to those news people."

Fine. I understood. An individual like him couldn't afford to alienate the media. But this was the last favor I was doing for him. I grabbed his hand. Don't ask me why I did that. I guess it was because that's what I would have done if it were anybody else who wanted me to get him out of sight and down into the subway system as speedily as possible.

Not the time to analyze how good it felt to hold his hand. I just started walking with him fast, head down, and he followed. When we came around the side of the building to Bloor Street I could see all the reporters and other folks still waiting anxiously at the door. Nobody noticed a young, unremarkable woman and a museum janitor head down the steps of the subway on Bloor Street West.

A blast of hot air encased us, and we clattered down the damp steps to the underground. I glanced up at him as we stood in front of the pay kiosk.

If you think you're getting a free ride, on top of everything else, think again.

He raised his hands palms up to indicate he carried no spare change. I shook my head to show my exasperation and dug into my pockets.

"You owe me four bucks," I said, and paid the fare for both of us with my last two tokens. He smiled and followed me into the waiting train.

"Where did you want to go?" I asked.

"Where are *you* going?"

"Home."

"That sounds nice."

I gawped at him. "You want to go to my home?"

"I can have my driver pick me up there."

My hands seemed to lift of their own accord in a gesture of bafflement. I muttered, "Fine. Whatever."

The car where we stood was packed with commuters, some soaked to the skin having been caught unprepared by the recent cloudburst. Most were headed for home after a hard day's work, and the ambience was noisy with the electrical hum of the train and the clacking of the tracks. The odor of hot, damp bodies and machine oil was the dominant smell. Very little chatter filled the car, as smartphones and other devices preoccupied most of the subway riders. There was nowhere to sit, so we each grabbed a pole and settled in for an uncomfortable ride. We were silent most of the trip north. As we passed each station I kept my eyes peeled for my stop.

I live in a small apartment on Oriole Parkway inside an old historic house on a tree-lined street. I was on the upper floor. There were two more apartments below me.

The wind had picked up and had already dried the streets with its hot breath. Luke followed me out of the subway and onto the sidewalk. I started homeward on foot and he followed. I felt like I had a lost puppy in tow.

At my place I expected him to say goodbye and call his limo to pick him up. He didn't; he stood outside on the straw-like grass, still wet from the recent rain, at the bottom of the peeling wooden steps, watching me on the front porch as I fumbled with my keys.

The humidity was increasing as the summer heat drank up the last remnants of the rain. He was sweating and so was I. There was no point in us standing here staring at each other.

"Did you want to wait inside?" I asked.

"If that's okay."

That was the first time Luke Trevanian had been polite enough to consider my feelings.

"It's okay."

We went up two flights of stairs to the top floor. I opened the door, and cool air washed out. I was determined not to be embarrassed by the modesty of my apartment. I loved my apartment, which was done up in pale blue and brilliant white. It had character and was neat and clean. It also had a lot of light from a number of skylights and long windows, and a small balcony with a glass door.

"It's heaven in here," he said. I imagined he was referring to the air conditioning, which I kept on even when I was out else the unit would heat up during the day to oven-like temperatures.

"This is nice," he added, looking around.

I grunted. I could only imagine what the billionaire archaeologist's mansion looked like. *Oh, wait.* It was probably a friggin' estate.

Suddenly, I was aware that he was on my turf and that he was wearing a janitor's uniform. I smiled. He grinned back. He would have to strip out of the disguise, so I could return it tomorrow.

He removed the cap, mopped his forehead with the back of his hand, and struggled out of the denim coveralls. I took them from him and folded them into a neat package.

"Aren't you going to call your gorilla?" I asked, setting the ensemble onto a side table against the wall.

He laughed. "He's not that bad."

"He's got arms like an ape." I glanced briefly at Luke's bare arms, remembering how they had engulfed me when *I* was the one in the janitor's costume, and stifled a moan. Frankly, he also had arms strong as an ape's, except in a more pleasing shape—*and* they weren't hairy. Or should I say, what hair he had on them was fine and bleached golden from the sun. I could feel myself getting hot again and I dragged my thoughts from his sunny tan.

This time he failed to read my thoughts. Thank God. His stomach rumbled and I laughed. "Are you hungry?"

He exhaled. "I'm afraid so. Didn't get much to eat this afternoon."

And why was that? Colleen and I had seen him in the Crystal Lounge with his ex-wife. If they weren't there to eat, why were they there?

"Here's an idea," he said. "Why don't we phone for a pizza?"

"Really? You want to eat pizza. Here? With me?"

Luke's eyes took on a gentle, almost tender look. It

made the green of his eyes resemble the reflection of the sea. "There is nothing I would like more."

"You don't like me," I said.

He stared. "What makes you say that?"

"Every second word you direct at me feels like an insult. What else can I think, Mr. Trevanian?"

"Let's try 'Luke.'"

"Okay, Luke. You don't like me. Why do you want to have dinner with me?"

"Same reason I want you on my archaeology team."

"And that is?"

A few framed prints hung on the powder blue walls of my living room. I glanced up, and saw that his eyes were already there. These were drawings of some of the archaeological sites I had worked at during previous summers, and some were of artifacts I had inked for my own pleasure. Most were from exotic locales like France, Greece and Italy. I even had one I had sketched in Syria before the civil war. My signature was scrawled on the lower right-hand corner of each. Did he really think I was a good artist?

His silence was a little unsettling. People accused him of being a treasure hunter. What did he know about art? Yet his services were in demand the world over. He must have some sort of expertise.

Why was he studying my drawings as though there was some major flaw in them? As my agitation escalated, I reminded myself that his opinion was irrelevant. After tonight I would never see him again. Until his face reappeared on TV.

He approached to examine the art pieces more closely. "You're very talented Ms. Lucy Racine."

The comment came as a surprise. I was prepped for another slight, and was stumped for a gracious reply.

"And that's why you want to have dinner with me?"

That pleasing chuckle again.

"You didn't know if I was a good artist when you told Shaun you wanted to recruit me. You knew nothing about me at all."

"I figured if you were the head of the art department you *must* be good."

It was my turn to exhale, but the sound I made was more of exasperation. His compliments always sounded like insults. Why was I simultaneously attracted and annoyed by this man?

"Pizza?" he asked.

Smiling despite myself, I went to call up my favorite place. I shook out the well-perused takeout menu from its drawer in the sideboard, my cellphone under my chin. I wagged the menu at him and waited for him to choose.

Turned out he liked the same toppings as I did: Pepperoni, mushrooms, green peppers, black olives and extra cheese.

I loved this pizza place because its policy was: Order is free if delivery takes more than half an hour.

It never took more than thirty minutes.

The pizza arrived. He paid for it with a credit card and added a generous tip. I stood rolling my eyes. I refused to get into an altercation over who should pay for dinner. This was not a date. And it was *his* idea anyway. Why *shouldn't* he pay?

"Got any wine?" he asked

All I had was a bottle of Chianti, not the most expensive, but a good standby with Italian.

He set the pizza box down on my glass coffee table, and opened the wine while I went to fetch plates, napkins and glasses. Was this really the world-famous, billionaire archaeologist Luke Trevanian sitting on my sofa, preparing to scarf down pizza with me?

CHAPTER

5

No kidding he hadn't eaten much today. He had an appetite like a fourteen-year-old boy and was making fast work of the pizza. Half of it was gone already and I had only eaten one slice. I sipped my wine and watched him chew. He seemed comfortable here with me and that was odd. Why was he really here? Other than the pizza, I mean. Obviously he was hungry. He seemed to be enjoying my finest cheap Chianti as well.

"I saw you in the restaurant," I said. "The Crystal Lounge."

From where he sat across the coffee table opposite me, he paused. Then sucked in a slice of pepperoni between his lips. How was that sexy? I leaned forward, and forced myself to focus on his response.

He patted the corner of his mouth with a paper napkin and winked. I felt the heat rise to my cheeks. Crap. So I was right. He *had* seen me. He said, "Sure. I was with Arianna."

I composed myself and waited for the stupid heat in my face to subside. I wanted him to explain about his ex-wife without my having to ask.

He laughed. "You're not one of them, are you? Please tell me you are not one of those groupies who are following our divorce."

I shook my head. "Not me. My sister."

"Ah, so that's who you were with."

My brows arched against my will.

"That's right, Ms. Lucy Racine. I noticed you in the restaurant."

We already established that. You don't have to rub it in.

"Why?" I asked.

"Well for one thing, I like a woman who's not afraid to eat with her fingers. And you, my dear girl, are not afraid to use your hands."

I giggled, and licked tomato sauce from my thumb and first two digits. "Oh. That's how I eat desserts. Give me a slice of cake, a donut or ice cream, and I end up sticking my finger in it."

He grinned. "You also almost knocked over my soon to be ex-wife."

"I did, didn't I? Hope she's forgotten. I need her signature on something..." I wished he hadn't reminded me of my latest failure to be assertive. "Oh well...."

"What is it? Maybe I can help."

"You know," I said, sitting up straight and setting down my wine glass. I was actually cross-legged on the floor. That's how I eat pizza. Usually in front of the TV. On the floor. I crawled to my knees and propped my elbows on the glass coffee table, my eyes turned up to him in appeal. "That's what puzzles me. How is it that you and she are on such good terms in real life, when all the media has you two scratching each other's eyes out?"

"In real life, we despise each other. We play nice because we don't want our catfights to be reported in the news. Fat lot of good it does, but we try. Besides—she needs the good PR for the museum. I still care about the museum, you know—whether you believe me or not." I was inclined not to believe him, and kept my opinion to myself. He added, "It's losing money you know."

I knew.

"So she's nice to me when she wants something. But she's still suing me for half of everything I own."

"Surely, she owns some of it, too?"

"Not really." His face turned hard. "She had the gall to ask for my yacht. What does she want with a yacht? She doesn't have time to use it. While I—It's how I run my archaeology enterprises. And she knows it." He shook his head. "I gave her a big fat 'No' to that. Now she's refusing to settle."

Maybe it was the wine talking, but my curiosity was winning. "I'm still surprised you had no prenup before you two got hitched."

"Interesting thing that," he said. "I wasn't a billionaire back then."

"Well, even a millionaire needs to protect his assets..." My voice trailed off. This stuff was private. How had I ever gotten onto the topic?

"Not that either."

"Seriously? I read about you. Well, my sister's read about you and reported it to me. Your family is worth a bundle. Your father—"

"Yeah, yeah, I *know* what my father is worth."

I looked down at my wineglass, reached out and took a quiet sip. "I'm sorry. This is personal. I shouldn't be asking."

"You are very sweet, Lucy. It's too bad you don't like me."

This was a totally different side to Luke Trevanian. The arrogant, overconfident, self-centered man was taking a backseat to the pensive, thoughtful, caring man I suspected was underneath. I ventured a shy glance upward.

"Anyway. You're right; my father is wealthy—as was *his* father. And now so am I, but it wasn't always that way." He finished his wine and refilled his glass. The bottle now hovered over mine and I signaled for him to pour me just a splash. I wanted him to continue his narrative. "Sure you want to hear this?" I nodded and he continued. "When I was in my late teens, ready for college I wanted to study ancient civilizations."

I sat back on my haunches. "What's wrong with that?" I had taken several archaeology courses myself.

"Nothing, unless you're the founder and CEO of a number of billion dollar enterprises. Daddy dearest wanted me to take over a couple of the companies. I said no. Business school prior to heading up one of his corporations was the last thing in my plans…. Dear old Dad has a bit of a temper. He's a control freak. They say it's what got him as far as he got, but that's not me. My dream was to be an archaeologist."

"And now you *are* one."

"I am…to my father's great shame and disappointment."

Although he omitted the specifics, he did elaborate slightly on why his father had cut him off from the Trevanian gravy train. It was simple. He disagreed with his father's choice of career for him and felt he had a right to choose his own. As far as the old tyrant was concerned, if he wanted to benefit from the family fortune, the son must follow in the father's footsteps. His mother sided with her husband to avoid any marital discord; and so Luke was left to fend on his own. Young, and fresh out of a private high school, penniless and naïve, he tried to pay his own way through college.

Lots of students did it that way (my sister and I, for example), but for once I resisted making a barbed comment. This career path was something he desperately wanted, enough to defy his domineering father. For the first time since we met I felt a smidgeon of respect for him. But there was something he was holding back. I sensed it in the way he hesitated at certain points in his story, as if he were avoiding some detail, something that would explain his frequent slide into boorish behavior. I began to see the bullying as a defense mechanism rather than pure arrogance.

"I'm sorry, Luke," I said softly.

"Why? What did *you* do? It's not your fault my father was an ogre."

"You talk about him as though he was in the past. Is he

still alive?"

"Oh sure. He's alive. And healthy, as far as I know...."

"But?"

He looked at me.

I raised my eyes at him.

"Why do I feel like kissing you right now?"

I almost laughed, the question had taken me so off-guard. Not that I would have minded. My thoughts occasionally shifted in that direction. But it was an obvious attempt to change the subject, and I wanted him to keep talking. I liked this side of him. It made me realize he was human and capable of vulnerability and compassion. I also wanted to know more about his relationship with his dad. Obviously, he respected and admired the man, no matter what he said. They were clearly estranged, and that explained a lot. It now made sense why he reacted like the world was against him. Attack before you're attacked. It was a method of protecting himself. If the people that were supposed to love and protect you were your greatest critics, then who could you trust?

"I take it you don't see him?"

"We speak when we have to."

"Holidays and birthdays?"

"Something like that."

His need to whitewash his answers made it clear there was more to it than that. But either the wine was wearing off or he truly was bored with the topic.

Some people seem to build walls between themselves and those that care about them. If the wall metaphor works it was true here. Not that I cared a wit about Luke Trevanian. Why should I? I barely knew him. He was practically a stranger. So what if he was something of a celebrity? That meant zip in my world. But the wall—what an apt metaphor, considering he was an archaeologist, because didn't they study ancient walls? And yeah, if emotional walls were built of brick, Luke Trevanian's was twice as thick as anyone else's. His was built of solid stone.

And yet I was tingling all over. He saw me as a woman, and not just as an instrument to manipulate. His gaze was on my lips, not my eyes. I must admit I've got lips on the fullish side. And so does he. I cupped my hand over my mouth. Thank God, my thoughts remained unspoken. Why was I thinking these things? That would be crazy. *I am just beginning to like him. I mustn't turn this night into a sex fest. If I sleep with him, if it's meaningless to him…?* I shook the questions out of my mind.

"What's the matter, Lucy? You look like you're going to be sick. Are you okay?"

"I'm fine," I said.

"Are you sure?"

Most of the pizza had been devoured, and very little of the wine remained. He rose from the sofa to pull me to my feet from where I still sat on the floor on the other side of the coffee table, and brought me around to stand in front of him. Did I say he was tall? He was *so* tall, and so strong and his shoulders were enormously wide. I nodded.

I was looking up into his face and his eyes were lingering on my lips.

His mouth came down gently at first and then with desperate urgency. He sucked in my lower lip and I felt his teeth sink into soft flesh. I gasped as he raised me bodily off the floor and high into his arms. Then he kissed me again.

I moaned, barely able to keep my breath in. We could only do that for a short while before we both needed to come up for air. I wanted desperately to peel off my clothes and crawl into a safe warm bed with him. But that wasn't the look he was giving me. His eyes warned that nothing was safe with him. If I gave in to my body's desires I'd be giving in to a dangerous man.

The phone suddenly rang, breaking the spell. We simultaneously came to our senses. He lowered me to the floor and now we stood staring at each other swallowing with difficulty, trying to speak. What was there to say? *Why did you kiss me?* He could ask me the same question.

"Excuse me," I said and went to answer the phone.

"Lucy!" Colleen squealed into my ear.

I held the phone slightly away from my head and said, "Hey, what's up?"

"You sound weird," my sister remarked. "Anything wrong? What were you doing just now? You sound... breathless."

"I'm not doing anything," I lied. "What's with all the excitement? You sound like something good has happened."

"Hasn't it?"

I shrugged though she couldn't see it. "Are you going to keep me in suspense?"

"Lucy, Shaun told me the exciting news!"

This time I frowned because honestly I had no idea what she was babbling about. "What exciting news?"

"You're going on an archaeological dig to the Amalfi coast, the Gulf of Naples, with Dr. Luke Trevanian!"

Whaaat? Did she say *Dr.?*

"He has a PhD you know."

I didn't know.

"Oh, good grief, Lucy, say something. You *are* going, aren't you? You have to. It's the seaside villa of Positano, the Gulf of Naples in Italy!"

"I heard you the first time."

"He's already made arrangements for you to take leave. I hear it's a two-month trip."

"*What?* I can't leave the museum for two months."

"But the arrangements have already been made. You leave in two days!"

I was stunned to say the least. Stupified. "Shaun made the arrangements? I never told him I wanted to go."

"Not Shaun, silly. Shaun doesn't have that kind of influence.... Luke Trevanian. He made arrangements with his ex, the director, Arianna Chase. Rumor has it that he agreed to give her their chateau in France if she would arrange to give you two months leave from the museum—"

Two months leave?

"I see…" I rolled my eyes toward the culprit who had taken my life in tow. I flinched to see a glint of mischief in his eyes. Talk about mixed feelings. He had assumed control of my life without my consent. This was unacceptable and I ensured he was aware of it by the scowling face I made at him.

When had he made these arrangements? We'd only met this afternoon. He just then learned I was an archaeological illustrator. My God, he moved fast.

A tiny smile played at the corners of his lips. He knew what we were talking about. Luke's voice grabbed my attention once more. "I can see you've got things to discuss with your sister."

How did he know it was my sister?

"I'm going to get out of your hair. I'm sure you have some arrangements to make of your own. Packing to do? I've called Norman to bring around the car."

I remained standing, stupefied, in the middle of my living room floor surrounded by the smells and debris of pizza, gripping the phone in my hand while my sister chattered away.

"The boat leaves at 1:00 PM sharp, at the marina. Thursday July 15th. Don't worry if you don't have time to get everything you'll need. The yacht is fully equipped. Whatever you need, it probably has. I'll send someone around to pick you up on the day."

CHAPTER
<u>6</u>

All right, I admit I have fallen under his spell. Even though I'm a little miffed that he went behind my back to ensure that I would take the job. I had a couple of days to finish up my work here, and when I got to my office the next morning I had a nice little surprise waiting.

On my cheap wooden desk was a beautiful bouquet of peach-colored roses, mingled with pale baby's breath, and green ferns. In front of the porcelain vase was a white envelope. I knew the name of the sender before I even opened it. There was a card:

> *Thanks for a great pizza night.*
> *Here's the 4 bucks I owe you for the subway.*
> *— L.T.*

He had signed it simply with his initials in capital letters, and had included four shiny one-dollar coins. I could no longer be irritated that he had manipulated me into accepting the job. The warm memory of his iron arms around my waist and his firm lips on mine destroyed every desire to be independent. I wanted him. God—did I want him. And every ounce of my being yearned for nothing more than to dig up frescoes by his side.

Were we even going to be doing that? I know he wanted me along as an illustrator, but oh, how I was hoping his motive for requiring my company was a little more intimate than that.

A knock came at my office door. Shaun was in the studio leaning on the doorjamb.

"Hey," I said, cheerfully. I ran my hands through my tangled hair, smoothing it out and preparing to bind it up and out of the way for when I went to work at my drafting table. "Well, I guess you get your wish after all. I've decided to go on Trevanian's expedition."

"Yeah," he said. "About that...."

I dropped my hands detecting his tone. My hair swung back down loosely around my face. "What. I thought you wanted me to go."

"I did." He paused and watched my expression for signs of emotion or some kind of reaction. But to what? He scratched his ear nervously. "That was before I knew you had a crush on him."

"Hey. I do not. Who told you that?"

He sighed. "You forget. I'm married to your sister. She tells me everything."

What had I confessed to Colleen last night, after Luke had gone? I had resisted, quite fiercely, the revelation of any feelings, whatsoever, for the billionaire archaeologist. Of that, I did remember. But she was my sister, and by that very fact had an intuition others might not. "He's okay," I said. "I decided it would be a great opportunity to work in Italy."

"You sure you don't have feelings for him? *Unrequited* feelings?"

What business was it of his if Luke and I wished to have a little fun? Now, I was becoming irritated. Rats, he was right. These thoughts were inappropriate.

"Nice flowers," he commented. "Who gave them to you?"

A lump formed in my throat. I swallowed tensely and

shoved the four dollars I was fondling in my hands into my pocket. "I helped Luke out of a jam last night," I replied rather tersely. "He was trying to escape the paparazzi. I made sure he left the museum unseen."

"Luke?" he said, voice rising. "Since when do you call him 'Luke'?"

"That *is* his name."

"He's used to being in the public eye, Lucy."

I pushed a finger in the direction of the flowers. "This was just his way of saying 'Thank you'."

He nodded, but instead of implying agreement I got the sense he was patronizing me. "I'm just thinking about your welfare…"

My neck was hot and so was my face. Not my favorite topic of conversation. Where was he headed with it anyways? Because I suspected he was verging on the truth. My frustration and the resulting conflicting feelings pricked me to the core. "Why? Why don't you think he'd be interested in me?"

"He was married to the museum's director." A pause. "Technically, still is."

"So?" I lowered my voice. "They're separated. And just because she's snooty, and fashionable and yeah, kind of beautiful, doesn't mean he wouldn't find someone like me attractive."

I shot a swift glance around. Were any of the museum's employees in earshot? Most were just arriving. They were totally oblivious to the argument, taking place inside my office. Shaun gave me a sad smile. He knew my track record with men.

"He wouldn't be good for you, Lucy."

"How do you know?" My fingers clenched into tight fists, an act I usually reserved for disagreements with my sister. I grabbed a scrunchie from my desktop and twisted my long hair into a bun. "We actually have a thing or two in common."

"Yeah? Like what?"

"Like antiquities. And why do you care anyways?"

"You're like a sister to me. I don't want you to get hurt. If you get hurt then there'll be hell to pay with Colleen. She'll blame *me*."

"*She* wants me to go."

"Right now, she does. She thinks it would be great if he *married* you. But seriously, Lucy, a man like that, he's out of your—"

"Hold it right there, buster. Before you say something you can't take back."

"You know I'm right, Lucy."

"So, you don't want me to go on this expedition? How will *that* look? Luke wants me there. He'll make things difficult if I'm not. What happened to: 'Our jobs might be in jeopardy'?" I mimicked quotes with my fingers as I repeated his own warning to his face.

"Okay, don't get all crazy on me. I'm just saying... I'm just looking out for you."

"Thanks, Shaun. But I'm all grown up now. Okay, yes, you knew me as a teenager, but I'm not that kid anymore. I know what I'm doing."

He smiled sheepishly. "You realize I think the world of you?"

"Sure, I do." I slid out of my chair and went over to plant a kiss on his cheek. "Don't worry about me so much. I can take care of myself."

"Just be careful."

He left me frowning. I stared at the empty doorway for a long time before I even noticed the activity of my illustrators and ceramics artists in the outer studio. That was strange. Shaun had never felt it his place to warn me about men before, why now and why Luke? Granted he was a billionaire, and maybe Shaun was right. Maybe Luke was just having some fun with me and would never let anything serious develop. Could be that he wasn't even capable of it. But last night when he opened up to me about his dad, and having to work through college, that really got to me.

Was it something else? He seemed suspicious of Luke. Why? What could Luke possibly be involved in that would trigger such mistrust?

Come to think of it Shaun had been acting a little odd these past few weeks. I had chalked it up to anxiety over Colleen's expensive habits. When school was out and she had summers off, that was when she tended to indulge.

I was frantic as it was, what with packing for the trip and delegating assignments to my artists. Good thing my passport was current and Colleen had already offered to check on my place while I was away. Should I ask Shaun if there was anything in particular that was worrying him? After tomorrow I'd be gone, and if there was something I could help with I'd like to do it. I owed the two of them big time for giving me a place to live while I was working my way through school. Our mom was a single parent. Our father was gone. Died in a hit-and-run shortly after I was born.

I should go to his office.

But first, time to deal with some unfinished business. I needed that signature from the director. That 3-D printer wasn't going to buy itself.

I rode the elevator to the top floor. It was entirely renovated and looked incongruously modern just like the Lee-Chin crystal extension. The floors were of polished marble and the offices had glass walls. The interior of every single one of the offices was visible from the corridor. Was that Dr. Chase's way of keeping tabs on her staff without appearing to do so?

Her office was at the far end of the hall. It was early. Not everyone had arrived at work yet. She wore a lovely white summer suit (Chanel, of course) and black blouse. She could have just stepped off the pages of *Vogue*.

A man stood in front of her in profile. I brightened. Was it Luke? At first I thought so. He was in top physical shape. But the silhouette was slightly off, and the clothes were all wrong. This man was casually dressed in khaki's and short-sleeved shirt with a baseball cap, set at a very steep angle to hide his face.

My smile faded. My next thought was: maybe it was Luke's bodyguard? Arianna was certainly attracting masculine types to her office these days. I was about to go forward with my forms for her to sign when I observed the fierce stance of her body. I guess not. She was busy. She was in a foul mood to say the least, and now was not the time to disturb her. Especially if she was bickering with her estranged husband or his bodyguard.

I know I was staring. I watched, perhaps too long. Like Luke and Norman the man was built like a firehouse. I was too far away to be sure of who he was.

A shiver tingled my spine. I approached. My curiosity had gotten the best of me. I *had* to look. The man leaned over the secretary's desk. Was he signing for something? His head was bowed, his face hidden. His shoulders were broad and his left arm visible. His sleeve rode up as he raised his hand. I caught an unusual tattoo. Where had I seen that before? A cupid riding a sea serpent? Did Norman have a tattoo? Did Luke?

The secretary's phone rang. Arianna's visitor turned. Before I could identify him, I whirled, and bumped into one of the young technicians I sometimes worked with.

"Hey, Lucy," he said. He hesitated as though he wanted to tell me something.

"Hi Tommy. You got something to show me?" I noted the camera in his hand. He often did photography for the art department.

"Um…. No," he said. "Not yet."

"Well, I'll be in the studio this afternoon. If you need me."

"Great."

A nervous glance darted in the direction of Arianna's office. Most of us were nervous when we had to speak to her. She was one of those kinds of people. Made you feel the size of a worm.

"She's occupied at the moment," I warned him.

"I can see that."

I hesitated, but he seemed preoccupied. His mind was on something else. The conversation that was taking place between our boss and the tattooed man? I shrugged. "Talk to you later," I said.

A nod before he watched me go.

It wasn't Tommy, the young tech, I was watching now. You know how there are people who kind of give you the creeps? Well, that man with the tattoo arguing with Arianna Chase was one of them. Why, I don't know. And I am not going to try to explain the feeling. It was just a fact.

I would try again later when the visitor, whoever he was, had left.

On my way back to my office I went to Shaun's, but he was away from his desk. Was he in the lab, maybe? I didn't feel like taking a trip down to the basement, and hung around a few seconds, and then happened to glance at the papers on his desktop. That was innocent, as I am generally not a nosey person. But I must have been primed for noticing weird things today.

This was a letter from the Italian government, which must have had something to do with his Roman acquisitions, and another one from Interpol—the International Police— who had jurisdiction over antiquities trafficking. I recognized the distinctive blue and white globe that was their symbol.

I glanced up briefly.

No sign of Shaun or any of his researchers or technicians.

My eyes lowered, and I skimmed over the letter.

It was a request for information about an Italian icon, a Black Madonna. The piece was a carving of the Virgin Mary with Child. The Madonna is a very common subject in the art world, but this particular Madonna was special. Instead of having pale skin, her skin was black and everything else, her hair, clothing, and background was rendered in gold.

Why would Interpol be asking about an icon from an Italian church?

"What the hell are you doing?"

Shaun had returned. I looked up to catch his cheeks flush and his eyes turn dark with fury at seeing me standing on the wrong side of his desk with a look of supreme guilt on my face. He ripped the letter from my hand.

"Sorry, I was looking for you... What is it, Shaun? Why are you so edgy?"

"I am not edgy. I just do not like people poking around my things."

"But this is museum business. Isn't it?"

"Yes, yes." He swung around to my side of the desk and nudged me in the opposite direction. Then opened a drawer and slipped in the letter and slammed the drawer shut.

I sat down in the guest chair. "Shaun. What has you so jumpy?"

At first I thought he was going to tell me. The sounds that began in his throat faded and never emerged as words. He sat down and stared at me. Then cleared the phlegm from his throat. "I'm just tired. With the baby coming and all."

"Of course you are. Anything I can do to help?"

"Actually, I've had second thoughts about you going to Positano. I don't think we can spare you. I need you to do the artwork for the upcoming Roman exhibition."

"Almost everyone in my studio is qualified to do the graphics. What's *really* bugging you?"

I watched him cautiously. He glanced nervously at the doorway as though he thought we might be overheard. I said, "I know Colleen's been spending a lot of money. She gets bored in the summertime. A trip to the Mediterranean might be just what the doctor ordered. Maybe she should come with me?"

"No," Shaun said.

"Okay, no need to get upset. I know you don't want her out of your sight while she's pregnant, but she's only three and a half months along."

"I'm sorry, Lucy. It must be the impending fatherhood. But I'd be happier if you stayed in town."

This flip-flopping was unusual for Shaun. He was normally so decisive. Was the prospect of becoming a dad really sending him over the edge? Maybe I should stay home and keep an eye on both of them. His behavior was a little worrisome. Colleen hadn't mentioned any trouble in paradise. And yet I was torn. What was going on? I was drawn to Luke and his project. Shaun, however, was family. He would only ask me to stay if it was really important to him.

I sighed.

Made up my mind.

I probably should stay until I knew there was nothing to worry about. There would be other opportunities.

"All right, Shaun. If it means that much to you, I won't go. But you'd better make arrangements for someone else to take my place. And I'm leaving it up to you to explain why I bailed."

CHAPTER

7

On Thursday morning I was just about ready to leave for work when I happened to glance out the window and saw a black limousine parked at the curbside.

What was that doing at my house? I went outside onto the porch, and Norman Depardieu stepped out of the front passenger seat. I forced myself to focus on his face, a face that would have been handsome if he would only smile more. His deep voice, despite being intimidating was unnervingly sexy. It must be that damned tint of French in the accent.

"I am here to take you to the harbor."

"I'm sorry?" I said, leaning over the rail. "Didn't Dr. Trevanian get my message? Dr. Templeton, at the museum, was supposed to tell him that I'm not going on the expedition."

"Yeah, well… and the boss he says otherwise. Get in."

I was not going anywhere with that gorilla. "I'm not packed. I changed my mind, I'm not going."

Norman rolled his eyes. He obviously cared little for me. The feeling was mutual. Although I felt a thrill every time he looked my way. Fear probably. Muscles or no muscles, I avoided eye contact. He must never know that I had *ever* noticed him.

He seemed to flex on cue as he fetched something out of his pocket. Now, he was on his phone talking to someone. I turned to lock the door of my house and head for the subway. "Just a minute," Norman said. "The boss, he wants to talk to you."

I hesitated, before I stepped down the stairs, and gingerly accepted the phone.

"Lucy?" the voice at the other end said.

"Hi Luke. Didn't Shaun give you my message?"

"He did. I don't understand. What changed your mind?"

"Well, to be honest I never fully committed myself, did I?"

"Oh? I thought you did."

"I can't go, Luke."

"Why not?"

"Shaun is worried about my sister—his wife. She's pregnant and he doesn't want me to leave her alone."

There was silence at the end of the line. I could almost hear the wind and the traffic on the miles of road that separated us. "Why don't all three of you come? There's room for two more, *and* you."

I laughed. "You can't buy away all life's problems."

"Why not? I always have before."

"Shaun can't come. He's in the middle of preparing a major exhibition. And he won't let Colleen out of his sight while she's pregnant. They've been waiting a long time for this kid." I decided not to elaborate on all the fertility treatments they'd had to endure.

"So how are you your sister's keeper? I want you, Lucy. I need you to come on this trip."

"You can't always get your way, Luke," I said. "I have to go. Or I'll be late for work."

"Lucy. Get into the limo. Your summer replacement is already at your drafting table. You no longer have a job."

A car sped past, and a woman with a stroller skirted me on the sidewalk; I barely noticed. I was having trouble processing his words. Was he saying what I thought he was saying?

"You got me fired?" My hands started shaking as well as my voice. "How dare you... you had no right! I'm going right down there and demand my job back, or I'll... I'll sue!"

"Hold your horses, honey. Nobody's fired. Listen to my words. Your. Summer. Replacement. She's only there for the summer until you return—if you *want* to return."

"Of course I'll want to return."

"Good. So you'll come? The car's waiting."

"How do I know you're telling the truth?"

"You don't," he said. "You can go to the museum and find out or you can phone them. Either way they'll inform you that you have a temporary replacement."

I was speechless.

"Are you there? Are you in the car?"

"No," I said.

"Stop being so stubborn, honey. Get into the car."

"No."

He was starting to irritate me again. Why did he think he could simply rearrange my life like that? After all his talk about how angry he was when his father did the same to him. Now the tables were turned and he was committing the same offense. I shoved Norman's phone back at him and hurried down the sidewalk towards the subway station.

I have to admit I was disappointed at not going on the expedition. I had this incomprehensible yearning to drop everything and dash off to his side. I was even willing to get into that big scary car with the gorilla bodyguard—if he hadn't been so damned pushy. I am not big on being bullied. Nobody tells me what to do. Just ask my sister. I would even go so far as to deny myself my heart's desire—if I believed that someone was bullying me into it.

Damn, I thought. Damn and damn and *damn.*

Nothing for it now. I couldn't turn back. That would make me look weak and I refused to give him all the power.

On the other hand, wasn't I just caving in to my brother-in-law's wishes?

Damn.

I got out of the subway and entered through the Michael Lee-Chin crystal extension. The elevator carried me to my floor and I entered the studio. A stranger was sitting at my drafting table working on some sketches. Everyone else looked up as I entered, surprised to see me. So, Luke was telling the truth. This person was for real. I couldn't exactly dismiss her. In fact I had no power to do that. I would have to go to the director's office.

Arianna Chase had made these arrangements as a favor to her ex in exchange for a pricey piece of property. That made me even angrier. How dare he play with my life like I was a character in a video game?

I had no doubt he played video games. He was a man, wasn't he?

My shoulders slumped. Now what? I couldn't think straight. I was not going back to my house to see if Norman was still sitting there waiting for me with the limo. I needed some coffee. I was about to bypass the Crystal Lounge, and head to the cafeteria where I could get a cheap cup, when I noticed an unprecedented disturbance. In startled disbelief, I stared at the glass doors, through the full length of the restaurant to the windows, out onto the rooftop garden.

The gall. That was a memorial garden! Then I laughed. Luke Trevanian was nothing if not persistent. He had landed his helicopter on top of the field of purple chive.

I located the private door that led outside. The garden was off-limits to visitors, and certainly to helicopters. I stood hands on hips, knee-high in purple chive, watching the intrepid archaeologist debark and duck his head.

"Hey!" he said, wind snatching at his hair and clothing.

"What are you doing here? Get that thing off this rooftop garden before the security guards send the police after you."

"Then come with me."

"I can't, Luke."

"You mean, you won't."

"You had no business replacing me in my studio."

"I made sure she was one of the best."

I shook my head, my hair flying around my face from the action of the helicopter's rotors, and my fingers fast and furious trying to control the unruly locks.

Why was he being so stubborn?

Why was I?

We were at an impasse. My throat was sore from shouting over the rumble of the helicopter's engine. He extended his hand. He was giving me no choice. If I left and returned to the museum through the Crystal Lounge, he would follow me, leaving his chopper running and making a commotion to wake the deadest mummy in storage.

Reluctantly, I slipped my hand into his and he gently but firmly locked his fingers around mine. We ducked under the whirling blades, trampled the vegetation beneath our feet, and then he lifted me into his arms and deposited me lightly on the deck of the chopper.

"Saddle up," he said, leading me to a luxurious, tan leather seat and handing me the seatbelt.

Why was I so helpless when it came to Luke Trevanian? It was like I lost all will and only followed his. Despite the urge to resist I found I didn't. Instead, I buckled up and watched the museum shrink into the distance and the clouds billow over the windows.

"I have no clothes, not even a toothbrush."

"No worries." He glanced down at his Rolex watch. Kidnapping me took all of one hour. We had three hours before the boat was to leave. "We'll go shopping."

***

When we landed at the heliport on the harbor, Norman was waiting for us in the limo. He sneered at me as we got inside, as though to tell me that my life was no longer my own. Luke instructed the driver to take us to the ritzy shopping district of Yorkville. "No," I objected, "I can't afford anything in those stores."

"You don't have to," he said.

"Oh, so now you're going to give me free reign with your credit card?"

"Only if I like what you choose."

I tried a different tack. "This is an archaeological dig. Won't I need work clothes?"

"Sure, but it won't all be work—I hope. Let me buy you at least one thing that's pretty. And let me choose it."

"I really should just go home and pack."

He grinned. "I'm not taking you home. If I take you home you might not come out again."

"That's the whole idea, Luke."

"But you want to come on this expedition, don't you, Lucy?"

I loved the way he said my name. Why was I such a wussy when he looked at me like that?

"Then take me home and let me pack. I'll also need to call my sister and Shaun."

"It's all taken care of. I've fixed it with your brother-in-law and your sister is delighted. I promised her if she wanted to visit you at Positano, I'd send my private jet to fetch her for a weeklong visit. As for your personal stuff, it'll be faster if we buy it. Just a few things to tide you over until we get to Positano. You'll love the shopping there."

"Oh, fine," I said. I sighed. I wondered how he had settled it with Shaun. I'm certain my sister was thrilled. I didn't have the energy to argue any further. One side of my brain, the impulsive, dreamer side was already on board. And I knew I wasn't about to win this one with my pragmatic side.

We went to a nearby shopping center instead of fighting the traffic to return downtown. I picked up a couple of pairs of Capri pants, lightweight skinny jeans, some t-shirts, tank tops, shorts, a miniskirt, a sundress or two, and underwear, and then cosmetics and pharmaceuticals. I was starting to have fun, snatching up whatever I wanted without worrying about the price, and beginning to regret not letting him take me to the high-end stores in Yorkville. I decided I was going to let the billionaire pay for all of this stuff. I was tired of fighting him.

As we headed out of the store, Norman's arms filled with my purchases, we sauntered past one of the few upmarket boutiques in the mall. Luke grabbed me by the hand and dragged me into the shop.

"One thing nice," he said. "You promised."

"Only if you promise to stop manhandling me."

He grinned. "I thought you liked it."

I punched him in the arm and left his side to find a nice dress. *I suppose there will be occasions when I'll need something fancier. Mustn't let my imagination linger on what that might be.*

Luke held out a beautiful black evening gown in shimmering silk. The front was cut deep in a V, to a fitted waist, and the back was scooped sexily low with draped fabric. Serendipitously, it was my size. He plucked a pair of black stilettos from an elegant chrome display stand, and ushered me to the posh, softly lit fitting room.

He and Norman stayed in the waiting area. Their voices drifted over. I hung the dress on an elegant silver hook.

Not my style. But what could it hurt to try it on? I stared at the very clean, very clear mirror. Whoever had designed the fitting rooms knew what they were doing. It was impossible to look bad in this lighting. My skin appeared utterly spotless and romantically backlit, my dark hair gleamed like I had brushed it a hundred times.

I wriggled out of my slim-fitting pants and blouse and removed my bra. One thing for sure: this dress was meant to be worn without a bra. The silk slipped over my bare skin fluidly, like gently flowing water. If only I'd had time for a manicure! And a pedicure. Pretty hands and feet somehow added to the allure.

Now the shoes.

I stood in the mirror, smoothing the half-zipped dress against my torso. Was that really me? I was stunned by the transformation. On occasion I had dressed up for museum functions but never spent much money on a gown. I twisted to look at the price tag. Nearly fainted. This dress cost more than three months rent!

"Come out," he said.

"Just a minute," I answered fretfully. "I'm having a little trouble with the zipper."

Why was I hot around the face and throat? Fortunately, the warmth gave my skin a nice glow. And my eyes seemed to sparkle. Was it excitement? Anxiety? Annoyance? Why did I care what he thought? Why did I want this dress?

I heard a phone ring. Luke's voice answered it. Then the curtain drew apart. I whirled, clutched the dress to my sides. Had the sales girl come to help with the zipper?

It was Norman. "Boss said you needed help," he muttered.

The French accent was practically inaudible now. Why did he do that? Switch back and forth? I was glad he was speaking more like an American. His real voice made me uncomfortable. I turned, indicated my back with a crooked finger. It was pretty hard to reach the zipper where it hid under a fold of silk without catching the delicate material. I was a little shy that he should see me half-naked. It didn't appear to bother him in the least. Maybe he was used to dressing Luke's ladies. I had no idea.

He came round behind me and gently drew the zipper up as high as it would go. That left my upper back bare. There was silence behind me for a long while. I grew nervous. Was something wrong? Did it not look right?

I turned back and caught Norman's eyes, wide and appreciative, and I knew the dress was perfect.

"Hey, you two. Whatcha doing, sneaking around on me?"

I suppressed a giggle and caught a glint of amusement in Norman's eyes and a quiver in his lips. Norman left first. He held the curtain for me to step out from behind the heavy, white, textured fabric and onto the plush carpet in front of a highly polished, oversized three-way mirror.

So happy I had decided to shave in the shower this morning. The movement of my leg in the shapely stiletto gave my calves definition. My knee parted the dress elegantly where it slit, exposing a smooth, silky thigh. The look on Luke's face told me I wasn't wrong when I thought the dress looked stunning on me. Even Norman's usual sneer had been thoroughly quenched.

"What did I say?" Luke smiled. "A body like a ballerina. And legs all the way to heaven."

"It's too expensive," I objected.

"The way you look in that, nothing is too expensive. Take it off. We're buying it." He pulled out his cellphone. "Time's ticking. Let's go." He handed Norman a credit card. "Pay for that and then we have to get down to the dock."

***

Things were moving too fast. I was given no time to think or make my own decisions. I was bundled into the limo with all my new possessions. The driver headed back to the marina. Luke had forgotten all about me now and was busy talking to his people on the phone. When we arrived, Norman and the driver took my purchases. I was left walking two steps behind Luke and his employees.

I was pleased to see that the team had been assembled and were waiting to be motored to the yacht. Tommy Buchanan was there and came rushing up to greet me. "Lucy!" We gave each other a playful hug. "So glad you're on the team too. Word was out that you almost bailed."

I pulled him aside out of earshot of the other team members. "Luke Trevanian can be convincing."

He grinned.

Was it just me or did he seem a bit overexcited for what the situation warranted? After all, I knew this wasn't his first expedition overseas. Of the current team members he was the one with the most outside experience. His photographic skills often took him away from the museum to document strange and exotic places. Wasn't his last trip only six months ago?

For minutes he was quiet. He gazed out at the lake view. The water was calm today. The sun sparkled on its surface like loose crystals. The high-rise condominiums fringing the street side of the shoreline towered, a massive wall over the park greenery. Numerous watercraft, many of them sailboats dotted the near horizon. The marina was bustling with amateur and professional sailors, and all types of boats were moored along the neat wooden docks.

Lake Ontario is the smallest of the Great Lakes water system, but that doesn't mean it isn't huge. In fact, it is a vast body of water that from shore gives the impression of an ocean. Yes, that was how enormous the Great Lakes were. It was the last in the massive lake chain that drained into the Atlantic Ocean via the St. Lawrence River.

Suddenly Tommy interrupted my musings. He tapped my forearm and urged me into the shade of a sprawling tree. "Hey, what gives?" I demanded.

Tommy adjusted his round-framed sunglasses. "Sun hurts my eyes. Damned nearsightedness. Had to give up swimming because of these things."

"You could wear contacts."

"Nah. My eyes are too bad. They don't make contacts that thick. And I'm a lousy candidate for LASIK eye surgery."

"Sorry, Tommy."

He shrugged. "I'm not. Not really. I wouldn't have such a great job if it weren't for these eyes. I'd still be trying to be an Olympic swimmer. And how far do you think I'd get with that? Not too many people make a living as Olympians."

True. A smile worked its way through the scowl. Tommy had a way of seeing the silver lining on everything. He was a pleasure to work with. We often collaborated on the reconstruction of broken pottery before I took up the illustrator's pen. He was a gifted photographer, and made step-by-step visual records of our work. The thick glasses did not affect this skill at all.

"Did you manage to reconstruct the rest of that cupid

fresco?" I asked.

I watched him pull out his smartphone from his back pocket. He tapped the screen, flipping until he landed on a completed image.

"Wow. That's perfect. You filled in the missing parts."

Tommy had taken a year of photojournalism but changed majors in his second year. His current specialty was computer metrics. He was one of those rare technological geniuses that compiled data from broken artifacts and digitally reconstructed the missing parts. He also reimagined facial features and body forms from dinosaur and hominid skeletons. I had been struggling with what this fresco might have looked like on its original wall. Tommy had made it happen.

"Look. Can you keep a secret, Lucy? I want to show you something. But you can't tell anyone about it."

"Sure. What's up?" He started to flip through his photos. Maybe he had a crush on some girl and was going to show me her picture? If I were to guess I would say it was Emily, the cute physics geek whose specialty was the molecular analysis of artifacts.

In the next moment I knew it wasn't Emily. The recruits were familiar to me, except for one stranger on the team. She stepped up to us.

It was Tommy's reaction that made me do a double take. Bright-eyed, he opened his mouth—and literally lost his voice. Tommy had a crush on the conservator? Wasn't she ten to twelve years older than him?

"Hi," she said, ducking into the shade. "Mind if I join you? That sun is brutal."

She was attractive in a stiff and formal way. She mopped her face not with the back of her hand, but with a neatly folded tissue. "Tommy." She smiled. "Aren't you going to introduce us?"

I had heard of this person—from Italy, wasn't she? The specifics failed me at the moment. But clearly she and Tommy were acquainted.

Words choked in Tommy's mouth, and the woman extended a strong hand. "Marissa Leone. I'm a conservator. Fresco expert."

"Lucy Racine. Illustrator. Nice to meet you." I turned to Tommy who finally found his composure. "How do you know each other?"

"Met last year at a symposium," they said simultaneously.

I secretly smiled. Did Marissa know how Tommy felt about her? Seemed not.

At the dock Luke was calling the team together.

Tommy quickly stuffed his smartphone into his pocket. Out of my corner vision I caught a quick exchange of glances between the conservator and the photographer. So—I was wrong. Their interest in each other had nothing to do with romance. Just what was it he was going to show me before Marissa interrupted?

The distraction was momentary. Some of Luke's yacht crew was guiding the team towards a pair of inflatable Zodiacs.

I got into one along with Marissa, Tommy and the six other team members. We were told that guides would meet us on arrival, and assign us rooms. After that we would assemble in the main meeting area where Dr. Trevanian would brief us on the expedition.

The wind and lake spray felt fabulous on my face. My hair whipped any which way like it had a life of its own. A strand caught in my mouth and I spat it out. My eyes teared from the blustery gusts, and sheer excitement. Small ragged clouds scurried across the deep blue sky. Seagulls wheeled and shrieked. The sound of the motor drowned out the voices of my companions. As we neared I shoved my sunglasses over my hair and caught the name of the yacht:

Madonna

Why would Luke name his boat after a nineties pop star?

I had no time to mull over the question in detail. The Zodiac pulled up alongside a retractable launching platform and we boarded.

CHAPTER

<u>8</u>

The yacht resembled a floating hotel. It was constructed from steelcraft and white fiberglass, with chrome fittings. The decks were of glossy cherry wood. The design was ultra-modern and all the furnishings were of the latest colors and design.

We were given stateroom numbers and were then divided up, two archaeology team members for every crewmember. Marissa Leone and I followed our guide, one of Luke's senior crew, down the companionway, through a corridor to find our individual cabins.

When I walked into my designated room I stood mesmerized. It was a spacious suite with a master bedroom, a sitting room and a marble and glass bathroom with both a standup shower and a spa-sized soaking tub.

Had I died and ended up in a dream?

The bedroom had a king-sized bed and was decorated with luxurious black, grey and white pillows overtop a thick duvet in white and grey. Pale, voluminous sheer curtains draped the oblong windows that let sweet, yellow daylight onto the bed and across the hardwood floors.

Surely, Luke had not intended this to be my room? It looked more like it should be *his* room. I suddenly had an uneasy thought. Did he mean for me to share a cabin with him? Oh, no. Not yet. We hardly knew each other. Yet, I have to admit part of me liked the idea.

I hurried to the wardrobe and swung open the double doors.

Nothing here but women's clothing. The beautiful black gown he had purchased for me today, and several unfamiliar though equally lovely gowns and dresses, hung from wooden hangers. Along the wall were shelves holding stylish shoes, hats and handbags. The ensembles were new and unworn. They were also insanely expensive according to the numbers on the price tags. And they were all in my size.

Inside an elegant white chest of drawers were my things, newly purchased. How had they delivered these items so quickly to the yacht?

Dr. Trevanian was full of surprises.

I breathed a sigh of relief when I saw no sign of his belongings, and then I experienced—maybe—a pinch of disappointment? I would have to get these contradictory feelings under control. Although, it did appear that he was less presumptuous than I had originally thought.

From a large mirror attached to an equally large vanity, the entire room was reflected back at me, making me feel small and out of place. I turned, dropped my handbag onto the bed, sat down beside it and fished out my smartphone to check the time.

A confident knocking sounded outside my cabin. When I answered it I saw Luke's long, trim form leaning against the doorjamb.

"Lucy," he said.

That one word—my name—sent thrills along my spine.

"Hope everything is to your liking?"

I nodded in wonder and then, perhaps even a little bit uncomfortably, answered. "Are all the rooms this big?"

He shook his head. "Only those for my VIPs."

I raised my eyes. "*I* am one of your VIPs?"

"Yes. I want you to know that everything is at your

disposal. The boat is outfitted with all the latest equipment and amenities. I have an on-deck swimming pool, multiple decks for sunbathing, a game room, movie theater, gym, spa and Jacuzzi. For shore excursions I've got jet skis, inflatable boats, a catamaran and a submarine. And of course a helipad in case of emergencies. It's going to be a two-weeklong trip before we reach the Amalfi Coast. I don't want you to get bored."

A submarine?

Holy cow.

I got my wits together and said, "I doubt if any of us are going to get bored. Actually, the only thing I'm really interested in is the lab."

"Are you sure?" he asked.

Of course, I was sure. It took me a second before I recognized the innuendo. At least he didn't wink at me. He remained standing at the door, didn't ask to come in, but also made no move to leave and show me the lab.

"I've missed you," he said.

"You just saw me an hour ago."

"That's what you do to me."

"Luke, you *do* realize that I don't believe a single word you're saying?"

"You're good for me, Lucy. You keep me grounded."

"Why, because I'm poor?"

He laughed. "Is that what you call it? The way you live? There must be something wrong with me then. You make me want what you have."

"And what exactly is that?"

"A family. Friends. People who care about you. Security."

"Security!" Maybe he *was* out of his mind. *Money* was what gave you security. And he had plenty of it. "If you call what I have 'security,' then you really *are* crazy."

"You *know* what I mean. You have people you can count on."

This was strange. Why were we standing in the corridor

talking about how lonely he was?

And yet when I looked into his eyes I could see that it wasn't entirely an act. There was something deep inside him that burned.

"Someone you can trust," he added.

I was beginning to feel uncomfortable. He talked about trust. *I* was the one who was unable to trust. I had no idea what his game was. Was there anything sincere in what he was telling me? Or was this a con game to get me into bed?

I was not averse to the latter. I just wanted him to be upfront. I wanted to know where I stood with him, but somehow I couldn't bring myself to ask.

He exhaled and smiled. "Sweet Lucy, I'm going to be quite honest with you. There *is* a reason I brought you aboard. I just can't tell you what it is right now. Come on, we're late. We'll talk about it later."

He turned to go and I grabbed his arm. He swung back to face me and I dropped my hand as I realized how the gesture must seem from an outside perspective. I hadn't meant to touch him.

He looked down at me, his lids lowered and his eyes anticipatory.

"You aren't into BDSM, are you?" I asked.

He jerked as though he were startled. "What?"

I blushed. I wouldn't put it past him. He was certainly keen on dominance and bullying. "Look, Luke. You made it quite clear, by buying me clothes and giving me this room—just *why* you want me here." I waved my hand spasmodically at the luxurious suite, pointed to the king-sized bed and the opulence surrounding us. I even had my own private deck, I suddenly realized, as a breeze swept in through the open window casting the curtain aside and revealing a beautiful, pristine cherry wood deck with deckchairs and potted palms and ferns. I was flushing furiously now, and I was furious with myself for doing so. I am not a prude. I've had my fair share of lovers but I usually waited until at least the third date before spending the night. I liked to know who I was sleeping with—in case they turned out to be weird or something.

But I wasn't about to go explaining this to him. No—what really got my goat was the fact that I couldn't figure out, why me? I was nothing like his ex, the sophisticated, gorgeous Arianna Chase. There were shiploads of girls—women—who could give him what he wanted. Why, in Italy, they were famous for their buxom, suntanned, cat's-eyed beauties. How could I measure up?

"Is that why you think I brought you along?" He laughed. "Well, okay, I'll admit, I didn't include you on my team because of your drop-dead, stunning good looks."

Should I be insulted?

"Although I have to admit you have enticingly creamy skin... As for the whips and handcuffs, well I guess that would be up to you."

Now, I wasn't only insulted but I was beginning to feel embarrassed.

"Do you want to sleep with me, Lucy?"

"I didn't say that."

"But everything you are saying, your body language is telling me: Yes."

"Well, you're reading it wrong."

"Am I?"

He stepped up closer to me so that I could almost feel the heat of his body. I could smell the sandalwood of his aftershave. He was dressed in t-shirt and casual slacks, and deck shoes.

"Just tell me why I'm here," I said, stepping back.

"I need you."

I hesitated. I was not going to make the same mistake I had made a moment ago. Was this about sex? I had no idea.

"For what?"

"To keep me grounded."

He turned and I was staring at his back.

"Coming?" he asked, swinging around.

CHAPTER
9

A few days later I was back at the lab alone. After the official tour of the boat the team had become quite comfortable, and as we weren't yet officially on the job, most were taking advantage of the yacht's amenities.

The lab facilities were impressive. Everything was shiny and new and state-of-the art. I had my own studio area for illustrating the finds.

To be honest I needed to find some clue as to why Luke Trevanian really wanted me here. I had thought that he just wanted a casual sex partner, but now that I had mused it over that answer seemed less likely. No matter how much I denied it, he was absolutely correct in assuming that I was attracted to him. And yet he was in no hurry to get me into his bed. He had made that perfectly clear. As a matter of fact he had practically humiliated me.

So it must be something else, something related to this expedition perhaps? The lab revealed no clues. After all we hadn't even arrived in Italy yet. We had only just left the St. Lawrence Seaway into the Atlantic. Luke had not been kidding when he said this yacht was fast. It was also remarkably smooth. I hardly felt like I was on a ship at all.

I was reviewing some literature about Positano when I

heard someone come in. I looked up and was about to say 'hello' when I noticed the furtive way the person was behaving. He was searching for something, opening drawers and cabinets ever so quietly. I would have risen to greet him if not for his odd behavior. What was he looking for?

From where I sat in the corner behind a row of computer stations I was hidden. But I could see the top of his head, and an occasional arm and shoulder as he poked through all the conspicuous places an individual could hide things.

The door opened and someone else came in. I debated whether or not to announce my presence.

"What do you think you're doing?" the second man said.

The voice caused the tiny hairs to rise along my arms. How strange. I raised my head just a bit to see who the voice belonged to, and caught a glimpse of a white captain's uniform and the flash of brass buttons.

The other person answered. "Just checking out my equipment."

I recognized the voice. I ducked my head around the monitor to verify the speaker. It was Tommy Buchanan all right. The captain had no reason to speak to Tommy that way. I was about to come to Tommy's defense, when Captain Spatz asked, "Why are you taking photographs of these cupboards and drawers with your phone? Your equipment is not locked away. It's on the counters."

"I'm just making a photo record of where I'll be working this summer," Tommy said innocently.

"If you want to remain part of this team, you would be wise to watch what you photograph."

Tommy fell silent; he looked nervous.

"Your friends are on the Lido deck. You should probably join them."

Tommy left the lab with the captain following closely behind him.

That was weird. Why would Luke care if Tommy was photographing the lab? Of course I was just as guilty as Tommy, having snuck into the lab to have a look around myself.

All was quiet now. I should leave. I suddenly felt the urge to be outside. Luke was hiding something from me. I knew it. And that strange scene in the lab between Tommy and the captain had me even more convinced. Leo Spatz seemed to involve himself closely in Luke's business. That in itself was odd. Was he one of Luke's closest confidants— next to Norman? It appeared so. Otherwise why did he think Tommy's photos of the yacht's lab would trouble Luke? The three of them were up to something. From what I had witnessed to date, Luke had an unusually personal relationship with his employees. As we got closer to Europe I suspected our trip to Positano would turn out to be more than a standard archaeology expedition.

I stuck my head outside the lab and looked both ways. If there *was* something they were hiding from the team, it would be somewhere other than here. The lab was unlocked twenty-four seven. What about Tommy? What did *he* know? Or think he knew? Surely it couldn't be anything bad?

Luke Trevanian was a well-respected archaeologist, albeit something of a celebrity. And since when was being famous a crime?

The coast was clear. I returned to the lab to straighten the books and pamphlets that I had removed from the library attached to the lab, and made my slow way back to the door. Along the way I checked out the cupboards and drawers that Tommy had photographed. Really, there was nothing suspicious about them or their contents at all.

I closed the door when I left and studied the empty corridor. Everyone was on the Lido deck. I didn't feel like swimming, sunbathing or drinking, so I climbed the companionway until I reached a door to the upper deck. A blast of fresh wind slapped me backwards, causing me to grab hold of the sides of the door. I hauled myself upright and braced against the gusts, then made my way outside. A quilt of white cloud sped across the blue sky, and I saw nothing beyond the rail except water.

I went to the rail to view the sea. It really was beautiful. Nothing for miles except sparkling grey-blue water. Someone came up beside me and I flinched.

"Hey," the man said. He was one of the crew, no one I knew or had been introduced to. He wore the standard Trevanian t-shirt emblazoned with a large T. He had a short, patchy beard and light grey eyes, and wore his hair shorn to the scalp. A gold ring hung from his right ear. "Haven't seen you here before."

"My first time on the yacht," I answered pleasantly. I was doing my best to keep my voice from betraying my nervousness. Something about this man made me wary.

"What are you doing up here by yourself? Passengers generally don't use this deck."

"Sorry. I'll leave."

"Oh, you don't have to leave." He put a hand on my arm. "The name's Spelnick. But you can call me Freddie. I like your body."

"What?" Reflex caused me to snatch my arm back.

"I like your body. You have a nice shape, like an hourglass. If you like I can show you around."

This man was creepy. Who said stuff like that to a stranger? He was beginning to scare me. The expression on his face was unpleasant. Why would Luke hire someone like him?

He leaned his bony back against the rail. He was medium height and thin. Wiry. His eyes were pale. Soulless. Completely without depth or warmth. People like this were unreadable. Or maybe there was nothing to read. What you saw was what you got.

"You're *pretty*."

"Look," I said, hoping to sound assertive. "I just came out here for some fresh air. If you don't mind, I'd like to be alone."

"What's bugging you? Shit, lady. I just said you were pretty. Don't you like it when people call you pretty?"

I was kind of speechless and flustered. I wanted to get

out of there. Clearly, this crewman had no idea that I was with Luke. I frowned at the thought. *Was* I with Luke? Where was he anyway? He'd made himself scarce since this morning.

"Look," I said. It's true the man hadn't exactly done anything wrong. Other than touch me. I was the one being rude. And yet gooseflesh was prickling up my arms. "I don't mean to be rude but I would like to be left alone."

His face took on a mean expression. His thoughts were masked behind a sneer. He was blatantly looking down my blouse.

"The captain is looking for you." The softly accented French voice had come from behind me, and I gasped as I felt a solid presence move up between us. I jerked my head to look. Luke's bodyguard Norman Depardieu towered over us. He shot an eye up towards the bridge.

"What the fuck did I do now," Spelnick grumbled.

Norman shrugged. "Maybe it's got something to do with your language. Better go up there and find out." He watched the back of the crewman disappear through the door, then turned to me. He studied my face. "Sorry about his potty mouth. You okay?"

I swallowed, and moved my head up then down.

"You probably shouldn't wander around the crew's decks on your own."

"This is the crew's deck?"

He nodded. "That jerk is a new recruit. Spatz hired him last minute to replace someone who was sick. Don't think Luke's even met him."

I squeezed my fists together to get the blood back into them. Funny how anxiety made your hands go cold. "Well, thank you for rescuing me."

"*Hé.* No problem."

He moved away and stood staring out over the wide expanse of sea.

Thank God he had appeared when he had. I know I was one of his least favorite persons but it was nice of him to save me. My impulse now was to return indoors. But his very presence stopped me. Why did the sight of him make me feel this way? Like something wasn't quite finished. I can't even describe what I was feeling, other than awkward. But I wanted to talk to him.

I inhaled. We should be friends.

His hand was resting on the rail and he had just lighted a cigarette when I approached. He blew out a puff of smoke as I moved up beside him and propped myself against the rail on my arms, looking seaward. He glanced down through his eyelashes at me. His expression was anticipatory as though he expected me to comment on his smoking. I made a sincere effort to resist.

"*Eh bien.* What happened?" he asked after a few moments of silence. "Did you get lost? How did you end up here?" His vision darted toward the spot where that crewman had accosted me. Norman Depardieu had incredibly beautiful eyelashes.

"No, I didn't get lost. I came out here on purpose."

"*Alors.* Were you looking for something?"

"Not particularly. I just wanted to be outside."

He looked away like that would encourage me to leave, and then leaned heavily onto the rail, with his arms crossed and chin down. "It would have been easier to go out onto the passenger decks. The exits are clearly marked," he said.

"I didn't know this deck was prohibited."

"It's not. But the crew uses it. You'd feel more comfortable where the sundecks and the pool are located."

I shrugged. I wanted to change the subject. "So, you like being on the water?" I asked lightly.

He grunted.

"I *love* being on the water."

"Yeah, I can see that."

I tapped his shoulder and when he ignored it, I left my hand on the huge muscles there. It was extremely hypocritical of me to be so familiar with him, because that crewman who was hitting on me gave me the creeps, but I wanted desperately for Norman's handsome face to turn to me.

His eyes flicked over and rested on my hand.

"Stop flirting with me, Lucy," he said bluntly.

I was appalled that he thought I was doing that. "I am *not* flirting with you."

His eye dropped to the fingers that were still resting on his massive shoulder. "Then what is *that* all about?"

I yanked away instantly. My face was red. I knew it. He was such a jerk. That was nothing. "People touch each other as a gesture of friendship. It doesn't mean anything." I was making a sorry attempt to recover my dignity.

His face was blank except for a hint of amusement in the eyes. His lips twitched as though he were trying to suppress a smile. He drew on his cigarette before crushing the remains on the heel of his shoe and casting it overboard. "*Alors.* You want to be friends with me?"

I *thought* I did. But now I was having second thoughts. If we were going to work together, wasn't it better if we were friends?

He continued to observe me beneath the lowered lashes. He was making me squirmy and he knew it. "I'm Luke's bodyguard. You are Luke's—what?"

That accusation had me speechless. I had no idea what I was to Luke. I would like to say we were dating, but except for that pizza night in my apartment he hadn't exactly taken me out on a date. He *had* bought me a bunch of clothes though, not to mention that he'd practically abducted me and given me a suite on his boat fit for a celebrity.

"Why are you so—so—difficult?" I blustered. I was trying not to snap at him. After all he had just rescued me from a very unpleasant situation. But dammit he was so aloof. Why did he have to be that way? And why did I care so much? I tempered my voice. "I just think it would be nicer if we got along."

"Ah... *Je vois.* I think we get along fine."

I huffed. He was not going to get away with this. He had

a way of pushing my buttons. I wished I would not react. So, that act of chivalry earlier, what was that? Just him doing his job? Was he just doing Luke a favor, and looking out for me in his boss's absence? Unfortunately my impulses always got their way. Words came out of my mouth before I could stop them. "Why don't you like me, Norman?"

His eyes went to mine and stayed there. "Why do you need to be liked, Lucy?"

"I do not *need* to be liked. I just thought since you and Luke are so close it would be nice to know you better."

He was silent for a moment. He waited as though I was supposed to elaborate. "So now that you do, what do you think?"

I frowned, frustrated. Norman Depardieu was impossible. "I think you are not a touchy-feely person. You hate being asked questions, and you especially hate being asked questions by me."

He nodded. "Correct on all counts…. Congratulations."

Okay, fine. That was the last time I would try. He was determined to shut me down. I threw up my hands like a drama queen. "What is your *problem?*"

I turned and walked away. But just as I did I swore he answered.

"*You.*"

I swung back, but he was staring out to sea.

I returned indoors. The man was infuriating. Was it so hard just to be nice?

Why did he have to be so complicated?

Why did *I* have to like him?

Well, one thing he was right about. I was totally turned around. And by that I mean definitely lost. Where was the lab again? Better yet. Where was my room? After my stint of eavesdropping I wasn't so sure I wanted to go back to the lab. Next time I would have to be more careful to announce myself. Sometimes the things you overheard were not things you wanted to know. All it had done was increase my suspicions of Luke. And I didn't want to suspect him of any wrongdoing.

I wandered around for about an hour, trying to retrace my steps. *Yeah, that is how big this yacht is.* And that was how distracted I had become. Norman Depardieu was exasperating. I was tempted to text Luke on my cellphone to ask directions. I wandered further and suddenly stopped. Finally, something looked familiar.

A door was ajar as I passed by and I could see the interior of Luke's office. It appeared to be unoccupied. I knocked.

Was Luke working inside? I felt the need for his company. I wanted his reassurance that he wasn't involved in anything unlawful. His twilight world of antiquities trading was sometimes borderline illicit. I had no idea how far he would go to get what he wanted.

I knocked again. When no one answered on the third try I shoved the door wider. I was curious to see his office.

I glanced around. I stood on the threshold, hedging. Should I go in? But then I heard voices around the corner and panicked.

Oh no, Norman again. And, I think, a woman. Her voice was vaguely familiar. Or maybe I was just imagining it. Of the male voice I was certain. I had left Norman Depardieu, not more than an hour ago, and recognized the slight French accent. I swear if I never had to face him again it would be too soon. And yet I could listen to his voice forever. That lazy foreign drawl was impossibly sexy.

They were getting closer. Any minute they would catch me like a peeping Tom.

I ducked into the office and hid behind the first piece of furniture I came to—a desk.

A rap came at the door. The last thing I needed was to make excuses to Norman one more time.

Norman spoke. "Hey boss, you in there?"

His head appeared for a moment, and then vanished.

To my horror I heard a *snap* as the lock shot into place. Now what? Surely I could leave even if no one else could enter? I started for the door and saw that it was one of those digital locks. That meant you needed a magnetic card key to get in, but merely had to depress the lever on the inside to exit.

I was about to do just that when I glimpsed something familiar on the nearby desk. I straightened and went over to investigate. Could it be...? I had seen this letterhead before. It was the same blue and white letterhead I had recognized on Shaun's desk back at the museum. And it concerned the same artifact. The Black Madonna.

I tried to rewind and recall the correspondence addressed to my brother-in-law. All I remembered was that it was an artifact stolen about fifteen years ago from a church on the Amalfi Coast, the church of Santa Maria Assunta. The artifact was never found. It was also valued at eleven million American dollars. Why did both Luke and Shaun have a letter from Interpol?

My eyes widened. Was it my imagination or was it odd that we should be headed to the Amalfi Coast to dig up frescos?

Then I noticed something else. The top drawer to the desk was slightly opened. The glint of metal caught my eye. I slid the drawer out and found myself staring at a bright, shiny revolver. I have never seen a real gun so what the make or caliber was I don't know. Nor did I want to know.

The only question on my mind was: Why did Luke need a gun?

Footsteps stopped at the door. Someone was coming in! I had to hide. Luke mustn't find me here.

A sofa sat at the other end of the room. I tiptoed quickly around the desk and darted over the plush carpet, nearly tripping before I slipped silently behind the oversized furniture. The door opened. Someone walked in, but the footsteps were light. So light that it made me think that whoever it was did not belong here. Come to think of it, they had made somewhat of a fuss entering. The locking mechanism had been tampered with. Had they owned a keycard, the lock would have snapped open immediately. Some rustling came from the far corner where the desk was located. I had to take a chance and see who it was. Not Luke. He wouldn't be moving around his own office so stealthily.

I recognized the shoulder-length brunette waves of the fresco expert who had introduced herself as Marissa Leone. What was she doing? Why was she snooping in Luke's desk? Whatever her business, her stay was short. The door *snicked* shut, and I lifted my head to make sure she was gone. The room was silent.

I crept out from my hiding place. That was close, too close. Now to get out of here without being seen. As I made to leave, curiosity got the better of me and I swept an eye over Luke's desk. The letter from Interpol was gone!

While I stood there in a genuine stupor, the door opened and in walked Luke. I remained where I was, dumbfounded and off-guard.

"Lucy? What are you doing in my office?"

My mouth was open. I froze. I literally froze.

He glanced at his desktop, frowned.

My heart was beating against my throat, my pulse rapid. My mouth was dry and my legs felt weak. I wished I were anywhere but here. All I could think about was the gun in his desk. He already had his hand on the drawer.

"Sweetheart, you look like you're going to faint. What's the matter? What happened?"

He led me to the sofa and sat me down. His hands felt like ice or maybe it was mine that felt like ice. All blood had drained out of my face and my extremities. My head felt heavy. A pounding reverberated inside my ears. How much did I know about this man, honestly? I was torn, had always been torn, from the beginning. I should have heeded the uncomfortable feeling in the pit of my stomach when I first met him.

Lots of people purchased firearms. It didn't mean anything. It was just that I had never known anyone who owned one. Except in movies and on book covers I had never seen a real gun.

Luke's surmise was correct. If I didn't calm down I was going to faint. I was hyperventilating.

"Let me get you a glass of water," he said.

At the bar in the corner, he opened a small refrigerator beneath the counter to retrieve a bottle of Perrier. The cap popped off. He poured half of its contents into a crystal glass. "Here, drink this. You'll feel better. I didn't mean to scare you. Are you all right? You're white as a sheet."

I was certain that I was. And that was no cliché.

I sipped the bubbly water, trying not to choke on the effervescence. Gradually, I felt more myself.

I was still suspicious of him, but it didn't appear he was going to shoot me for breaking into his office.

"Were you looking for me?" he asked.

He was giving me an out. If I were smart I would take it. I nodded.

"About anything in particular?"

My head wagged back and forth, almost of its own accord. My ears were ringing and the hand I gripped on the glass was slightly trembling.

"Poor Lucy," he said. "It's okay, honey. I'm not angry. Stop looking like I am going to hurt you." He paused. "How did you get in here?"

What could I say? That I was snooping around because I suspected he was up to no good? What would my excuse for jumping to such a conclusion be? And what had I intended to do about it anyway had I learned it to be true? It made no sense.

The water in the green, glass Perrier bottle began to swirl impatiently in his hand. I had to give him an explanation. I had none. I had to say something. *Anything.*

Nothing was better than the truth.

"It was unlocked," I stammered. "I knocked and when no one answered I went in."

"Fair enough," he said. "You were curious. You wanted

to learn something about me." He paused. I waited. "Did it change your mind?"

I frowned. "Sorry?"

"Did it change your mind about me? You saw something that scared you." His face suddenly softened in enlightenment. Briefly, his glance flickered toward the desk. As it landed once again on me I observed just how green his eyes were. His head nodded slightly. "Oh, I see. You saw the gun... It's okay, Lucy. I'm not a terrorist." He laughed.

My breathing was coming easier now. It was not like there was a body anywhere. I took one last sip of the water, and placed the glass down on the coffee table. "Why do you need a gun?" I asked.

He shrugged, set the bottle down beside my water glass. "I don't know that I do. But it's always better to be safe than sorry."

That didn't make me feel much better.

"Now answer my question."

"I didn't mean to snoop, Luke. I..." I was going to explain about the letterhead, but then I realized I'd have to explain what drew me to it in the first place. Instead I asked, "Why is your boat called the 'Madonna'?"

He watched me swallow. I reached forward and took another sip of the fizzy water. He seemed to muddle something over in his mind. It was as though he suspected I knew something. He just wasn't sure what it was. I saw again that hint of vulnerability that had made me trust him in the first place, when every nerve in my body had warned me not to.

"You saw the letter," he accused.

Unblinkingly, I stared at him, said nothing.

His eyes flickered briefly to the desk. "Did you take it? It's missing."

I shook my head. I felt dizzy. The vibrating of the ship's engines seemed to have stopped. Or maybe I just thought they had because all of the blood in my body had drained to my core. A horrible wave of vertigo threatened to topple me.

It felt like the yacht was changing tack.

Luke's head jerked faintly, like he had noticed something too, before he glanced back at me. "What are you afraid of, Lucy? I told you I am not going to shoot you. I'm not even particularly upset that you were snooping in my office. I have nothing to hide from you. I don't *want* to hide anything from you. What do you know, or think you know that has frightened you so much?"

At that moment Captain Spatz appeared at the door.

"Leo," Luke said, glancing up.

"Sorry, Luke. Am I interrupting anything?" He appeared disturbed, controlling some frustrated emotion.

Luke answered sharply, "A little. What is it?"

"There's been an accident. One of your team has fallen overboard."

CHAPTER
10

The yacht's engines were cut before we arrived on deck. The ship was as still as it could be with the water moving under her. Most of the archaeology team bunched up at the rail. The sailing crew was busy lowering an inflatable Zodiac into the open ocean, with Norman Depardieu overseeing the rescue from the deck. Life preservers had already been tossed overboard. The orange lifesavers were floating loose.

I scanned the vast, aquamarine sea.

Who was it?

Snatches of conversation drifted over to me, and my heart gave a flip. I learned that the figure overboard was Tommy. Tommy Buchanan from the museum!

Fortunately, he was a fine swimmer. He used to be on the university swim team. Now that my head had cleared of hysterics and I was thinking more rationally, I noted that he was moving.

He managed to swim to one of the floats and clung to it. I imagine he was frightened out of his wits. Yet he possessed the presence of mind to save himself and keep afloat. From this distance and with the sun in my eyes it was impossible to see his expression, but by the frantic way he was waving his free hand I knew he was close to panic.

He was in the middle of the Atlantic. He might have been abandoned in the cold waters, the yacht sailing swiftly eastward, sending him west had he not been spotted. He was drifting further from the ship with every passing moment due to the backwash. That creepy crewman, what was his name? Freddie Spelnick, had a pair of binoculars fixed on him, and everyone else was doing their part to keep him in sight. Except for the waves from the yacht's last maneuver the sea was calm.

"What happened?" Luke demanded of the captain.

"Not sure," Spatz answered, his voice authoritative amidst the confusion. "From what I was told, your team was having drinks on the deck. Just a few beers and light cocktails. Maybe your boy had one brew too many. You know how these jokers can be. Showing off to the girls, probably sat on the rail and fell off."

Luke frowned. I frowned too. Captain Spatz's off-the-cuff explanation was harsh.

I turned my attention away when I felt Luke's eyes land on me. I reddened at my thoughts. How could I think he was Tommy's assailant? And what reason would he have to push one of the museum techs overboard? And why did I think Tommy was pushed? His steady gaze on my face wasn't helping. Finally he turned back to the rail. He stared solemnly seaward. Clearly he was disturbed. Who could blame him? I was ready to believe the worst of him—

The yacht's crew was down on the water in the inflatable Zodiac motorboat. Each was equipped with red life vests. No matter how expert a swimmer any of them were, everyone in the Zodiac in open water was required to wear a vest.

They headed toward the victim who was continuing to wave a hand. They reached him, and hauled him on board. He was settled into the bow, the life preserver looped over his head to hang around his neck. They were taking no chances of losing him again.

The pilot effortlessly spun the rescue craft around. They made it back to the yacht.

In the shadow of the hulking craft, Captain Spatz returned to his post to watch. Norman reached down. His massive sun-browned muscles helped Tommy climb the ladder from the launching platform to the yacht's deck. Spatz ordered the two rescuers back to the water to retrieve the lost life preservers.

"Are you okay, son?" Spatz asked, as Norman released the young man's arm. "Get this boy a towel!"

"I'm fi…fi…fine," Tommy stuttered.

The young man was breathing roughly, his teeth chattering, legs unsteady. His dark hair was plastered to his skull making his eyes appear enormous and bright. His skin was disturbingly pale.

His clothing, a short-sleeved shirt and mustard khaki's, was heavily waterlogged. They clung in wrinkled folds to his body. Seawater dripped down his arms and legs forming a messy pool on the floor. He was barefooted and standing in the puddled water.

He was still shaken. Who wouldn't be after an accident like that? His eyes moved from the captain to Luke. His vision stayed fixed there, and it was obvious he wished that someone other than himself had the spotlight.

"Glad you're okay" Luke said. "After you towel down and get into dry clothes, go to my office. Do you know where that is?" He gave brief directions.

Tommy wiped his wet hair out of his eyes, and answered, "I'll find it."

The entire assembly waited on deck. All of the crew and the archaeology team were present. "Did any of you see what happened?" Luke demanded.

A few members of the archaeology team nodded.

"Okay. Talk. You first." This was aimed at a young woman in a neon pink bikini top and white shorts. She had caught Norman's attention. His watchful eye had swiveled simultaneously with mine but lingered longer than necessary. It was virtually impossible to ignore the screaming bright color of her top, and yet politeness required that we focus on her face. I recognized her from the museum. She had a physics background and was a specialist in the molecular analysis of artifacts.

"What's your name?" Luke asked.

"Emily. Emily Chow."

"All right, Ms. Chow. What happened?"

"We were all sitting over there—" She pointed to poolside where yellow-striped upholstered, white-painted, cast aluminum deckchairs were neatly arranged around the oval of the turquoise swimming pool. She hugged the frosted glass she still held in her hand. The drink looked like orange juice poured over ice—or if it had alcohol in it, it was a screwdriver. "Tommy was the only one not sitting with us. He was over by the rail."

"How did he fall in?"

She hesitated. She twirled a lock of her shoulder-length, black hair around her finger, her confidence fading. "Um, that part I didn't see." She glanced at her colleagues for confirmation. "Some sort of fog drifted in. It didn't last long, but the next time I looked he was gone."

"We heard a splash," someone else said. I turned to see who it was. The person whose name was Jackson Shriver was a museum technician who worked for Shaun, my brother-in-law. He studied material science and did analyses of old paintings, ceramics and frescoes. He told Luke that he was probably the person nearest to Tommy when he went over. "Then I found this on the floor." He held an iPhone in his hand. It was the latest version. "It's Tommy's."

"So, none of you actually saw him fall in?"

The captain leaned forward. He seemed particularly keen on their answers at this point.

They shook their heads.

Luke frowned. He was only just beginning to accept how green some of the recruits were. They ranged in age from twenty-three to thirty something, with me one of the oldest at thirty. Many had never worked in the field; they were museum technical and computer specialists from the ROM.

The only member of the team who was a stranger to me was Marissa Leone. She came from a different museum. She was mid thirties, possibly older.

"Let's get this clear, right now," Luke said. He confiscated the phone from the young man and shoved it into his pocket. "This is not summer camp, nor are you in a hotel. We are on the open ocean. We were lucky this time. The quick thinking of Captain Spatz stopped the boat before we got too far out of range. We were fortunate the weather was in our favor. The backwash alone could have sent Tommy so far out to sea we'd never have located him without aerial surveillance. By that time it might have been too late."

Everyone was cowed. Luke was clearly frustrated that he had to put a damper on things. As Luke continued his tirade—he was clearly upset by the incident—I realized that Captain Spatz had retreated to the sidelines to stand beside me. Leo Spatz may be the captain, but the yacht and all of its passengers were the billionaire's responsibility. We were behind Luke facing the audience of team members, resting our backs against the bulkhead in the shade. Spatz wore a short-sleeved, dress uniform shirt that came almost to his elbows. He shot a reassuring smile at me beneath his captain's cap and I smiled back. All that was visible because of the shadow of his cap was his mouth.

Luke's agitation had me unnerved. All the while he was talking and the tech team was explaining, I had a queer sinking feeling. I barely knew Luke Trevanian. What was he doing with a gun? When Captain Spatz came to his office to report the accident, my first thought was that the victim had been shot, then tossed lifeless into the sea. Why did my mind keep returning to the gun in Luke's drawer? What was the connection with the two Interpol letters? The adrenalin in my system was escalating to high alert…. If he had involved Shaun in some black market activities…

I slammed down hard on that thought.

I should have touched the gun to see if it was hot. If it was hot that meant it had been fired. Why did I think it had been fired? Why was I speculating that Tommy had been shot at and that that was how he'd ended up overboard? But none of that had happened. No one heard a gunshot. No one was dead.

"Are you feeling all right, Ms. Racine?" the captain asked. "You're looking kind of pale."

"I'm fine Captain Spatz," I said. "It's all the excitement. It was just a shock that someone fell overboard in the middle of the ocean."

Spatz's capped head bobbed slightly. "Shouldn't have happened. Those kids are going to have to be more careful. This is a goddam ship, not a hotel."

"I'm sure he didn't mean for it to happen."

Spatz gave me a gentle nod. "Didn't mean to sound harsh. It's just that we have enough to do around here without having to babysit, too."

"Well, I'm sure after this incident, the team will be more careful."

"Hope so."

He went silent. He returned his focus to Luke. Luke had finished his reprimand and was looking around for us. His eyes landed on the captain and me, before he swung back to his subdued audience.

"Okay, I want you to enjoy yourselves, but please refrain from climbing on the rails. That's what they're there for—to keep you from falling into the sea."

Some low grumbling began. Luke ignored it as he made to return indoors. His head turned sharply to the right. He glanced at me. "Lucy. Come with me." His attention switched to the left. "Norman. You too…. And Leo, if you wouldn't mind," he said to Captain Spatz, "I'd appreciate your presence in my office as well."

The others followed Luke indoors. I hesitated still experiencing the residual thrill of fear. The fear was morphing into a distinct feeling of foolishness. How could I think Luke had shot at Tommy? What motive could he possibly have to shoot him? I felt I owed him an apology.

But unless I confessed what I had suspected, an apology would be absurd. Besides, I was curious to learn the real reason Tommy fell overboard.

I'll admit I have a soft spot for Tommy. He's such a nice boy. I probably shouldn't call him a boy. He was a young man. But there was something very boyish about him that brought out the 'mommy' in me, despite the fact that I was only seven years older than him. He had soft features, almost unformed, with a body to match. Too much computer time had atrophied his muscles. Now that he had given up swimming because of vision issues, the oversized eyeglasses gave him a Harry Potter look. It also didn't help that he personally perpetuated the nickname of Tommy rather than graduating to the more mature 'Tom' or 'Thomas.'

He was very talented and not at all prone to recklessness. I knew, for a fact, that he did not drink. His mother was an alcoholic.

So, how had he fallen overboard?

CHAPTER
11

Even though Luke had left the door wide open Tommy had not entered, and was waiting for us outside the office door. He was in dry clothes, another short-sleeved shirt and, this time, dark green cargo pants. Although his hair was still damp and lay slightly rumpled from being towel-dried, clearly, no comb had touched it.

Nothing appeared unusual concerning his behavior until he saw us approach. Only then did he stiffen. His eyes shifted from Captain Spatz to me, like he was attempting to relay some message that I failed to receive.

"Go in," Luke said, and gestured with a hand for the three of us to precede him, while Norman waited for his boss before he followed.

Tommy entered the office and shot quick, sharp glances around the spacious room. Luke waved him toward the sofa and armchairs at the far end by the bar. The sofa was one of those huge over-stuffed pieces of furniture with a collection of decorative, neutral-toned pillows layered systematically in a neat row. I sat down among the plump cushions of the sofa, and Tommy and Captain Spatz each took one of the armchairs, while Norman remained standing within hearing range.

Tommy's lips looked a bit blue. He was probably still cold from his recent submersion in the Atlantic and, like most males, refused to admit it.

"Do you want a hot drink, Tom?" I asked.

"Yes, please." His eyes pleaded with me but I had no idea what they were trying to say. I glanced around for a coffeemaker.

At the bar Luke was busy pouring two fingers each of expensive scotch whiskey into a trio of crystal glasses. He added a splash of water to all three and raised one toward me and one at Tommy. He did not offer Norman or his captain a drink; I suppose because the bodyguard and Spatz were both considered 'on duty.'

"This'll warm you up."

The young man lifted a hesitant hand at Luke in objection.

Luke arched a brow. "No?"

Out of the corner of my eye I caught the boxy shape of a Tassimo coffee maker on the bar. I rose, and placed my whiskey glass onto an end table. I said, "I'll make you some coffee."

Luke set Tommy's glass, untouched, back on the bar out of his sight. "So, can I take it that you *weren't* drinking out there?"

"No, sir. I mean… I mean I wasn't drinking. Not alcohol anyways."

"You don't have to call me 'sir'."

"No, sir… I mean, No," he said.

"How did you happen to fall off the boat?"

Several creases lined Tommy's forehead. "Well, that's the strange thing. I don't really know." He took in a deep breath. The boy was nervous. He was avoiding eye contact with everyone. Especially Captain Spatz. Something was bothering him. Was he humiliated that he'd caused the yacht to change course to pick him up? It was true he had inconvenienced the expedition and made something of a fool of himself—since the last thing Luke Trevanian needed was to chaperone a group of feckless young folk—but Tommy's reluctance to speak seemed more like fear than humiliation.

"Were you on the rail?"

"Not exactly."

"Exactly what *were* you doing?"

"I was taking some pictures with my phone. I saw a really huge bird, thought it might be an eagle. Unusual to see something like that so far out to sea. And yes, I admit I was leaning slightly over the rail, but not far enough to fall over. And then... it was really strange." He paused to catch his breath. A barely imperceptible glance darted in the direction of Spatz. Beyond the captain was Norman's muscular form blocking the exit. Was he looking at him?

He continued explaining, his voice puzzled. "A sort of mist came in from the sea, blinding me. Then I felt something...I'm not sure what...like something hit me. Or maybe it was vertigo. I blacked out. That's when I must have fallen overboard. Luckily the cold water woke me up instantly—or I would have drowned."

"Tommy was on the swim team in university," I elaborated. I was trying to explain his proficiency in the water, why he had beaten the odds of drowning. I should have said more, delved deeper. His response sounded worse than unlikely. A mist? In the middle of a sunny day? Vertigo? Well, I guess that was possible. I myself was queasy with heights. Still, there was something uncharacteristic about his behavior. Everything pointed to a major secret, and I would give my eyeteeth to know what it was.

"Are you prone to fainting spells?" Luke asked. "Do you have some kind of medical condition?"

I understood why he was asking these personal questions. As leader of the expedition and owner of the yacht, he was responsible for every person on board, and was in fact legally liable for any harm that came to them. But did he have to be so cold?

"No. I don't have any medical problems. That's why it was so strange. Actually—it was a little scary."

"Don't worry about it," I said warmly to counteract Luke's lack of warmth. My hand reached out to reassure him. "It happens all the time. Especially when you're looking down from a great height." The yacht's sundeck was a fair height from the water.

"Is this your phone?" Luke asked. He dragged it out of his pocket and raised it.

Tommy reached out to reclaim it with unusual urgency, but Luke jerked it back. Out of my peripheral vision I saw Captain Spatz react.

"Mind if I keep it for awhile?"

"Why?" Tommy asked.

"I need to look at what you were photographing."

"If you give it to me I'll show you."

Our Tommy was an excellent photographer, and worked miracles at the museum, recording artifacts for posterity.

By now the coffee was ready and I brought the hot mug over.

"Thanks," he said. He took a few sips. His color returned and he was looking much better. His eyes lingered on me just a little longer than was comfortable.

I felt for certain that he wanted to talk to me, but was intimidated by the presence of these men. I hoped my encouraging expression confirmed to him my support.

Tommy opened his device, did something too quick for the eye to catch and surrendered the phone.

Luke was seated on the sofa, muddling over the photo gallery on Tommy's phone, while Spatz and I strained to see what he was doing. There were pictures of his dog, some selfies with friends, and the hurried snapshots he'd taken of the yacht's archaeology lab. A few sky shots with a large bird. So he was telling the truth about that. Luke's thumb flipped back and forth through these images swiftly and without interest. Suddenly, he stopped.

"What's the matter, Luke?" Maybe it was my imagination but I could swear Spatz moved in closer. "See something?" the captain asked.

To Tommy Luke instructed, "Send this photo to my device."

Tommy accepted his phone, glanced at the image. "I don't remember taking this picture."

He was lying. Why? He glanced up swiftly. His thumbs tapped away and I heard the distinctive *swish* as the item was sent.

"You can go," Luke said. "Take the coffee with you. And shut the door."

When Tommy was gone, Luke turned his attention to Spatz. "So, what do you think?"

The captain was silent a few minutes. "It was obviously an accident. The kid had a dizzy spell." He shrugged. He hesitated as though he wanted to say something else, thought better of it and rose. "Need me for anything else, Luke? If not, I should get back to the helm."

Luke shook his head. Spatz left.

Norman spoke up. He deliberately avoided my eyes and focused on Luke. "Do you want me to stay, boss?"

"No," Luke said, and the bodyguard slipped through the exit but before he closed the door behind him, his gaze landed on me.

I was glad Norman was gone. He did strange things to my body. I was always too aware of his physical presence. So I never felt free to speak my mind.

Luke was deep in thought.

"What did you see among the photographs?" I asked.

He hedged for a moment then showed me.

CHAPTER
<u>12</u>

It was nothing as far as I could tell. He had opened his phone and selected the photo, a blurred image of someone's tattoo. A serpent or a snake? There was also a vague figure seated on top of it. Riding it? It must have belonged to a friend of Tommy's, and then I remembered Tommy's attempt to lie about having taken it.

"He must have slipped," I suggested. "And snapped that accidentally. Look how out of focus it is."

Luke shook his head. "No. I believe this was taken on purpose."

"You think so?" I frowned. "You should have asked him why he took that picture."

"I don't think he would have told me. I think he was in a hurry. And he wanted to keep it a secret."

I took the phone from him and examined the photograph again. It reminded me of something. Oh my God. It reminded me of that man in Arianna's office. If that man wasn't Luke or Norman, who was he? Why was he there? Arianna Chase, the director of my museum, was Luke Trevanian's estranged wife. What was she up to? One thing was certain. If Tommy had taken this picture deliberately, it had been done in a rush. And he had tried to avoid getting caught in the act.

No logical connection sprang to my mind, and I was afraid to discuss my suspicions with Luke. Who did this tattoo belong to? And why did it matter? The tattooed man in Arianna's office flashed in my memory once more. I trusted Luke less than I trusted Tommy. Until he gave me a reason to trust him I must remain cautious.

I passed over the phone. "Can I ask you something?" I asked.

"Sure."

"Why *did* you name your yacht, 'Madonna'?"

It was just the tiniest movement—and I was sure no one else would have noticed it, had there been anyone else to see—but he visibly flinched. He took so long to answer that I was able to slip in another question before he had formulated his lie. "Are you going to tell me why the name 'Madonna' bothers you so much? And since it does, why on earth did you name your boat after a nineties pop star?"

"I didn't."

"The Virgin Mary then."

"Who says it bothers me?" he asked.

"Your twitchy body language."

It was a nervous laugh that came out, a laugh that was meant to distract, and divert attention away from his true feelings. Then he realized that I wasn't fooled. "It's that obvious, is it...?"

I swear he almost wrung his hands. Only decades of practice and strict self-control prevented him from acting on his emotions.

"Only to me."

"God, I hope so."

"What's the matter, Luke?" He slumped against the plump cushions of the sofa beside me, disturbing the pillows. "You're wound up tighter than a guitar string."

He glanced over. "Tell me about it."

I twisted to see him better. He took my hands. His grip was firm and commanding. I tried to wipe my mind clean of the thoughts his touch provoked.

"You look pretty," he said.

I glanced down at my Capri pants and my tank top. "Are you mocking me?"

"No, I mean it."

His hands reached out and pulled me towards him. I stiffened. Why did this man simultaneously arouse me and frighten me. He brushed his knuckles down the side of my face, then along my throat. I was lost. Resistance was futile. No matter what my brain told me, my body believed the opposite.

Sensations of pleasure began to overtake common sense. To be truthful, I secretly ached for his attention. His domineering style was a turn-on. And by that I mean how he did what he wanted and took what he needed without asking first.

All of my earlier misgivings vanished. At the moment I longed to be told what to do. A quivering racked my body, and it thrilled me as much as it baffled me. For the first time in my life I forgot to question my impulses.

The time for talking had passed. Our lips locked in ecstasy and our tongues discovered each other's. Time stood still and I disappeared into the wonder of his kisses.

We broke free of one another at last and he looked darkly into my eyes. Then he lowered his head, and his lips crawled thrillingly down my throat to the space between my collarbones. His tongue played with the indentation there before continuing its exploration.

His mouth filled with my breast after he pulled the slipping strap of my tank top down to my ribs. I was not wearing a bra and maybe that was what had enticed him in the first place. I felt his leg slide between mine as his hands traversed my lower back. He rubbed his lips against my nipple and raised his head.

"You're right, I'm wound up tighter than a guitar string. And I have an idea how to release it. You have only to say the word, and I'll stop. If you don't stop me now, I won't be able to in the next few minutes."

He was not asking my permission. He was telling me that I had already consented.

He was right.

It was not the first time I had made love on a sofa. But it was the first time I had made love with a billionaire.

"Your skin is so soft," he murmured.

From my thigh all the way down my calves to my toes his hands travelled. He followed the same route with his lips and his tongue. When he reached my toes I gasped as the warm wetness of his mouth enveloped my first two digits.

It was all uphill from there. By the time he slid inside me with a force I knew he'd been containing, I was all his.

***

We lay spooned together on the plush cushions, my backside pressed into his groin while he nibbled my ear, before reaching over me to the coffee table to take his scotch glass. He downed the amber fluid in one swallow, and reached for mine and offered it to me. I took a small sip. It was velvety smooth and rich like candy. Our clothes were scattered on the floor.

"Penny for your thoughts?" he said.

"Only a penny?" I rolled over to prop myself up on one elbow and look him in the eyes.

"Okay, a million dollars. I'm sure your thoughts are worth at least that much." He grinned.

I smiled back.

"Well?"

"Well, what?"

"Why so pensive?"

I swallowed nervously.

The charming smile on his face masked so much of what I wanted to know. But one thing had set my mind at ease. He had no tattoos. "Why me?"

"Why not you?"

"You could have any woman you want. Why me?"

He sighed. "Because I find you easy to talk to. And I like

you, Lucy. I really like you."

I sat up and looked down at him. I had read somewhere that physically positioning yourself higher than someone else gave you more power. He was so beautiful with that suntanned skin and those rippling muscles that I wondered if it were true. He didn't seem to be under my power.

He sat up, forcing me to sit up further. I was suddenly conscious that I was naked and grabbed a pillow to cover myself.

"A little late to be bashful, Lucy."

I slugged him playfully with my fist right in the abs.

"Ouch," he said. "Remind me not to get on your bad side."

"I can't talk to you when we're naked. Get dressed."

"Not yet." He took a long swallow of the scotch whiskey that remained in my glass then pulled me over and turned me to lie against his chest. His lips teased my hair and he forced me to relax against his torso. "This is nice."

I had to admit it was. I released my hold on the pillow and let it fall to the side.

He nuzzled the top of my hair and rubbed a stray lock out of my face while the other hand rested flat against my belly. "I trust you, Lucy," he said. "Why do I trust you?"

I twisted around so that I could see his face. He looked truly confused. There was also a hint of strong emotion, just barely masked. What was it? Frustration? Anger? Why should trusting me make him angry?

He kissed my forehead and I could smell the liquor on his breath.

"*Should* I trust you, Lucy?" he asked.

My hand went to his cheek. "You can tell me anything, Luke. I promise whatever dark secret you have, it stays between us."

I was half-joking, half serious. Most people had secrets, but their secrets were nothing life-scarring. When plucked out of their hiding place and exposed to the world, these secrets were usually something quite mundane, and had more to do with feelings of humiliation than anything else. They were something one could get past if one would simply own it. Luke's secret however seemed darker than this. Why? I don't know. I've said this before but his very presence shouted 'danger!'

For a long minute he hesitated. I could almost hear the wheels and cogs spinning in his head as he muddled over the pros and cons of dragging me into his shady world. He gently nudged me away and I stood up. His legs swung to the floor and he got to his feet. All this time he remained silent and I knew he was weighing the consequences of unburdening himself to me. I was no longer self-conscious of my nudity. He had all of my attention.

He went to tug on his pants, before he tossed me my clothes and I, in turn, tackled button and zipper. We finished dressing almost simultaneously. He was tucking in his shirt when he finally came to a decision. The muscles of his jaw tightened. It was a struggle, and I vowed not to disappoint him.

"Interpol is after me for a crime I did not commit," he said.

CHAPTER

13

Alarm bells rang in my head. My gut told me that Luke Trevanian was a dangerous man. Was that why I had kept Tommy's strange behavior to myself?

"What do you mean?" I asked.

"Interpol thinks I stole a valuable artifact." He paused, quite aware that this wasn't how he had meant to confess his story. He was testing the waters, and when I remained standing in front of him, rather than fleeing in the face of the disturbing news, he continued. "Well... let me try this again."

He went to pour himself a stiff drink from the expensive scotch bottle. The alcohol was having a sobering rather than an intoxicating effect on him. He glanced at me, but I shook my head. I was going to need a clear head if I was to absorb what he said next. "Okay, so I'll try to explain. Bear with me, Lucy.

His green eyes appeared artificially green in the dimming light of his office. The muscles in his jaw worked. I could see the tension in his face. I was tense myself.

Why he had decided to divulge his troubles to me no longer mattered. I wanted to know; I waited while he collected his thoughts.

"The International police are on the trail of a thief who stole a rare and ancient—and almost perfect—Black Madonna from a church in the seaside town of Positano. The theft occurred about fifteen years ago, but only now have they got an inkling as to where it might be stashed."

My eyes widened.

Positano was where we were headed for the archaeological expedition.

"They believe they are getting close. They have leads and clues. They are near to discovering the identity of the thief and by tracing the thief they believe they will retrieve their Madonna. They want my help. They want the help of Luke Trevanian, international archaeologist." He paused. "But what they don't know is that—I—am the man they are after."

He took a gulp of his whiskey and set it back on the coffee table.

"But I didn't steal it, Lucy."

This was more than I could take in or accept all in one go. Shivers crept up my spine. Why would they think *he* stole it?

He sighed, nodded. "I know. All right. There's something you need to understand about me." He paused, weighing his words. "No one is aware of this."

I stared at him, a cold feeling of dread rising through my chest.

"Remember I told you that my father cut me off when I was ready to attend university? I had no money and I really wanted to go to school. I desperately—or maybe stubbornly—wished to become an archaeologist. More than anything in the world. Well, I had no financing and no job. My father made it impossible for me to get any sort of employment that would pay well enough for me to meet my tuition. All I could get was service jobs. And being a barista at Starbucks just didn't pay the bills. So, when I got an opportunity to smuggle artifacts to private collectors… I agreed."

My uncontrolled reaction must have said it all. First horror. And then pity.

"Don't look at me like that, Lucy. It's hard enough to tell you this as it is. Let me finish then judge me if you must."

I tried to soften my expression. The struggle of emotions in his down-turned face was heartbreaking. He had decided to reveal all to me and it was coming out fast.

"I got myself involved with a bad lot. Remember, I was only eighteen. But I was good with boats. I learned to sail by the time I was ten years old. That made me an asset. I smuggled ceramics and pieces of paintings, nothing big and nothing from museums. The stuff came straight from archaeological sites. I convinced myself that I would atone for my illicit activities after I got my degree. I would make up for it, somehow, if only I could finish school. I had to show my father he was wrong. But my God, Lucy, *I* was wrong. And, I stupidly continued to help the smugglers. We usually operated by sea. The objects were little things, often broken pieces—until the Black Madonna. I had nothing to do with that. By the time the gang vandalized the church, and made away with it, it was over for me... You have to realize these people knew my identity, but I was totally ignorant of theirs. They wore masks. Only my contact allowed me to see his face.

"So anyway, I was never in any real danger. They used me because I was safe. No one would accuse the son of a billionaire of smuggling. But then I got caught. I almost went to prison. My father got me off. He had money and influence and he managed to get my criminal records sealed. Inside those sealed records I was accused of stealing the Black Madonna.

"No one bothered to discover the truth. It didn't matter. The case was closed and everyone forgot about it.

"By that time I had finished my Bachelor's degree and was well on my way to obtaining my Masters. My father was ashamed of me but my mother finally convinced him to help me to get my PhD. I think he agreed because he blamed himself for my idiocy."

At first I was too stunned to make a sound. I was too stunned to even think. But as his explanation sank in, my thoughts travelled through various scenarios coming up with the easiest thing. I was beginning to understand the complicated relationship between father and son. They both felt guilty and they were both too proud to admit it.

Just as quickly, I knew that this was not what Luke needed to discuss with me, and it was not the reason he was confiding in me now. He was worried, desperately concerned. And so was I. If it were discovered that Luke was the criminal behind the theft of the valuable icon, his records would be opened. His shady past exposed. His future destroyed.

"My God, Lucy. I could go to prison."

There was nothing I could say to quell his angst. But I did need to know one thing. Would I believe his answer? Regardless, I had to ask.

"Did you do it?"

He was silent.

"Did you steal the Black Madonna?"

"I told you I didn't."

I wanted to believe him. But he had hidden so much from me. And why shouldn't he? This was not something he was proud of. Sure, I might be making a mistake. But I had always followed my instinct. That instinct was telling me to believe him. I would worry about whether he was still a crook later.

How protected were those records? What kind of situation had to exist before a court order could be demanded and his records unsealed?

The growing fear escalated and I tried to nod with confidence and reassurance. "You say you didn't steal the Black Madonna. Who do you think did?"

"Technically, I stole nothing. I simply moved the goods in my boat to secret locations. It was, shall we say, a 'summer job'. I spent the holidays in Italy. That's how I met the smugglers. Well, that's not even exactly true. I never knew who the head honcho was. No, my contact was a local fisherman. He'd done these runs for the gang, but wanted out because he had a wife and family to protect. When I met him it was serendipitous for both of us.

"Honestly, Lucy, I had no idea how serious a crime it could be. These pieces of art and pots looked like junk to me. I was young and stupid. I did what I was told because they paid me well and I knew a thing or two about boats." For a long while, he mused over what he had just told me. "You know? I never even saw the Black Madonna. The authorities attributed the theft to me out of convenience. That way they could close the case." He smiled sadly, waiting for me to accept that he was a fugitive from the law.

"That was over a decade and a half ago, Luke. Why are they reopening the investigation now?"

"Because they think someone aboard this boat stole it." And here it was. He was finally answering my question. "The only person that it could be is *me*. And they know it. They want to trip me up. Get a confession to past crimes. They suspect me—or if they don't, they soon will. Most of the people on my yacht are too young to have been involved, and of course, the museum team is innocent. They're new. The only possible culprits are Marissa, Norman, the captain—" He paused here as though something else had occurred to him then shrugged it off and tapped his chest "—and yours truly." He glanced down for a second. "Captain Leo Spatz joined my crew a few weeks ago. He was recommended to me by my estranged wife."

"Where did you meet Marissa?"

"She contacted me a year ago. We worked on the preliminary assessment of the Positano frescoes. She's an affiliate of the National Museum of Rome."

"And Norman?"

"We met in school. He was also taking archaeology. We remained friends. He went into the military for a short time. And then I employed him…"

"I see," I said.

He smiled. "You really do, don't you?" He took my hand and kissed my fingers. Then he dropped them, and I recognized the tightening of his jaw. It was a fight stance. "It's time I set things right. And I need your help, Lucy."

"How can I help?"

"You're in the museum business. Once we get to Positano I'm going to station you inside the excavation. I want you to keep your ears and eyes open. But mostly, I want you to keep an eye on Marissa. I saw you talking to her. You two hit it off, didn't you?"

I shrugged. "I guess."

"I want you to become best friends with her."

"Why?"

"Because she's either the thief or the cops. I'm not sure which."

Yes. Yes, it made sense. Of all the members on the team and of all the sailors crewing for the yacht, only Marissa seemed anomalous. Sure she was a fresco expert, or so she claimed (I had yet to see any evidence of her expertise), but she stuck out like a sore thumb. If you were to ask me what I meant by that, my explanation would be flat. It was simply that she didn't ring true. And not just because I'd caught her in a suspicious act.

I asked, "What was in that letter, Luke? The one from Interpol."

"A request for me to meet with the authorities when we dock."

I paused, then said, "I know who took it. I know who took your correspondence from Interpol."

He regarded me severely. "You do?"

"It was your fresco expert. Marissa Leone."

***

Marissa was seated in front of one of the yacht's fancy computers in the lab when we walked in. As soon as she heard us, she switched out of the website that she was so deeply perusing, but not before I caught a glimpse of it. We had been coming up behind her and now she swung around sharply.

"Hey, wasn't that the new website for crowdsourcing stolen artifacts?" I asked.

Marissa was smart enough to know that it was pointless to lie. "That was WikiLoot."

WikiLoot was a database of artifacts that posted photographs and documents from unresolved cases of valuable stolen objects.

"What were you looking for?" I asked.

"Oh, nothing in particular. Just browsing."

Browsing? Oh, I don't think so.

Luke decided to forgo the civilities and went straight to the point. He accused her of stealing his letter from Interpol.

"What are you talking about?" Marissa asked innocently. If she was insulted by the accusation she masked it well. Her behavior was cool and indifferent rather than offended. Despite my better judgment, I found myself believing her when she denied participation in the theft of Luke's letter. "Why would I take *any* thing from your office? Why would I go into your office without your permission? You must be mistaken."

"*She* saw you," Luke said, aiming a finger in my direction.

"That's not possible," she countered. "I don't even know where your office is. Besides, I was up on deck with everyone else. Ask any one of them."

She was admitting to nothing and she was calling me a liar. Why had we thought she would confess so easily? Had she taken it, she would simply deny it.

There was nothing to do but interrogate the others.

We found most of them still outside on the deck. Luke queried the tech team: Alonzo Acosta, Emily Chow and Jackson Shriver, and all three admitted to seeing Marissa reclining in one of the deckchairs for most of the afternoon— until just about fifteen minutes ago.

Luke decided to save time and quit while we were ahead. This line of questioning was getting us nowhere. We returned to his office, and as I preceded him through the door I stopped short.

We had been gone for almost an hour—plenty of time for Marissa to return the stolen correspondence. But why would she do that? I pointed to the desk. There on the top, mostly buried under some files was a corner of the blue and white letterhead.

I shoved the files off to reveal the distinctive symbol fully. "Do you think it's been here all the time?" I asked.

Luke slid it out from its hiding place and raised the letter. If Marissa had taken it, then she had replaced it immediately following our inquisition. I could swear it was missing when I went to the desk after seeing her standing there. Had I been mistaken? But Luke had also noticed that it was gone. He should know. It was *his* desk. And he was the one who had arranged the items on top of it.

He grunted. "Just puts her higher on my suspect list. Here—I want you to read it." He passed the letter to me. By now the fine-quality paper was well handled with small dents and a slight dog-ear. I smoothed it out.

Dear Dr. Trevanian,

On behalf of the International Police (Interpol) I would like to request your expertise on a matter of great cultural importance to the country of Italy and particularly to the town of Positano. As an expert in Italian artifacts and those especially pertaining to the catastrophic events of AD 79 when Mount Vesuvius erupted burying much of the Amalfi coast villas as well as the famed sites of Pompeii and Herculaneum, I believe you are in a position to aid us. I understand that you are funding an excavation of the ruins beneath the church of Santa Maria Assunta and therefore are familiar with the layout of the church and what lies beneath it.

Our records show that you have had business dealings with a Signor Marco Ferri. He is a person of interest in this case. We have interviewed Signor Ferri and he has referred us to you. We understand you are familiar with the case of the stolen Black Madonna. It was appropriated from the church September 2, 2002 and was allegedly recently spotted in the home of a private citizen.

I would like to meet with you at your earliest convenience. I have been told that you plan an expedition to Positano in August. I hope we can meet then.

Thank you in advance.

Yours truly,
Alessandra Piero
ICPO–Interpol

Phone: 39-(081)-xxx-xxxx
Email: APiero@Interpol.int

Nothing in the letter explained why Marissa or anyone else should care about its existence. It politely requested the help of Luke Trevanian in his capacity of archaeologist and expert in Italian art. The Black Madonna was purported to be carved in ebony, and painted with gold. Because it was flat, in the art world it was called 'high relief'. It was rare because of its age, and the perfection of its preservation. Most artifacts of this age (13th century) were badly deteriorated, but this one apparently was as bright and unmarked as the day it was created. After having gone missing for fifteen years, its current condition was yet to be verified. Unless it had been badly handled, the authorities expected it to have remained pristine. That was what made worshippers of the religious icon believe that it had supernatural properties. And that it truly was protected by some higher power. In my opinion 'seeing was believing'—and I had yet to see this artifact because it was still missing.

Originally the investigators had assumed the priceless icon had been sold to some wealthy private collector in the United States. Interpol now had reason to believe the object never left the European continent, and that in fact it was somewhere in a private home in Italy. It was seen in a cliffside villa, the home of a wealthy businessman named Marco Ferri.

"I spoke to Piero after she sent me that letter," Luke said. "Marco happens to be an acquaintance of mine. And that is the connection Interpol has linking me with the stolen goods, although it is couched in all sorts of niceties to hide the fact that they"—he jabbed a finger into his breastbone—"suspect *me*."

I reread the letter but found that my interpretation of the letter was the exact opposite. "It doesn't seem to me—not from this letter anyways—that Interpol suspects you of stealing it at all. Don't you think you might be seeing accusations where there are none?"

"Why didn't the police charge him?"

I shrugged. "Not enough evidence?"

"Actually none. When they arrived at his house, the piece was nowhere to be seen."

"How did they know it was even there?"

"Last summer, a snoopy reporter who managed to crash one of his frequent patio parties found his way indoors and claimed he saw it in the master bedroom. He recognized it from photographs released by the police long after it was stolen from the church in Positano. The reporter snapped a few shots and posted it on that crowdsourcing website set up by some whiz kid who is hell-bent on locating stolen objects."

I fell silent to process this new information. Then I reversed gears to mull over all he had told me earlier. "Why do you suspect Marissa?" I asked.

"She's in the museum business. She would have contacts

for buyers. But I only really suspected her after you told me she had taken the letter."

"And yet it's right here." I rattled it in my hand.

"It is, isn't it? And yet you were so certain you saw her snooping around my desk."

Of that I was positive. Could it possibly have been anyone else? I had also noticed the website she was navigating when we interrupted her so abruptly. The same one Luke had just referred to.

I decided to keep my suspicions to myself. This business of the Black Madonna had come out of nowhere, distracting me from my mission to get Tommy alone. What exactly had him so worried? Certainly it had nothing to do with this? But now it looked like Marissa might be involved.

I needed to think.

Who could I trust?

I told Luke I needed to return to my stateroom for a shower. He agreed and suggested we meet in his room for a private dinner.

"Would that look suspicious to the team?" I asked.

"Who cares if it does? Do you?"

"I guess as long as you aren't paying me a whole lot more than you're paying them." I chuckled.

"Oh, don't worry. You're getting the perks in lieu of extra pay."

He hauled me into his arms to demonstrate exactly what he meant.

CHAPTER
<u>14</u>

The yacht sailed into the lovely blue Gulf of Naples to magnificent weather. Bright sunshine blazed down over the water glancing off the mountain peaks, casting elongated shadows. In the summer months this corner of the Mediterranean dazzled with super yachts and luxury boats of all shapes and sizes. It was a breathtaking achievement of nature amalgamated with the best that human engineering could offer. The towns were carved out of the cliffs with steep stone steps and cascading greenery. Set against a backdrop of the soaring Lattari range and picturesque villages in deep valleys, the Amalfi coast was an artist's dream.

There is no marina large enough to berth a yacht the size of the *Madonna* in Positano, but the forecast for the next few weeks was for calm and settled weather. Luke had made arrangements in advance to rent a buoy for open moorage.

By the time we were anchored every one of us was itching to get off the boat and onto dry land. Three Zodiacs were launched from the side platform and we landed at the dock on the beach.

I stood on the street with Marissa staring skyward at the network of winding roads and steps ascending the hillside.

The sharp rise was clustered with pretty bungalows in multiple tiers, painted in colorful pinks and peach tones, and ivory—and draped in clinging, blossoming vines of deep purple and red. The town gave the sense of being dug right out of the cliff along the nearly vertical rock face.

Everywhere I looked I could see the signs of luxury and affluence. From sprawling private villas set among fragrant lemon, lime and olive groves to the premier restaurants whose outdoor patios teetered over pearly beaches and turquoise sea. Diners had exquisite views of the Li Galli archipelago, home of the sirens of Homer's Odysseus, and Capri, where I'm assuming the Capri-style pants were born.

The rustic Italian seaside town was more or less divided in half by a large cliff upon which sits the Torre Trasita, an ancient castle-like tower, totally renovated inside with the most up-to-date style, and which belonged to the Italian businessman Marco Ferri. On the western flank of the tower was the Spiaggia del Fornillo beach. This was the less expensive part of town where artists and writers liked to hang out. On the eastern side sprawled the Spiaggia Grande, and the town center. Here you could find actors, filmmakers and the nouveau riche enjoying the amenities of Positano. I have to say I was quite speechless staring up at all of this beauty. I had never seen anything quite like it before.

Marissa turned and I followed her gaze across the incredibly silky blue water. In the distance were some islands. "It's amazing how this place with all its modern conveniences and luxury can't shake off the past."

I nodded. I knew exactly what she meant. Staring out across the sea and its exotic landscape the imagination quickly brought up images of the old gods, like Neptune and the sea nymph Amphitrite. It was a love story to beat all love stories. Neptune the Roman god of the sea fell in love with Amphitrite who wished nothing to do with him.

The myth in many ways reminded me of my own relationship with Luke. Neptune was persistent and when still the obstinate nymph refused him he sent one of his servants, a dolphin to convince her, and this he managed to do (in my story Norman would play the role of the dolphin). She changed her mind and the mighty sea god rewarded his faithful servant by placing him in the heavens as the constellation Dolphinius.

Halfway through my dreaming, Luke joined us and said, "Today is a free day. Do whatever you like. I have some business to take care of in Florence. I'll be back tomorrow morning. We'll start work then."

The team split up into small groups and drifted away. Luke took my hand. "Sorry, Lucy. That means you too. I can't take you with me. Besides you'd be bored. Business with my ex."

"Arianna's here? In Italy?"

"Yeah. On business."

Their business just happened to coincide?

Fine. It was none of mine.

"All right. I'll see you tomorrow. Are you taking the helicopter?"

He nodded. "Norman will keep you company."

"Oh, that's not necessary—"

But Norman was standing right there and I didn't want to say anything that might insult him. But honestly? I'd rather not spend the day with him. His expression seemed to mirror the sentiment. What had I ever done to make him dislike me so much?

"Sure you don't need me, boss?" he asked.

"I want you to look after Lucy."

"I doubt that she needs looking after."

"Show her around. Seriously, what's up with you two?" He turned to me and kissed me full on the mouth. "Honestly, honey, he doesn't bite."

Oh, I wouldn't be too sure about that.

Luke took one of the Zodiacs back to his yacht where the helicopter waited for him on the helipad.

Norman and I stood staring at each other. It was late afternoon. Shops had just reopened after the midday siesta. In

Italy they called it *riposo*, the hours between 1:00 pm and 4:00 pm when shops and services closed so that merchants could go home for a long lunch and a nap during the hottest hours of the day. The strip along the beach was bustling with the sounds of businesses opening up for cocktails, early suppers and souvenir shopping. Honestly, it was like the world had come to a halt. It was that awkward. "I don't know about you but I could do with something to eat," he said to break the silence.

I avoided eye contact with him. "Fine by me. Where to? Someplace not too fancy, I'm not dressed for it."

I wasn't. I was clad in pale blue Capri pants and a loose, white crop top.

"You look nice."

His voice had that slight French accent, and was soft and quiet, almost like he had spoken to himself. I glanced up at him but his sight was fixed on the restaurant strip along the cliffside. He muttered, "There's a place I like, not too expensive, with a great view."

Not that cost ever entered into the equation since Luke paid for everything but it was kind of endearing to see that such things still mattered.

I followed him to the open patio. It was early by European standards for dinner. But the deck was crowded with people starting the cocktail hour. The waitress managed to locate us a table for two. We sat down beneath a red and white umbrella, by the rail, overlooking the marina. The sun was angling, sending a flood of pink and orange across the beach. The low light cast blue shadows of beach umbrellas, sailboat masts and streetlamps in long dark stretches.

I looked at the bar menu and ordered a bottle of Chablis. Norman ordered us two glasses of sparkling water with lime and a plate of fried calamari, olives and hearts of palm and artichokes all bathed in the local olive oil with fresh lemon and tomato garnish.

The waitress smiled at Norman. He returned the obvious flirtation with an amused twitch of his lips. It was hard to figure out this guy. Something about him was so macho masculine, but he also displayed a veiled—what— sensitivity? It was impossible to describe. This part of his personality, when he showed it, I liked. For example, at the moment the young waitress was using her eyes in that way women have when they want a man to notice them. Have *I* ever done it? Probably. I recognized the move when I saw it, and I was definitely seeing it.

Norman however was not taking advantage of her. He was clearly aware that she found him sexy. Seriously, who wouldn't? But she had to be in her late teens. A little young for someone in his mid thirties.

This was the first time I had found myself alone with Norman since our unwieldy encounter on the upper deck of Luke's yacht. I was scrambling for a topic of conversation. What I came up with was kind of lame. "Italian girls are so pretty," I said.

His reply was swift. "There are pretty women everywhere."

Good answer.

"Why don't you have a girlfriend, Norman?" I was trying to keep things light.

"How do you know I don't have one?"

I laughed, a little uncertainly. "All right. None of my business."

The waitress returned with the wine. She set out two glasses. She began to pour into his but he raised his hand to stop her. "*No, signore?*" she inquired.

"*È solo per la signora.*"

She bent over my glass and filled it with a pale, clear white. I sampled it. It was delicious.

"Just the water, for me," Norman said, indicating the lime and ice-filled glasses on her tray. The clinks of the beverages punctuated the clumsiness of our conversation.

I was fearful of another tense silence so I asked, "Are you never off-duty?"

He shrugged. "Mostly not."

"But surely escorting me around isn't part of the job?"

"Actually, it is."

I paused. "So—I'm supposed to drink this entire bottle myself?"

This time he couldn't suppress the amusement. "*You* ordered it."

I guess I did. I lifted the glass and held it out to him. He raised his sparkling water and smiled. "*Santé.*"

"That's French isn't it?" I knew very well that it was, although I decided to keep my aptitude for French hidden. "You speak Italian too. I heard you." Like Luke he was multilingual.

I took a long gulp of my wine. The Chablis was delightful. Cool and refreshing... and... I glanced at the label...with a higher alcohol content than usual. I took another deep swallow before I picked up my water glass. Being alone with Luke's bodyguard made me twitchy. I should probably quench my thirst with something less powerful before I chugged this, and it all went to my head.

I swirled my glass, my gaze never leaving his face. "How many languages do you speak?"

His eyes took on a slight twinkle. "How many *should* I speak?"

"Fine. Don't tell me. You like to keep your secrets. Though I don't know why it matters. Who cares how many languages you speak?"

"Exactly."

I smirked. "You can be annoying."

He smirked back. "And *you* can ask a lot of questions when you're drinking."

"Is that why you're *not* drinking?"

His broad shoulders lifted. "People say a lot of things under the influence."

Ha. I laughed. What would *he* say under the influence, eh?

I finished my first glass. The waitress came around to flirt with Norman some more. She asked if he wished a refill of his fizzy water before she remembered to refresh my glass. I leaned forward. "Somebody's got a crush on you," I teased.

"She's eighteen. Luke knows her parents."

I shot a quick, appraising glance at her. "Ah. So *that's* the barrier."

He scowled. And the sensation, that he only tolerated me because of Luke, returned. I mimicked his expression and his eyebrows rose. He suppressed a smile. "You better eat something, Lucy. Alcohol on an empty stomach, not a great idea."

Fine. I will eat something if that will make him happy. By night's end I was determined to change his opinion of me. I playfully poked the calamari with my fork and raised it to my lips. I realized as I popped it in that Norman was observing my technique.

"Mmmm. This is delicious. Try it." I forked another piece and waved it in front of his lips. His nicely shaped mouth stayed closed. He took the fork from me and fed himself.

I have to admit I was feeling the Chablis. It felt good to be here on the beach with the thunder of the sea, the crowds chattering around us, and the wind in my hair. All thoughts of Luke's cryptic past melting with the wine. If only life was always like this.

Why did Luke have to abandon me and leave me in the company of his Holy Grumpiness? Oh yeah, Arianna. It had to do with Arianna, the ex-wife. Did *she* know all about Luke's mysterious past? They had been married for at least a decade. Of course, she knew his past.

And why did he have to remind me that his divorce wasn't final? I shouldn't be with him. Technically, he was still involved. And yet, I enjoyed his company... and all the perks that came with it. Especially the sex. And this—

Norman ordered a couple of more dishes. My mind was on other things. I think there was more seafood, some kind of savory fish stew, and a salad and lots of crusty, warm Italian bread.

We ate in silence and I had finished half the bottle of wine. The sun was setting, all aglow in every shade of rose.

Norman paid the bill and the pretty waitress stood above him returning the credit card. "*Grazie, bellezza,*" he said and rose to his feet.

The girl did the hair thing and made eyes at him. He gave her a small smile and watched appreciatively as she walked away. I grabbed the bottle and my glass, and climbed over the rail and onto the beach.

"Lucy!" Norman chased after me. "What the f... *Merde.* What are you doing?"

"Going to the beach," I shouted over my shoulder. The wind flapped my crop top, exposing my midriff. That twinge of jealousy when Norman eyed the girl's swaying behind irritated me.

"Get back here."

I ran. What choice did he have but to follow me? Well, maybe that was only wishful thinking. His boss was away. He had free will. But he chose to follow me. I collapsed onto the beach in front of a cement block and leaned my back against it. How long had we spent at that bistro? Must be hours. Norman had even managed to squeeze in dessert—a luscious-looking strawberry flan. Myself, I had chosen to stick with the wine. Hindsight is 20/20. If I were psychic and sober I most definitely would have made the opposite choice. I was not a smart drunk.

The light had changed radically and would soon disappear. I inhaled, spread out my arms. "This is perfect." I poured another glass of Chablis and took a long, lingering sip. "Paradise."

He slumped down beside me. "*Mon Dieu.* You are crazy."

I delivered him a sidelong glance. "I'm just having fun."

"I can see that."

I nestled the wine bottle into the sand beside me and tilted the glass to my lips. "Sure you don't want any?"

He shook his head.

The sunset was mesmerizing. There were still some people on the beach but it was steadily darkening. Most of them were heading to the restaurant strip now alight with strings of incandescent bulbs for cocktails and dinner.

I suddenly turned to Norman. "Why aren't they divorced yet? Why aren't Luke and Arianna divorced yet?"

His French drawl returned and he relaxed. "Ah. So *that* is what is bothering you. It's a lengthy process, divorce. I *don't* recommend it."

My eyes rose to his face. "You've been married then?"

A soft, humorous sound escaped his lips, almost a snort. "No. Never. I just meant Luke and Arianna's divorce has been going on for well past a year."

"What's holding it up?"

"They can't agree on a settlement."

I slumped back against the cement block. "That's what Luke said."

"You don't believe him?"

"Do you?"

He turned away and exhaled. I sensed tension in his voice as he replied. "Maybe we should change the subject."

"Fine. What do you want to talk about?"

He turned back and something mimicking a smile was on his face. "What do you want out of life?"

"A digital 3-D printer."

He sat up straight. "What?"

"I would really like to get a state-of-the art, digital, 3-D printer for my art department."

He rocked backwards and laughed.

"Why are you laughing? You asked me what I wanted."

He clamped his lips shut but humor danced in his eyes. "So tell me. Why is this 3-D printer so important?"

"It might save my job at the museum."

He frowned.

"The museum might be facing cutbacks. I figure if I can show the director how updating to state-of-the-art tech can put our museum back on the map, she won't cut my department. All the big museums have them. They enable us to replicate artifacts so that the really valuable ones don't have to be put on display and risk damage or theft."

I was doing everything in my power to maintain a coherent discussion with him. My thoughts, though, were fluffy and oh so very jumbled. Between the 3-D printer, the wine and his masculine presence my brain was doing a balancing act trying to recall what his name meant in French and why I needed a 3-D printer. Norman from Normandy. Uh-huh. Viking origins. Norman meant man from the north. Yeah, he was an awesome, ripped, Viking. Was any of this coming out of my mouth for him to hear? Did I care? Nah. That part of my brain swimming in alcohol suggested I dump some of this delicious wine down his throat. Then maybe he would feel the same.

I giggled and forced myself to concentrate on his face. The amusement in his eyes turned serious. What did I say? Can't remember now.

He lowered his eyes. "How much do 3-D printers cost?"

"Too much. The best ones cost over three thousand dollars. Add tax to that and it's closer to four."

"Did Arianna turn down your request for a 3-D printer?"

"She hasn't heard my request yet. I chickened out...." That last emerged as a mumble. A giggle? Were we still discussing 3-D printers? "What about you? What do *you* want?"

He shrugged. "Most things I want I can't have."

Like what? "Isn't that true for most things in life? Most of us can't just take what we want. Unlike *some* people."

"Some people? Ah, you mean Luke."

"Yeah, Luke. And you too. I'm sure he pays you a six-figure salary. After all, you have a dangerous job."

"What do you mean by that, Lucy?" He sat rigid, alert, forcing me to alertness too. "What do you know about my job?"

"Nothing. Except, well... Luke is a billionaire. And he

didn't become one by chance, did he?"

Silence. Impenetrable, unquestionable silence. Norman was doing his best to misunderstand. He was quiet, but even through my inebriation I detected a multitude of thoughts tumbling about in his brain. In general, the eyes did not lie. And I looked into his to see if it were true. It was. Trouble stirred there. And secrets. He knew exactly what I was talking about. His conundrum was in deciding what I knew and what I didn't.

"Luke obviously trusts you," he said.

I shifted to catch his expression. But it was too dark to decipher. "You think that's a bad idea. Why?"

There was an edge of anger to his tone now. "Stop asking me questions. If there's anything you want to know, ask Luke when he returns."

I twisted so that we were face to face. Norman was also a very mysterious man. What secrets did *he* have? He was incredibly sexy, too, and I shouldn't be having these thoughts. The way that young waitress kept flirting with him, how could she help herself? But it was the way he handled it that was so sexy. Without acting inappropriately, he never made her feel rejected. Not once.

"Do you think I'm pretty, Norman?" *Oh good grief. Where did that come from?* Must be the Chablis talking. Tomorrow all of this will be a blur. But for now the liquor was playing Truth or Dare with my tongue.

"I should take you back to the yacht, Lucy. It's getting dark."

It was. But did I feel like going back to the yacht? No way! I wanted to…. I wanted to… skinny-dipping!

I took another slug straight from the bottle this time. I had no idea where the glass had gone. I jumped to my feet. I ran down the beach in the quickly descending darkness, kicking off my sandals and tugging off my top.

I threw the crop top in his face as he caught up to me, and yanked down my pants. I stood in the sand in my bikini underwear. The expression on his face was bold-faced startled. "Good Lord, Lucy. What are you doing?"

"Come on. You too. Take that shirt off. I want to see what's underneath it."

He grabbed me by the wrist. The anger was real now. "Get your clothes on."

I jerked my hand out of his grasp and unhooked my bra. He was paralyzed at first because he wasn't expecting that. I shoved it at his chest.

I turned and ran towards the pounding surf. It was totally dark now and the moon and stars silvered the surface of the sea. His footfalls padded across the soft sand. Then he tackled me and dragged me away from the water. Entangled together, we fell. He rolled me over to face him. He was lying, half on top of me. His breath was warm and smelled of strawberries from the flan he'd eaten for dessert. His tongue almost touched my earlobe as he whispered. "You need to sleep it off."

My arms collapsed around his neck. He seized both of my wrists and disentangled them, pinning them to the beach. "From here to eternity," I sighed into his ear.

"You'll regret this in the morning. If you remember any of it at all."

My knee hooked his hip. He laughed and murmured cynically under his breath. He went still for an immeasurably long moment. The reason for his amusement hardened against my thigh. He growled, released me, and rose. My head was really spinning now, but in a good way. I opened my eyes and saw him gather up my clothes from the beach. "Sit up," he ordered.

I thought I was.

"I can't believe I'm hooking your bra *on*… instead of *un*hooking it."

"Huh?"

"Never mind. Arms up." I raised them obediently like a child and he pulled my top down over my chest. "Now where are your shoes?"

He gave up on trying to get them onto my feet, and

hooked the straps around his fingers. Then he hoisted me into his arms and marched up the beach.

After that, I don't remember much except that I woke up in bed wearing his shirt. My mind was still spinning, but slowly reality was breaking through. I turned my face on the pillow and saw the shadowy form of the bodyguard next to me. It wasn't quite morning and I was horrified at what I had done. My mouth felt furry, and my head was hammering. I rolled, and fell hard onto the floor at the realization that Norman was sound asleep beside me. The loud thump of my falling woke him.

"Lucy, are you okay?"

"Uh-huh."

"What are you doing on the floor?" His voice sounded sleepy. His eyes I imagined were too, although it was too dark to see. The whole idea was incredibly erotic. He rolled over to look.

I rose to my feet without his help. "What are you doing in my bed?" I demanded. I tried to look vengeful but I felt like a puddle of jelly.

He propped himself on one elbow. "This *isn't* your bed."

"Then what am I doing in *your* bed?"

His tone was edged with annoyance. "It's not my bed either. We're in a hotel. I didn't want to take you back to the yacht, drunk like that. People would talk."

And they're not going to talk now? But no one knew. *I* didn't even know. What had happened? Oh my god I didn't…. I didn't…. Norman switched on the nightstand light so that I could see my surroundings. His eye caught the mortification on my face and he sat up. Lines of exhaustion appeared on his brow. Just exactly what had I put him through? He sighed and his voice softened. "Lucy. Don't worry. The hotel was completely booked up except for this room, so I took it. You were sound asleep by the time I dropped you on the bed."

I glanced down, then up, raising my hands that pinched the hem of a large t-shirt. What was this? Where were my own clothes? The shirt was soft and oversized and hung halfway to my knees. "Yours, I presume? Why am I wearing your shirt?"

I watched the possible explanations jostle in his head.

"Yours was kind of wet."

"Wet?"

A pause. "You don't remember?"

My frown grew deeper. He hesitated for a moment. "After dinner we went for a walk on the beach. You... you walked into the water. Got splashed..." I glanced hard at him. *Really?* How could I forget that? My memory was foggy. I recalled sitting on the sand with him, sipping wine. He wasn't drinking. Oh my God, had I drunk that whole bottle myself? I *never* did that. But then there was a first time for everything. I turned away to use the bathroom and to rinse out my mouth. I glanced in the mirror and saw myself in his shirt. Oh...oh hell. The beach. Clothes flying. Mine. Complete or partial nudity. I glanced at the door. It was all coming back to me. Why had he kept that from me? And then I wondered. *Did I have sex with Norman?* I still had bra and panties on. If we'd had sex they'd be off, wouldn't they?

I crept out of the bathroom. Maybe he had gone back to sleep and I could flee this embarrassing situation. But no. He was sitting on the edge of the bed in his khaki pants, shirtless. Feet bare.

He looked amazing. I forced my eyes to look elsewhere.

"It happens, Lucy. Don't feel so bad. You didn't do anything. Not with me."

I stood in front of him. He had dressed me, and then undressed me and then dressed me again. In his shirt. "I don't think I'm ever going to be able to face you again."

He laughed. For once a real laugh, not just that twinkle of amusement. "Too late, sweetheart, you're already facing me."

I cupped a hand to my mouth. What did people do in a situation like this? Mutually agree that the whole night never happened? I mean what he was virtually saying to me was that he hadn't felt the least bit unable to resist. So I should forget about it. *Forget about it?* This was going to go up on the board as one of the most humiliating nights of my life. The hunk of man meat had rejected me.

"Lucy. What's wrong?"

I shook my head.

"I mean it. Nothing happened. There's nothing to feel bad about. Luke doesn't need to know that you had a couple of drinks too many."

Luke wouldn't care because nothing had happened. I had torn off all my clothes and Norman had put them back on me. He was so turned off that he had put my clothes back on me. And not only that: he lied about what *really* happened. How humiliating was that?

Why did nothing happen? Why did I feel bad *because* nothing had happened?

Did I have feelings for Norman? No! That was absurd!

Norman rose from the bed and pulled the drapes slightly aside. The dull gleam of dawn shot in. His voice was cold when he spoke. "We should get back to the yacht before anyone gets up." He darted an arm towards a chair and said, "Your clothes are over there."

He had become the indifferent bodyguard again.

CHAPTER
<u>15</u>

"Well, what would you like to do first?" Luke asked. "Go shopping?"

Positano was home to *Moda Positano*, a fashion that emerged in the fifties to symbolize freedom from the strict dress codes of the time. The town was always a home for the creative thinker and doer, and its galleries, theaters and expensive boutiques reflected this philosophy. Luke had returned as promised and the expedition was back on track. Since he hadn't arrived until early afternoon he was willing to give us another free day and officially start work tomorrow.

"Actually, I would like to visit the church," Marissa said.

"So would I." I was particularly anxious to see the famed edifice not because I was in a hurry to start work on the excavation, but because it was inside this church that the mysterious Black Madonna had gone missing.

Others in the group agreed. They all wanted to see where they would be working.

"All right," Luke said. He glanced over at Norman. "Lead the way."

Norman had accompanied Luke on all of his expeditions. Luke had been here once before to do a preliminary investigation and to make arrangements for this larger project, so Norman knew everything necessary about the Church of Santa Maria Assunta. Luke gestured for us to precede him in the wake of his bodyguard. Before complying, I darted a glance up the nearly vertical gradient of colorful villas stacked one on top of the other, then down to the beach. Norman and I had silently agreed that we would not speak of last night ever again. When Luke asked me if Norman had taken good care of me I'd said yes. And he had. Although I still had a residual headache. Except now I couldn't bring myself to act normal with him. So I didn't.

We walked along the beach. We climbed a narrow cobblestone staircase lined with boutiques. Most of the staircases leading from the Marina Grande Beach pass behind or through a small piazza in front of the church. From here I was exposed to a lovely view of the church's dark yellow façade and the bell tower. Above us I glimpsed a walkway strung with deep pink bougainvillea and artists' stands selling their wares.

The church was only about a quarter of the way up the hillside. It was clearly a focus of the community's cultural, religious and architectural landscape. It was located in the town center just a few steps from the beachfront. Even without being told, I had recognized the church by its famed Majolica tiled dome. The sun currently danced off the distinctive blue, yellow, and green patterned tiles, reflecting the colors of sky, citrus groves, and sea.

The excited group gathered at the main door. We entered to a sensation of open coolness. The ceilings were high and the floor spacious. My pulse increased slightly as I took in the beautiful gold and white interior, restored in the Neo-classical style. In the apse the remains of a Byzantine floor were still visible.

I left my friends. I wandered along the central nave to the front where, overhead, a conspicuous blank space drew my eye to the wall. That, I was fairly certain, was where the Black Madonna should have hung.

"Not long ago the church of Santa Maria Assunta housed a 13th century icon of the Virgin Mary with child," a voice spoke into my ear.

I turned to look and saw that it was Tommy. Somehow he had come up from behind me without my hearing him. That sent a shivery wave up my spine. I chose to ignore it. My decision had been made back on the yacht. Not only was I going to help Luke catch the culprit who had stolen the icon, but danger or no danger, I was also going to trust him. The question now was: how did this concern Tommy? What was *his* interest in the missing artifact?

"The Black Madonna," I queried. "How do you know about that?"

"I'm not the only one on the yacht that knows about her."

I swung around to face him fully. He was quiet and then he asked, "Do you know the legend?"

"No," I said.

"It was first stolen centuries ago and smuggled by pirates. I'm not sure where they stole it from, but they were trying to take it across the Mediterranean. When a storm rose the terrified sailors heard a voice in the gale screaming, *'Posa, posa!'* In the local tongue this means 'put it down, put it down!' The priceless artifact was unloaded here, at the mouth of a cave, at Positano, and the storm stopped."

The silence that followed was apt. Unnerving. I needed to break it. I also wished that Luke were nearby holding my hand.

"How do you know so much about the icon, Tommy?"

He shrugged. "Ask Marissa."

I meant to. But first I wanted to ask *him*. Exactly what did he mean by that cryptic suggestion? There was something else. His strange behavior in Luke's office returned to my memory. There was something he wanted to tell me, but he was afraid to. I had not managed to get him alone after that interview with Luke. Now was my chance.

I looked around for the others; they had split into small

groups and were gathered at the other walls admiring the paintings there. We were out of earshot.

"Tommy. What is it?" I coaxed. "You can tell me."

Tommy's eyes flitted nervously.

I suddenly noticed that Captain Spatz was in the doorway. What was he doing here? His sudden appearance sent a chill over my body for no apparent reason, but the next time I was alone with Luke I was going to ask him exactly why his ex had recommended this particular captain. Clearly, he had a similar effect on Tommy.

My hand reached out to calm him. The boy slipped an envelope between my fingers. "Hide that," he whispered. "Don't open it until you're back inside the privacy of your cabin. You're the only one I trust, Lucy."

He started to slip away. "Tommy!" I shouted in a tight whisper. This was a church after all. "Tom, wait. You can't just run away. You have to explain."

"Not here," he mouthed at me.

He had already rejoined the team. Captain Spatz was now consulting with Luke over some matter with the yacht. That wasn't so unusual but what *was* odd was that Tommy moved as far away from Spatz as possible. I was about to join the team when I turned back to have one last look at the blank space on the wall above the altar.

A priest in cassock was standing in front of me.

"*Buongiorno*, my child," he said. It would be rude to just turn my back on him so I stayed put, fighting the urge to excuse myself and chase after Tommy. "You are curious about the icon that once hung there? I overheard your friend tell you of the legend. What is it that you would like to know? Perhaps I can answer your questions."

His English was very good, although he had a strong Italian accent. I assumed he was used to accommodating English-speaking tourists. Perhaps if Tommy wouldn't tell me what I wanted to know, the priest might. "Do you have any idea who stole it?"

The old man shook his head. He started to speak in

Italian then switched to English. "One rainy morning it was gone. The space on the wall has been waiting for its return ever since."

"Why don't you hang a substitute there, meanwhile?"

He chuckled mildly. "You think that we have not tried? We commissioned a portrait to be mounted in its place, but every time the painting was hung, it would fall within the hour of its hanging. It did not matter how many nails were used, it refused to stay in place. Finally we gave up. It is as though the Holy One is telling us that the space is reserved for the Black Madonna, and *only* the Black Madonna."

He paused in his explanation before he asked, "Are you of the Catholic faith, my child?"

"No."

He studied me silently for a moment. "I was watching you before your friend came over to speak to you. What is your interest in our Madonna?"

I shrugged. "I understand that she was very rare and an exquisite work of art."

"Indeed, she was. Was that what your friend was discussing? He left in a great hurry, and he seems to have upset you. Something he said troubles you deeply. And if it has to do with the missing icon it is of the utmost interest to the church." He paused. "But perhaps it is something else? Are you in need of guidance, child? Should you feel the need to lift the burden you can talk to me. Anything you tell me is in confidence."

Hesitation paralyzed my voice. How could he understand the tension I was feeling right now when I didn't quite understand it myself? By sheer force of will I broke through it, and spoke with confidence. "Not really."

His warm brown eyes were all-seeing, and he did not believe me.

"You do not have to be Catholic to seek advice or forgiveness from our church." With a subtle gesture, he indicated the confessional in the alcove around the corner.

I was a little taken aback. Across the room Norman

caught my eye. It took some effort to ignore him. "Ah…Thank you, but no thanks. I can deal with this problem on my own."

He smiled a kindly, fatherly smile. "We are always open to those in need." He turned his head. "It seems your friends are calling you. You are part of the archaeology team?"

"I am. I'm their illustrator, Lucy Racine."

"Nice to meet you, Lucy. My name is Father Carmine. And now it seems you must go. Your expedition leader beckons."

Luke signaled to me from across the room to band together otherwise I might get left behind—or worse—lost.

"What time are your hours, father?"

"This time, everyday."

I bade the priest goodbye before I realized what the item was that remained firmly gripped in my hand. My eyes dropped to the envelope. I was so distracted I almost *did* get left behind. I gathered my wits about me, clutched the envelope, and hurried across the floor.

The team was heading through some doors into a back room.

"When we get inside, you'll be astounded," Marissa said, excitedly. She had turned her head so that the entire group could hear her comment. The acoustics were amazing in this church. Marissa had been here once before with Luke. I jostled my way between Jackson and Alonzo and tried to get to Tommy who was now chatting off to the side of the line with Emily. The space was too narrow and the people were tightly packed together. I sent Tommy an anxious look and he shook his head. Luke was out front with Marissa and Norman. I gave up for the time being, and slipped the envelope into my purse and zipped it shut.

Norman opened a small door to what appeared to be a crypt. He switched on a flashlight and warned us to be cautious descending. I am nervous around heights but this did not feel the same as standing outside on a narrow bridge over a steep gorge. Even so I would breathe more easily once we were on the ground. A labyrinth of ladders and scaffolding appeared out of the gloom and we followed Norman, single file, to the easiest path down.

We landed at the bottom of what was the only well-lit area. There were bare light bulbs strung from the scaffolding and Norman had pulled a switch to turn them on. We were nearly thirty feet under the church Luke informed us.

We continued into a dazzling room of brilliant frescoes. The greens, yellows, reds and blues were almost as bright as the day they were painted and seemed to emit a light of their own. This was the extraordinarily preserved remains of a lavish *villa marittima*—or, in simple English, a seaside villa. It was once a luxurious retreat for ancient Rome's wealthy to escape the summer heat and the rat race of urban life. The crypt led into the villa's stunning *triclinium*, a dining room.

The eruption of Mt. Vesuvius had caused the villa to entirely collapse. An engineer had discovered the buried villa during the restoration of the crypt and bell tower, and I could see where a previous team had removed mud and lapilli (the small stones ejected by the volcano), which had buried this ancient settlement. A piece of mud held the impression of a door that had disintegrated over time and where the intricate decoration in muted gold was still visible.

The edges of wall paintings and frescoes emerged from the debris.

"What do you think?" Luke asked, slipping up beside me.

"It's magnificent." I paused, and turned to him. Then I darted a quick look for Tommy but failed to sight him. "Luke, I need to talk to you about something. It's about Tommy."

He nodded. "Not here. And not now."

I understood his resistance to tackle the topic at this moment. But I wanted desperately to consult him on Tommy's strange behavior.

"Don't worry," he said, stroking my arm with his knuckles. "We'll talk. Later."

Marissa was explaining some things of interest to the team. "Thanks to an ancient system of artificial terraces cut into the hillside on which the town sits, the old villa before the eruption of the volcano may have covered more than 2.25 acres. It might even have been as large as the entire town is today," she finished.

"Or possibly not," Luke cut in. "The villa may well have been perched on a terraced platform with ramps leading to other terraces below, and might have stretched over two or more levels along the cliff, as houses presently do, but I doubt that it occupied the entire village."

There was a second of silence and I wondered if Marissa intended a rebuttal. Her lips parted as if to speak, then clamped shut.

After we toured the site, a few of the team and Marissa remained to admire the partially exposed frescoes. I remembered Tommy's words when I had questioned him about the Black Madonna. He had answered: 'Ask Marissa.'

Just exactly what was I supposed to ask Marissa?

When the crowd had thinned out I searched the cavern for Tommy. What could possibly be in his envelope? I was annoyed by his secretive behavior, and more than that I was frightened. But he was gone. I asked Emily if she had seen him. She shook her head.

I left the group and searched the other underground caverns. Most of these were not accessible. Some were partially opened and had piles of rubble and earth semi blocking the entryways. A large collapsed fresco painting showed clear colors in red, yellow and blue, and was partly embedded in the ground. Scattered roof tiles and iron implements poked through the volcanic ash. There was no sign of Tommy.

I had managed to negotiate one of these entryways and was standing in a dark, cave-like space fully prepared to open his letter right here and now, when I sensed a distinct presence. I jerked my head up from where I was concentrating on digging out the envelope. I caught a sound behind me and craned my head to look; at the same time I shoved the envelope deep inside my handbag and zipped it up.

"You shouldn't wander into unlit places," Captain Spatz said.

I slipped the purse strap across my chest tourist fashion, and spun to face him. "Isn't this part of the excavation?"

"Not yet. It hasn't been set up. The walls need to be shored up. And the scaffolding hasn't been tested."

I could see that. It looked as though the contraption had been hastily assembled and then the worker had been called away without adjusting the boards and steel beams. On the floor below it were disheveled piles of dirt and rubble. Just how did Luke's captain know so much about excavation techniques?

He took a step closer to me. I could smell salami on his breath. The heat of his body reached me and I found the intimate warmth disturbing. I sensed he felt the same. "I saw you talking to Tommy Buchanan, Ms. Racine. Did you learn anything new about his accident aboard ship?"

I took a solid breath; the question was reasonable after all. So why did I feel this sense of apprehension from him? "No," I lied.

He shrugged. A controlled smile tightened across his face. "Are you sure? Luke and I would like to get this whole mess cleared up. Litigation, you know."

"Don't worry about that. Tommy would never sue Luke. He's not that kind of person." I back-stepped and tripped over the unevenness of the floor, which sent my feet flying out from under me. If not for Captain Spatz's quick action I would have fallen and hit my head against the rear wall. He shot forward and caught me around the waist, slamming my cheek into his shoulder as he hauled me upright.

Suddenly the doorway darkened and a figure walked in. I exhaled in relief and Spatz released me.

"That's where you are." It was Norman's voice. He made no comment on the scene he'd barged in on—*if* he had seen anything at all.

I wiped the sweat from my forehead. My fingers were cold. Despite the coolness of the cavernous space, I was unbearably hot. Norman didn't ask why I was in the captain's arms because he had already stepped away when the bodyguard arrived.

"You shouldn't be in here."

"I was just warning her," Spatz said. "Parts of the wall could cave in. This section of the site has only been recently opened."

I believed him. My fall was testimony to the unseen dangers of subterranean excavations.

Norman extended his hand for me to precede him. I cannot describe the comfort his presence gave me.

"Luke wants to go get something to eat," he said. "He's waiting for you."

I nodded. Maybe some food would make me feel more myself.

CHAPTER
16

Captain Spatz returned to the yacht. Norman and I joined Luke outside. We decided to try a lovely outdoor café, situated on a cliff bluff, overlooking the sea. Most of the team was hungry by the time we left the church and accompanied us. Where was Tommy? I glanced down the street. He may have joined Emily and a couple of the younger team members to explore another part of town.

I was obligated to dine with Luke, Norman and Marissa. Because of this mix of company, Tommy's envelope would have to wait. Did the young technician's mention of Marissa mean that I could trust her?

My mind was so distracted lunch was a blur. I wanted to tell Luke about my conversation with Spatz. I had no chance. Most of the discussion revolved around the upcoming excavation, and the removal and restoration of the paintings, pottery and frescoes from the church. I vaguely remembered sipping chilled Limoncello from a ceramic glass and nibbling on fresh, savory seafood (shrimps, calamari and scallops) and a salad with black olives, tomatoes and a very white and piquant cheese.

Luke ate quickly. Clearly he wished to get moving on his investigation. He gave Norman the afternoon off even though the bodyguard insisted on accompanying us. Luke suggested he drop us off at our destination, and then pursue whatever activity he desired for the remainder of the day. Marissa announced that she had some shopping she wanted to conduct in town.

Luke had hired a car for the short drive to the Torre Trasita, the residence of his colleague Marco Ferri.

"I want to meet with him before my meeting with Piero," he said.

"Are you sure you want me to come with you?" I, myself, wasn't sure I wished to get involved with Interpol. Piero as I recalled was the name of the agent that had contacted Luke. It was *her* name that was signed on the letters—the one to Luke *and* the one to my brother-in-law, Shaun. "After all, this is your private business and nothing at all to do with me."

"Do you mind, Lucy? I really would like an objective ear at this interview."

"Interview?" I queried.

"Well, I can't exactly call it an interrogation. I want to know if Marco is hiding anything. And whether I can trust him."

***

The trip was short. In fact a car was unnecessary. I could have done with a walk. Norman delivered us to the garden path, which wound through native flowers and shrubs towards the house. After the bodyguard drove away, Luke led me down the rocky steps at the side of the Torre.

"Careful," he said as I stumbled on some loose stones.

The Torre Trasita is a former guard tower which looks, from the outside, exactly like a castle keep. Built of solid stone with long windows on every level, it had a very interesting history. In the 14th century it served as a lookout point to warn against Saracen attacks. When pirates were spotted at sea, the guards would light a fire on the top of the tower to alert the villagers—to which they would respond by running for the hills. It was later purchased for commercial use, and entirely renovated. A few years ago, Marco Ferri turned it into a summer home.

Luke was studying the exterior walls of the structure. It was built of the original mortared stone and had elongated, narrow windows at each level. To meet fire codes each level opened onto either a concrete or black cast iron balcony, linked by stairs that ran in a zigzag up the height of the building. The stairs appeared to stretch from what looked like a rooftop patio, to a garden of tall ornamental grasses, bougainvillea, and fragrant roses at ground level.

What was he looking for? He gave no explanation. When he was finished, he wandered downhill in the direction of the beach. I followed to the water's edge where waves lapped the pebbles. A couple of old pylons stuck out of the water about twenty meters down the shore. At one time a dock probably stood here. Now nothing remained but rotting stumps. Why hadn't Signor Ferri built a private dock?

But then the marina was not far and that was probably where he berthed his boat, if he had one.

"Are we looking for something in particular?" I asked.

Luke hesitated for a moment, then shook his head and gestured for me to follow.

The front door opened to boisterous laughter and high spirits. The man standing there was clearly happy to see Luke. "*Ciao, amico mio,*" the portly gentleman said. He was expensively dressed in designer casuals with deck shoes. His age was anywhere between forty-five and fifty-five. His blue eyes had that far away look you often see in airplane pilots and seamen, as though so many years of staring into vast distances had somehow faded their color. I had been told that he had made his fortune in custom yacht building. In fact, he was the builder of Luke's current luxury vessel, the *Madonna*.

"Marco," Luke responded. They hugged in the Italian way.

"And who is this beautiful young lady? Your latest,

Luca?" Marco used the Italian form of Luke's name.

"Lucy Racine. This is my old friend, Marco Ferri."

"*Ciao*, Marco. Nice to meet you," I said.

"Come in, come in. You would like a drink, yes, *Lucia?*"

Somehow Signor Ferri managed to make my name sound so much prettier in Italian. "Nothing for me, thanks," I said, "We just had lunch."

"But it *is* the cocktail hour," Marco said. "Come. *Prego.*" He led us through a beautiful hallway to the living room. The Torre Trasita was circular. All of the rooms in the building accommodated the circumference of the tower. I wish I could describe adequately the stunning splendor of this place. It had multiple iron-railed, curved staircases and ceramic floors in polished tiles that reflected the greens and blues of the sea. The living room was furnished with lovely white sofas and armchairs. They looked like no one had ever sat in them. The pristine white walls were hung with modern art and a few traditional pieces. I saw nothing that resembled our missing icon.

Before our arrival Luke and I had hatched a plan. The idea was for me to excuse myself to use the bathroom, and find my way upstairs and into some of the bedrooms. It was unlikely, if Marco really owned the stolen artifact, that he would have rehung it anywhere obvious. It had already been recognized. I asked Luke if he knew the name of the photographer who claimed to spot the object. Apparently his identity was secret. He had, however, posted the photograph on WikiLoot, the website for crowdsourcing missing artifacts. He had used an alias.

"It's a beautiful day. Why don't we sit outside?" By 'outside' Marco meant his rooftop patio.

It was a wonder in itself. Still, I avoided standing too close to the rail. The entire top portion of the tower had been transformed from a historic watchtower to a lovely blue and white patio, surrounded by a concrete and iron railing. The floor tiles reflected the sky and the lounge chairs were white with royal blue pillows. The dining set was of black cast aluminum and royal blue fabric upholstery.

Our host brought with him a chilled bottle of white wine and three glasses. These he set upon the glass tabletop. Over our heads a turquoise and white awning provided shade from the late afternoon sun. All around were splendid views of the sea.

"And where are Isadora and the kids?" Luke asked cordially.

"The boys are all grown up," Marco said, chuckling. "They only come home to eat now. Soon they will go to college, I hope. But for now, they are on summer vacation with their mother in Naples visiting their grandparents."

"That's too bad, I would have liked to see Isadora again."

Luke shot me a look and I interpreted it as my cue to use the lavatory. I asked Marco where the nearest one was, as I understood there were four bathrooms in his home. He gave directions and I returned down the iron staircase that ran along the exterior of the tower to a glass door on one side. Fortunately it was short. I have not suffered from vertigo in a while and I was not about to start now. Under cover of an enormous cypress growing out of the side of the cliff, I stopped on the small, shaded balcony to look up through a curtain of hanging wisteria. I unlatched the door and ducked inside.

I had to hurry. I peeked into the bedrooms, starting with the top level. Each had its own en suite bath. The bedrooms took up the entire floor. They were huge suites with not only king or queen-sized beds, but also sitting areas replete with sofas and tables, and private balconies looking out onto the water. The intricacy of each suite's unique design reminded me of the interior of a seashell.

The floors were inlaid with ceramic tiles in variations of the aquamarine theme. In keeping with the color scheme most rooms had bold white walls with plush furnishings in bright blues, greens and yellows. It was dazzling.

Unfortunately I saw nothing resembling the Black Madonna.

Marco had told me to use the first bathroom I came across. At level three, I walked into a lovely, pristine blue and white marble bath. I could have stayed in there all afternoon. There was something so soothing about the sea colors.

Without looking down, I returned to the rooftop patio. Luke gave me a bare glance of inquiry. I responded with the slightest shake of my head.

"Your home is exquisite," I said to Marco.

He smiled. "I adore how almost every room has a view of the water."

"You love the sea," I said, seating myself at the round glass table across from him.

"I do. When I was a boy I used to go on the sea often."

"Ah, you're a sailor, like Luke. Do you have your own boat?"

He nodded. There was a hint of amusement in his face that I couldn't quite understand. "But of course, you must stay the night. You and *Luca*."

Simultaneously we exchanged glances. It was getting so that I could read Luke's mind. "Be delighted, Marco," Luke said. "What do you think, Lucy?"

"I would love it."

Marco took us out to a fine restaurant for dinner. We ate heartily of the delicious local fare and drank perhaps a little too much wine. I was so thrilled to be in this exciting town with the most stimulating man on earth that I completely forgot my reasons for accompanying Luke to visit Marco. Luke never mentioned the Black Madonna. I guess he didn't want to make Marco suspicious. But the friendly Italian noticed nothing amiss or irregular. He seemed genuinely pleased that Luke was visiting.

In the end it was Marco who brought up the topic of Interpol's interest in his art collection but this didn't happen for another two hours. By that time everyone was safely home and in bed. The archaeology team, after a night on the town, returned to the yacht after Luke contacted Norman to inform him that he and I were staying with his old friend. From what I could hear of their phone conversation, Norman wanted to return to the Torre with us. His job after all was to keep Luke safe, but his boss assured him he was in no danger whatsoever. Not from Signor Ferri.

It was then I began to have doubts. Not just about Marco Ferri. My doubts concerning Luke were returning.

It happened that I was sleeping beside Luke in the bedroom with the aquamarine floor tiles, white bedspread and turquoise pillows, when I awoke to find myself alone. I had reached out to feel his hard abs on my groping fingers and found only soft mattress.

Pale moonlight filtered through the white curtains turning the beautiful circular bedroom suite into a seaside wonderland. It was perfect, except that Luke wasn't here. I remember making love with him, half drunk with good wine and food and half giddy from pure desire and pleasure. The freshness and coolness of the sea air had danced in through the partially opened window cloaking our naked flesh in its delicate touch. He had taken me as wildly as Neptune might have taken his sea nymph. I was all his, down to my very toes. When his tongue reached my nether regions I thought I should die from the pleasure of it, and when I opened my thighs to allow him to explore further I felt his lips and the warmest of pressures as he worked me toward ecstasy.

I was getting myself worked up just thinking about it. Where was he? I blinked the sleep out of my eyes and looked around me. I was moist and yearning and ready for him. But no sound came from the bathroom or the connecting balcony.

I had borrowed one of Signora Ferri's satin dressing gowns, and donned this now. It was a deep purple color, luxurious to the touch, but more, the dark hue helped me to blend in with the shadows. Marco had promised me that his wife would not mind.

Barefoot, I crossed the room to the sofa. Luke was

nowhere to be seen. My purse was there and I dug out my phone. Maybe he had left me a text message.

No message. The door was slightly ajar. He had left it like that so that he could leave silently. Was he having trouble sleeping? A shiver along my arms told me something was wrong. I took the curving staircase to the next floor and waited in the shadows. No sounds came from that bedroom. When I arrived on the main floor I halted on the staircase. A light was below me and I detected quiet voices. I should have been able to just walk downstairs like I, too, was suffering from a bout of insomnia and needed a nightcap or something to read. The tone of their voices warned me that my presence would not be welcome. They were speaking in a mixture of Italian and English.

"What did you do with it?" Luke's voice.

"I hid it somewhere; no one will find it."

"Marco, that was completely reckless of you. How could you let someone see it?"

"I thought it was okay. That no one would dare walk into my private studio. It is just off the master bedroom. Even Isadora does not go inside there."

"She doesn't know?"

"She does not."

"I always wondered what happened to it. And when they thought that I had stolen it…." He made some expletive in Italian that I failed to grasp, but knew it for a cuss word just by the way he said it. "When I got that letter. When you implicated me—"

"I did not mean to implicate you. I was scared. They wanted names. Your name came out. I did not think—"

"We're just lucky there were no other witnesses. I can have the object's image removed from the website. But the thing itself—"

The next bit was in Italian, most of which I found incomprehensible. My Italian, while workable, was not fluent. Then I caught this:

"There is the matter of the boy." Marco's voice.

And then: "I'll take care of it." Luke's.

All at once a violent vibration stirred in my hand. I'd forgotten that I still held my phone. I quickly muffled the device and tiptoed as quietly and as fast as I could up the shadowy stairs and back to my dark room. Oh my God. Had Luke been lying to me all the time? I ran into the adjoining bathroom and shut the door. The caller ID showed that it was Colleen on the line. I was relieved and worried at the same. What time was it there in Toronto?

6:00 PM.

"Colleen," I whispered. I was standing in the dark on the cold tiles in my bare feet, the borrowed robe in disarray. "Is everything alright? Has something happened?"

"No. I'm fine, Lucy. I just missed you. Why haven't you called?"

"It's midnight here."

Silence, and then she said, "So it is. Sorry, did I wake you? You never go to bed until after midnight. Why are you so upset?"

"I'm not upset. I'm just...."

"Lucy? What's wrong? I know you. Something *is* wrong. Why are you whispering?"

I hedged around whether or not I should tell her what I'd become embroiled in. The last thing I wanted to do was worry her. But I needed to know if Shaun was involved.

"Colleen," I said. "You're right; something is going on here, but I can't tell you about it right now. All I can say is that I need you to do something for me. Please don't ask any questions. I'll explain everything when I get a chance. Right now, I need you to go to Shaun's office and find a letter. It will be from Interpol and will have the signature of an agent named Alessandra Piero... Yes, that's right. Piero... P-i-e-r-o. Can you do that for me?"

"Interpol? Lucy, what have you gotten yourself into?"

"It's the museum I'm worried about, Colleen. Don't fuss about me. I'm fine. I'm quite safe." Even as I said these words I hardly believed them. What if Luke was mixed up in some present-day smuggling racket? What if he had involved my sister's husband? It was crazy to think that, but she was a bit of a spendthrift. He was drowning in debt and maybe he needed the extra income. *I don't know. I'm just inventing this as I go along.* My mind was whirling a mile a minute. It was one thing for Luke to use me, but I refused to let him use my brother-in-law! "Please Colleen. Will you do that? I know it's late, but the service door at the back, that the janitors use, will be open. Find the letter. And don't, whatever you do, let Shaun catch you. It's in his desk drawer—the top one. I know it is. I saw it. When you find it, snap its picture and email it to me. Then put it back exactly where you found it."

"Lucy, is Shaun involved in some shady dealings? You're asking me to steal something from his office!"

"No. I'm pretty sure he's not involved." God help me I was lying to her, but I had to get her to cooperate. "It's just that there might be a connection with some artifact that's gone missing from a church in Italy, and the museum might know something about it."

"Well, if you suspect some shifty goings on with the museum, shouldn't Shaun know about it? In fact, doesn't he already know since he's in possession of this letter?"

"No." I scoured my brains to figure out how to explain this to her without incriminating her husband. I knew nothing for certain. So I mustn't jump to conclusions. "Sometimes museums end up with stolen property. They just aren't aware that the objects were stolen because they acquired them from a legitimate auction or dealer."

"So why can't I tell Shaun why you want the letter?"

"He thinks I have an overactive imagination. You know what he'll say. I don't want him jumping all over me until I know for certain there's nothing to worry about. If it *is* something, then for sure I'll want him to know. I'll tell him myself."

That seemed to satisfy her. She agreed to fulfill my request. However, before she hung up she asked, "So how's it going with the billionaire?"

I laughed and that lightened things up a bit. But beneath the bravado I was trembling.

CHAPTER
<u>17</u>

The next morning I was terrified I'd be unable to act normal when I woke up. I needn't have worried. Luke had already showered and shaved and was rapidly talking to someone on his phone when I crept out of bed. He blew me a kiss, and gestured to me that the bathroom was free. It was obvious that something was wrong. He hardly paid any attention to me, even when I came out of the shower wrapped only in a towel with wet hair. When we sat down to breakfast, he informed Marco we had to leave immediately.

"What happened?" I demanded. My fears from my midnight excursion were crushed by my present curiosity. And to be truthful, neither Luke nor Marco Ferri seemed, in the cold light of morning, to be capable of the illegal activities I had overheard—or was it *imagined*—last night.

He hesitated as though he wished he could leave me out of it. "There's been an accident at the church."

"What kind of accident? Was anybody hurt?"

"Yes," he said. He glanced at me gently. "Look, Lucy, maybe you shouldn't come with me. Go back to the yacht. Or better yet, take Emily and go shopping in town."

"I don't want to go shopping," I said, shaking. I was simultaneously insulted and pleased that he was trying to

protect me. I wasted no further time analyzing my hypocrisy.
I still did not really understand why he wanted me here. It
seemed I was more of a hindrance than an aid if he were truly
a criminal. "Tell me who was hurt."

He shoved a croissant into my hand. He took a quick
gulp of the coffee that Marco had poured into his cup, and
apologized to our host. "We have to leave, Marco."

The Italian understood. The warmth in his dark eyes
suggested empathy. Apparently everyone was in the know
except me.

Marco led us to the front door. I thanked him for his
hospitality. I followed Luke to a black sedan that was waiting
for us. Inside it, Norman sat in the driver's seat, clean-
shaven. He was smoking a cigarette. The hard line of his jaw
showed tension.

He tossed the stub out the open window without
acknowledging me. It took an extreme effort of will for me
not to tap him on the shoulder and force him to smile. After
that infamous night on the beach we rarely spoke. We were
like two powerful magnets balanced at opposite poles forcing
us apart. To him I was just another one of his boss's flings. I
coughed. It was a deliberate effort to let him know what I
thought of his smoking in the car. Did Luke even notice?
Maybe it was no concern to him because the car was a rental.
I had never seen Norman smoke in the limo. He only smoked
on deck aboard the yacht. Luke had strict rules about
smoking on the yacht. In fact, as I recalled, Norman
Depardieu rarely smoked. Whatever was going on had him
agitated.

We boarded. I sat silently in the back seat with Luke.
Norman asked for instructions. Then Luke turned to me. "A
body was found inside one of the crypts."

My hands shook. I felt my body trembling. I could
barely form words. "Who was it?"

"Tommy."

Oh, God.

"His body was discovered half buried under some fallen

rubble. A temporary scaffold had been erected. Apparently, something jarred it. It was unstable and it collapsed. The boy was slow to get out of the way. A board struck him on the back of the head. He was dead before he fell."

Poor Tommy. If only I had gotten to him before he so recklessly returned to the worksite under the church. What was he looking for?

I was quiet, shaking uncontrollably. Luke's arm came around me in a gentle, reassuring squeeze. It was strange. While Luke's gesture of comfort was welcome, it was Norman's obvious concern over my distress that soothed me most. He sat behind the wheel, his eyes flickering every now and then at the rearview mirror to catch my expression, a tender look of empathy on his face. I buried my cheek in Luke's chest to avoid eye contact with Norman. The depths of his concern for my feelings made me want to burst into tears.

After that, we spoke little. I had myriad questions I wanted to ask him but he had told me all he knew.

"I'm sorry, Lucy. I know you two were friends."

Luke handed me his cup of coffee. He really never knew what to do when people were upset. That was okay. Norman's eyes had flickered my way again and I lowered my head. "It's okay, Luke." I swallowed. "I'm okay."

"Do you want to go back to the yacht? I can have Norman take you back to the yacht."

"No. I want to go to the church and find out exactly how this happened."

"Are you sure?"

"Yes."

He nodded. He removed his arm from around my shoulders and turned away. He was on the phone again. Business or the police? Could be either. In the driver's seat, Norman's gaze flickered once at me, and then back to the road.

I sipped the coffee Luke had given me, in silence, and when the mug was empty, set it down on the car floor.

The drive to the church was short. Because of the traffic, we could have walked it in less time. Norman parked the car and we made our way up the staircase to the piazza in front of the church. The police were already there. Yellow crime tape stretched in front of the building. No one was allowed inside. Luke and Norman left me to talk to the officers stationed at the door. I was in a state of shock. My brain could barely contain all the questions that were spinning inside it.

Marissa and the rest of the team were waiting outside near the bell tower. I made my way to them. Around the base of the bell tower the plaster was decorated with motifs in low relief. Eyes lowered, I forced myself to breathe to remain calm before I could speak. I turned my attention upwards to see Marissa watching me.

The reason my eyes had been drawn first to ground level was because of her shoes. Even from a distance she had appeared different in stature, taller and more authoritative. Gone were the running shoes of yesterday. Her feet were shod in classy medium heels. She stared at me for a full minute after I had raised my eyes. Exactly what was she thinking?

"Is there any more news?" I asked her. "Do they know what Tommy was doing in the crypt alone?

"No," she said.

I shut my eyes to control the emotion. Now was not the time to cry. Later, when all of this was explained I could cry. Right now I wanted to know why he was dead.

Although no one had mentioned foul play, I could not rule it out.

He was trying to tell me something. Yesterday. If only I hadn't let him slip away. The envelope! I still had his envelope. I fumbled at my purse and noticed Marissa observing me. My hands went still, and I matched her gaze. She was not dressed like a museum worker or an archaeologist. She was wearing slacks, a fitted red shirt and a blazer. There was something quite different about her today, other than the shoes, and her clothing. It was the thing I had noticed about her before even approaching. She displayed a manner that I could only describe as officious.

There is something to be said for intuition. Explaining how it works is a quest in futility. But when it happens you trust it. I suddenly knew who she must be.

"Your name isn't Marissa Leone is it?" I said.

A crease broke the smoothness of her forehead. She nudged me aside, a few feet away from our colleagues.

"How did you know?"

I swallowed. "You're not a conservator, are you? You have nothing to do with frescoes. You're with Interpol."

She nodded, and removed a badge from inside her jacket, hiding it from the sight of passersby with her lapel. "My name is Alessandra Piero."

"I know."

She smiled. "Of course, you do. I slipped up somehow aboard Trevanian's yacht. Does Dr. Trevanian know?"

"I don't think so."

"Good."

I felt awkward now that she had admitted her true identity. It left me with a dilemma. "Did you find what you were looking for?" I asked.

"Yes—and no." It was clear she had no intention of elaborating. "But you... *you* appear to have found something, yes? You look like you have something you want to share."

"You're searching for the Black Madonna," I accused.

"I am."

"Do you have any idea where it is?"

She shook her head. "Do *you* know where it is?"

I mimicked her gesture, my chin swinging to and fro. I was still unable to decide what to do. I wanted so much to trust Luke. What was he into? And could he possibly have anything to do with what had happened to Tommy?

No. NO. I refused to believe it.

"Look, Ms. Racine."

Why so formal, I thought. We'd been sharing close

quarters aboard ship for almost two weeks. But I supposed now that she had revealed her true identity, formality ruled. Did she expect the same from me? Her voice had changed too. She now had an accent. An Italian accent. This was her real voice, not the Americanized one she had been using when we first met. "If you know something, you had better tell me about it. It may be related to why Tommy Buchanan was murdered."

"*Murdered?*" Now that the word was spoken aloud it seemed absurd.

"The collapse of the wall and the scaffolding was made to look like an accident. It was no accident."

"But who? Why would anyone want to kill Tommy?"

"He had information, yes? He knows or should I say, he knew about the Black Madonna."

She touched my arm and drew me aside, to a wall dripping with bougainvillea. I stared at the small pink lantern-shaped flowers as though they would somehow make everything clear to me. There was a scent in the air that at first I attributed to the flowers, but then I realized the fragrance was more like citrus and it was coming from her.

Everyone had an identifying scent; hers was citrus. Was it her shampoo? It didn't really matter. It was a nice smell and made me like her. How strange that smells could do that. It made me less suspicions and more curious.

I returned my attention to her and listened closely. Everyone else's attention was drawn to the cordoned off front doors. No one was eavesdropping. We could speak freely. Luke and Norman had disappeared inside the church.

"The icon... she is very important," she continued. "And the gang of smugglers... they are still at large. They are still active. They have taken much more valuable artifacts than this religious object. It is suspected that this racket is responsible for billions of dollars worth of stolen artifacts. I believe they continue to this day. I wish to bring them to justice." When I remained silent, she added, "This boy, Tommy Buchanan. He was a colleague of yours, no?"

"Yes. He worked at the same museum. The ROM."

"You were friends?"

"Well, it depends on what you mean by friends. We've known each other for years. We were more than co-workers…. So yes. Yes, we were definitely friends."

"And your brother-in-law, Shaun Templeton. He also works at the Royal Ontario Museum?"

"You *know* he does."

Her eyebrows rose.

I decided to say nothing further. She appeared to have no suspicion of Arianna Chase, the museum's director. But she had raised the name of my brother-in-law. I refused to implicate Shaun in anything until I had all the facts.

CHAPTER
18

It was then that my phone chimed. It was loud enough to startle the both of us. I wished I had set the ringtone to low. I had deliberately increased its volume to ensure I received any message from Colleen the second it hit my Inbox. Now I realized that the email was irrelevant. It was obvious from Alessandra Piero's expression and what she had already told me that the letter was from her.

"Aren't you going to answer that?" she asked.

"It's just an email."

"From your sister?"

I raised my head, not startled exactly, but alert. How much did she know? And just what did she suspect of Shaun? I decided this cat-and-mouse game had to end. "How is my brother-in-law involved?" I asked, point blank.

"I'm not certain he is." She moved a little closer to the wall to allow some tourists to walk past and out of hearing distance. The on-duty officers had turned them away from the church. "Ms. Racine," she said. "You are going to have to trust me. *I'm* the good guy."

"Then why did you have to come on board Dr. Trevanian's yacht as Marissa Leone? Why the disguise?"

It struck me at that moment. Luke was correct, and even

honest, when he guessed that Interpol suspected him in the theft of the Black Madonna. But worse. They suspected him to be involved in a modern-day heist of the priceless artifact. What was *even* worse was that, after overhearing Luke's conversation with Marco Ferri last night, I realized her suspicions were justified. What other explanation was there? What could he possibly have been referring to in that whispered dialogue except the church's stolen icon...? And... oh no, oh my God, no. Ferri had mentioned a boy. *There is the matter of the boy.*

Alessandra Piero watched my expression with the utmost interest. "You remember something... something I should know."

The body belonged to Tommy. Then another piece of last night's eavesdropping threatened to shatter my mind. *I will take care of it.* Luke's voice.

I darted a frightened glance at the church doors.

No. I refused to believe it.

"What's the matter, Ms. Racine? What has you so distraught?"

My hand pawed involuntarily at the soft leather of my handbag. The email chimed again.

I opened my purse for something to do, and to distract her from pursuing her line of questioning. I withdrew my phone. Two emails. Both from Colleen. The first was the photograph of Shaun's letter from Interpol. It was almost identical to the one Piero had written to Luke. No need to expand the image to know that it was the same. The other email was a chatty update.

Could Shaun be implicated in any wrongdoing by the museum or by his association with Luke? No. She had read the letter. She insisted that he was unacquainted with the man, Marco Ferri.

"Dr. Trevanian is a enigmatic man," Piero said.

I allowed her to distract me from my musings. "Yes, he is."

"Look, Lucy. May I call you Lucy?"

"Why not? You've been calling me Lucy until today."

"I am now here officially in my capacity of a representative of Interpol—as far as you are concerned."

"Do any of the archaeology team or sailing crew of the *Madonna* know who you really are? The captain perhaps?" Why did I ask that? Except that it seemed logical to me that if she were to inform anyone on board it would be him. For some inexplicable reason I hoped she had not.

She shook her head. "For now—I would like to keep it that way."

"So, you're trusting *me?* Why are you trusting me?"

Her silence irritated me more than my own mixed feelings, more than my own belief that I was not trustworthy. I had slept with her number one suspect. I had not only slept with him, but in official terms I was what the authorities would deem his mistress.

"You think Luke murdered—" I blurted out the accusation without thinking.

I had to take the focus off myself, and my own guilt. But I could not bring myself to use Tommy's name. If I did I would be admitting that he was dead. That he was killed in cold blood. Possibly by Luke. I almost cupped my hand to my mouth. Instead, I crushed the thought.

"My job is not to determine whether Tommy Buchanan's death was accidental or a homicide. The local authorities will take care of that. Until I am called in otherwise, my job is to rout out the member of the gang who is hiding the Black Madonna."

"Why is that artifact so important?" I fumed.

"Why does it distress you so?"

"I am not distressed. It's just that it keeps coming up."

"How so?"

I wanted to tell her how Tommy had mentioned it in the church yesterday. My conversation with him replayed itself. I had asked how he knew so much about the stolen artifact. His answer? *Ask Marissa.*

"It's a religious icon," Piero said. "But *you* tell me why

it is so important. You are the expert."

"No. I am not. I'm just an illustrator."

She looked down at the phone that remained in my hand. "Your sister?" she asked.

I showed her the letter: her own letter, with the Interpol insignia, signed by her own hand.

Dear Dr. Templeton,

On behalf of the International Police (Interpol) I would like to request your expertise on a matter of great cultural importance to the country of Italy and particularly to the town of Positano. As an expert in Italian artifacts and those especially pertaining to the catastrophic events of AD 79 when Mount Vesuvius erupted burying much of the Amalfi coast villas as well as the famed sites of Pompeii and Herculaneum, I believe you are in a position to aid us. I understand that your museum is affiliated with an expedition to excavate the ruins beneath the church of Santa Maria Assunta and therefore you may be familiar with the layout of the church and what lies beneath it.

Our records show that your museum has had business dealings with a Signor Marco Ferri who is a patron of the church. He is a person of interest in this case. We have interviewed Signor Ferri and he has referred us to you. We understand you are familiar with the case of the stolen Black Madonna. It was appropriated from the church September 2, 2002 and was allegedly recently spotted in the home of a private citizen.

I would like to meet with you at your earliest convenience. I have been told that you are assembling a technical team for Dr. Luke Trevanian's expedition to Positano in August. I hope we can set up a telephone meeting to discuss it.

Thank you in advance.

Yours truly,
Alessandra Piero
ICPO–Interpol

Phone: 39-(081)-xxx-xxxx
Email: APiero@Interpol.int

"What were you trying to prove with that?" she asked.

"I just wanted to know what the connection was between Luke and Shaun. I thought there might be something in the letter."

"Will you feel better if I tell you that I believe there is no connection? That they are acquaintances? That's all?"

"Yes, that would make me feel better."

"Then that is what I am telling you. Do not worry about him anymore."

"And Luke?"

"Dr. Trevanian is another matter."

I stared at her. I had to trust her. I had to trust someone. I glanced down at my purse. Tommy's envelope was inside. I had not looked at it.

Ask Marissa.

"You were working with Tommy," I accused her.

She did not confirm or deny the accusation.

"You don't have to pretend. He as much as told me that he was working with you."

She frowned. "What did he say?"

I unzipped my bag and fumbled for the sharp edges of the envelope. The corner pricked my thumb and I withdrew it. "Let's find out, shall we?"

I looked at Piero. I still thought of her as Marissa.

"Call me Marissa," she said. "It will make things easier."

She had the power to read minds. I would have to be careful around her.

I nodded, and opened the envelope.

Inside were photographs. I understood why he had not sent me digital images, why he had printed them instead. Digital images were easily stolen, passed around, and deleted. What I failed to understand was why he had given them to me for safekeeping. Why not give them to the Interpol agent instead?

There were two photos. One was of the Virgin Mary with Child. Every part of her skin, her face, her throat, her arms and hands were dark, almost black. Everything else, her clothing and background, were gold.

The photograph was taken inside a room I recognized. It was the same room—the divine, concentric, seashell-like turquoise and white room inside the Torre Trasita that Luke and I had shared last night.

So it was true. Marco Ferri was in possession of the stolen artifact.

Piero pointed to the image of the Virgin and Child, "This one was posted on WikiLoot. It's how I found it. And how I found Tommy. He was the genius behind the website. If you haven't figured it out." She removed the other photo from my sweating fingertips. This one was the photo of the tattoo Luke had shown me on Tommy's cellphone. She stared at it and I could see that it troubled her.

"Do you know who that tattoo belongs to?" she asked.

No. But I knew someone who did. I looked up swiftly and shrugged. "No. Why would he take a picture like that?"

"Does Trevanian have a tattoo?" she asked.

"No," I answered, a little too quickly. She studied my face as though she thought I were lying, then shoved the photograph behind the other, and raised the one of the Black Madonna.

"This one I asked him to take down from the website. But unfortunately, it did not save him. The killer had already seen it and knew he was on their trail."

I had to get her mind off of Luke. "You think the owner of the Torre Trasita killed him? Or had him killed?" Marco Ferri had been the epitome of the friendly Italian but the look on the Interpol agent's face was giving me second thoughts. Surely, it was impossible to mask harmful intentions? But must I remind myself that I had just met the man? For all I knew he *had* no wife or children and he hated Luke's guts. I shuddered to think that I had spent the night in a murderer's home.

"Perhaps," she said.

If it were true, then Luke was implicated. But something inside me refused to acknowledge his guilt.

"There is something else inside the envelope. A message?"

I unfolded the scrap of paper. It was scrawled by hand in black ink and obviously scribbled down very quickly before being torn from a larger sheet of paper. It said simply:

> *When you read this I will probably be dead. The Black Madonna is not what she seems. I can't say more in case this message falls into the wrong hands. But you know me; you know what to do with it.*

Nowhere was *my* name mentioned.

Piero nodded. "Good, he did not identify you. That will keep you safe. And…"—she took the paper from me, as well as both of the photographs—"I will keep *these* safe."

I started to object, but then I saw the logic in her actions.

I looked up at Piero. Although I knew her real name I continued to think of her as Marissa. "Do you know *any* thing about conserving artworks?" I asked.

"As a matter of fact, I do. I have a degree in classical art, and a diploma in art conservation."

"So, we're going to continue with this charade."

"We are." She studied my face. "Are you up to it, Lucy?"

I shut my eyes. I was in it too deep to say, No. And I would never forgive myself if I decided to step into the sidelines at this point. In fact, I knew I couldn't turn my back on this mystery, not even if my life depended on it. Luke, *my*

Luke, was somehow involved. I sighed. Piero knew even before I nodded that I was committed.

How had I gotten so waylaid by the archaeologist? Could I even call him an archaeologist? It was looking more and more like his story was a con and that I was the victim. Why, then, did my heart deny it?

People say that you know when something is real, that you have a gut instinct. I had that now. Luke may have been a petty criminal when he was a teen, but not at present. He was a billionaire. Why would a billionaire risk involvement in something so shady, so dangerous? For kicks? Was he so bored that he'd lie and cheat, steal and smuggle for the thrill of it? I have to say I have not known a lot of billionaires. Actually none. So I'm a virgin when it comes to what makes them tick. But from what I had learned of Luke over these last weeks, he never did things for kicks. Something else was going on and I had to get him alone, had to get him to tell me the truth before the day was out.

"What do you want me to do?" I asked.

"You have a relationship with Luke Trevanian."

I shrugged. "You know I do."

"He trusts you?"

"I think so."

"There is something dubious about Trevanian. He is hiding something. Do you know what it is?"

I shook my head. I could barely breathe and that was my punishment for lying to the Interpol agent.

She said, "Tommy took that photograph of the tattoo for a reason. From the looks of it the work was done on a man's upper arm, near his shoulder. I believe if we find the man who wears that tattoo we will find the killer." My blood ran cold. My hands felt clammy. I was certain my face was drained of color. Had she noticed? I raised my eyes as she pelted me with yet another question. "Who aboard the yacht has a tattoo?"

I answered honestly. "No one among the team or the yacht's crew has a tattoo, as far as I know. But then I haven't seen all of them shirtless."

"No. Just Dr. Trevanian." Her eyes flickered knowingly.

I recognized the innuendo and scowled. "I told you. He has no tattoo. *Any*where."

By the expression on her face, she understood my meaning. She chose to ignore my reaction. "The only way to find out if anyone among our acquaintances possesses that tattoo would be for me to do a strip search. I doubt I would receive any cooperation, as I have no authority to demand that anybody remove their clothes. Nor do I have any evidence to insist that they do so." She paused. "Besides, it would mean my having to expose my connection with Interpol. And that is out of the question."

I had one more piece of information that I was keeping from her. I should have mentioned that Arianna Chase knew the identity of the tattooed man. I did not.

CHAPTER
19

"If you are so dead set on no one discovering your real identity, why the getup?" I was referring to her clothes. She did look more like a police detective than an archaeologist or tourist.

"I need to get into that church. They won't let me in to see the body unless I'm here in an official capacity."

"Who found the body?" I asked.

"It was the watchdog. Depardieu."

So, Norman was first on the scene? My suspicions escalated. But when I thought about it, why not? It was his job to open the doors to the crypt for the archaeology team.

"He called the police?"

She nodded again. "We all left for the church from the yacht at 8:15 am. He opened the doors to the *villa marittima* and we descended down the ladders to the *triclinium*. The boy was found inside an antechamber, one of those not yet opened to excavation. Some rubble had been cleared and dirt removed to expose the edges of a fallen fresco and some roof tiles."

It sounded like the room I had found myself in yesterday when I left the group to seek a quiet place to open Tommy's envelope. That was when Captain Spatz materialized, scaring me half to death, and forcing me to delay the task.

"Did Tommy tell you anything else?" Piero asked.

I got a grip on myself and whispered, "No."

We looked up as a commotion came from the church's front doors. The team was being ushered away. Luke and Norman had returned outside and were telling our colleagues that there would be no work done today. The police were busy recording the crime scene and statements would be taken from everyone who knew Tommy Buchanan. The police were already pretty much certain that the death was an accident. All of the team could vouch for each other's whereabouts between last night and the approximate time of death early this morning. Even Luke and I had alibis. We had been seen with Marco Ferri at the restaurant and he would confirm where we had slept last night. Besides, none of us had motives. I glanced briefly in Luke's direction.

"Do the police know of Tommy's connection with the Black Madonna?" I asked.

"No," she said.

The team had left and Luke and Norman were coming towards us. Luke looked tired today and harassed. Who could blame him? This was the opposite of how he had imagined his expedition to begin. "Are you going to let him know who you are?" I asked.

She thought about it. "How close is he with his bodyguard?"

"Norman? I think he pretty much knows everything."

"And you. How much do *you* know?"

"About Luke?"

She nodded.

Not as much as I would like.

I answered, "Not a lot."

She seemed to muse over my response, and then her head rose and her eyes aimed over my shoulder. Her entire demeanor changed. I turned to look.

"The police are scanning for evidence of foul play," Luke said stepping up to join us. His eyes landed on mine.

He took my hand, which was cold as a slab of meat. "You okay, Lucy? I know this news about Tommy was a shock."

I nodded, withdrawing my icy hand and warming it inside my pocket. I did not want the Interpol agent to know how distressed I was. "It's just so incredible. Honestly it's hard to believe. It feels surreal. Do they have any clues as to how it happened?"

"They're looking. But they don't think they'll find anything." He sucked in a sudden breath. Slapped his chest. "Jesus. Just occurred to me that I will have to inform his parents." Lines creased his forehead. Then he turned back to us. He sighed. "I'll take care of that tonight when we know more. Meanwhile the police are pretty certain it was an accident. They tell me we can probably start work in a day or two."

"I would like to make sure none of the frescoes were damaged in the mishap," Marissa said.

Gone was the Italian accent, replaced by a more American twang. Yes, the voice that had spoken *was* Marissa's. The Interpol agent was in disguise once more. I turned to look at her. The persona of Alessandra Piero had vanished. She had decided not to trust Luke.

"They won't let you in until tomorrow. What I could see didn't look like anything important was damaged. I identified the body," Luke said.

Marissa nodded. "Well, Lucy, since we have the day off, how's about you and I go shopping?"

My eyes widened with just a hint of surprise. I felt confused. How could she think about shopping when Tommy—I flinched as the reality suddenly hit me—Tommy was dead! True, Tommy was probably only an acquaintance to Marissa, but still…. I glanced at Luke. Even Luke was behaving incredibly nonchalant. Only Norman caught the concern on my face but he swiftly turned away.

I stared through the sheen of tears that threatened to break from my eyes.

"It's a good idea, Lucy," Norman said, raising his head.

Luke nodded. He gave me a thumbs-up without so much as twitching a hand.

I sighed, swallowed the emotion. I could no longer help Tommy. But maybe I could help Luke. This was what he wished. He wanted Marissa and I to become best friends.

As far as the Interpol agent was concerned, she wanted my allegiance—and possibly my help to bring Luke down. She would have to provide a hell of a lot more proof before she swayed me to her side.

All right. I would go. Spending an entire day with Marissa was on the bottom of my list, but I was torn between pleasing Luke and helping Interpol. Luke's eyes begged me to humor her, and so I did. We said our goodbyes like casual acquaintances—employer and employee—rather than intimate lovers. What I really longed for was Luke's company, his strong protective arms around my shoulders, convincing me he was a decent, honest man. Another side of me yearned for the truth. So, I went with Marissa into town with the full intention of doubling back and revisiting the site of Tommy's accident, and to examine the body itself. I shuddered. That was not a task I looked forward to.

We left the men, and scaled the stone steps to the cobblestone alleyways where the shops were located. A magazine article I'd read when I was researching Positano came to mind. The description was published in an old *Harper's Bazaar* magazine by the famous American author John Steinbeck. Apparently he had spent much of his time in this lovely portion of Italy, which was, and still is, a favorite haunt of artists and writers.

He was accurate in the way he had described the town. This place was a place of magic, not murder. Bad things *never* happened in Positano.

I followed Marissa into town. The boutiques clung to ledges along the mountainside just as the houses did. We stopped to study the maze of alleys and steps crowded with interesting shops. I poked my head into one of the open store doorways and saw rows of crisp linen dresses, stylish,

French-cut swimwear and trendy leather sandals. Next door to this was a boutique selling rustic pottery and finely glazed ceramics.

We spent about fifteen minutes browsing. Marissa bought a small vase and told me to make a purchase. We had to have something to show for our excursion when we returned to the yacht.

I backtracked to the first boutique and chose a red one-piece swimsuit, high-cut at the thighs and with a neckline that plunged to the navel and double spaghetti straps. Subconsciously, I was thinking of Luke, and how he'd react if he saw me in this. But consciously I just thought it was pretty. I also found a pair of nice leather sandals.

When I stepped out of the shop Marissa was waiting for me. She had her back to the shop and was staring at the horizon, a hand over her eyes to shade them from the blinding sun. Behind us the boutiques sat stacked one on top of the other. As I looked down, a little nervous from the breathless height, the cluster of quaint structures reflected back to me in the sea below. The air was fresh with the scents of salt, lemon and bay trees. Despite the unsettling events of the morning, sun and sea air had a way of calming the nerves.

I stood unnoticed behind Marissa. I raised my eyes, squinted. What was she watching that had her so mesmerized? I got the distinct impression that she wished she'd had a pair of binoculars with her. But neither of us had thought to bring a pair. Why would we, when our purpose this morning was to descend into a dark crypt of a chamber, and examine some ancient Roman frescoes?

Some sixth sense told me she wished to be left undisturbed. I let my vision follow the direction of hers.

Out in the bay I recognized Luke's yacht. Someone had lowered a Zodiac and was now speeding across the distant harbor. As they neared land, the inflatable watercraft slowed then disappeared behind a rocky promontory. For the life of me I could not begin to guess at what had the Interpol agent so transfixed. Had she identified another suspect aboard

Luke's yacht?

Something in her manner as she studied the yacht roused my suspicions. Did she really think Luke was the leader of some kind of modern-day smuggling ring?

When I finally decided to announce my presence by rattling the paper bags bearing my purchases, Marissa turned and smiled.

***

An hour later we were back at the church. The police were finishing up and were ready to move the body. Marissa flashed her Interpol badge and explained that she was investigating a cold case involving a missing religious icon, and that it might be connected with the accident. The officers bought her story, and let us in. We were allowed only ten minutes.

"I'm not sure I can bear to see this," I whispered to Marissa.

"All right, stay here. But if you notice anything suspicious let me know." She left me at the door.

The dark chamber was strewn with rubble and broken planks, and metal beams from the collapsed scaffolding. A shovel and some other tools, as well as a battery-run lantern lay on the ground, lit. The body was recovered from the wreckage of fallen planks. Even where I stood in the semi-dark I could tell he was lying facedown. He had been hit on the back of the skull. Marissa switched on a flashlight and aimed it directly on the victim. His head was twisted to the side, his face quite clear in the bright light. Yes, it was Tommy.

Why did she want me here? I turned away, afraid I might gag. I have never seen a dead body. To me he looked quite dead. I sent my eyes up to the ceiling, then down the wall to the floor. Nothing was out of place. All excavations looked like this at the start, when they were just beginning to be unearthed. Mounds of dirt and rubble rose like mountains at the far corners of the floor. Where the reliefs and frescos had been discovered, bright color and animate images peeked from their coverings of ancient earth and volcanic ash.

Then I saw a dark gap in the wall. At first I thought it was part of a mural because of the surrounding darkness. Marissa busied herself examining the body. She searched Tommy's pockets, or so I thought. I would imagine that was a job for the local police? Of course, I was no homicide detective. What was she looking for?

The dark irregular shape in the wall beckoned me. I moved closer to see. Indeed, it was a gap and it was bigger than it had looked from where I was standing previously. The pile of rubble had hidden it. The impact of the fallen scaffolding must have shaken the room to its foundations, jarring loose this portion of the plaster wall. If I could clear away some of the debris I might be able to find a way inside. I was certain it led to another antechamber.

"Did you find something?" The sound of Marissa's husky voice bursting suddenly into my ear made me jump. She appeared irritated, almost annoyed. I pointed to the gaping hole in the wall. She came quickly at my beckoning and shone her flashlight within. There was a room on the other side.

The footsteps of the police officers returning got our attention. Marissa swiftly straightened. She brought me up with her by seizing my elbow as though to hide our discovery. I turned. She hurried me back to the site of the accident as four uniformed officers entered with a stretcher.

"I trust you have seen what you wished to see," said one of them. He seemed to be in charge.

"*Si, grazie,*" Marissa said.

"Okay, we take the body, now. You must leave also."

The officers proceeded to lift the body. They laid it on the stretcher. Then two of them hoisted it, one at each end and they awkwardly filed out.

"We can't leave yet," I insisted.

Marissa shrugged. "You wait here. I will speak to them." She handed me the flashlight. I almost dropped it. I found myself alone in the silence. I glanced at the gap in the wall, then down at my hands. Was I prepared to get dirty? Because that was what it would take.

I needed some gloves. There was a box of surgical gloves in the outer chamber, the *triclinium*. It was partially illuminated by a battery-powered lantern. Luckily nobody was present. I managed to steal a pair. I also made off with a trowel.

Inside the dark antechamber once more, protective latex over my hands and with the flashlight, I aimed the beam at the gap in the wall. I only needed to move about a foot of the rubble to get inside.

It was dirty work. It took almost no time at all before I was able to crawl through the gap. I left the trowel on the floor and rose. A pillow of cold air embraced me.

Here was another chamber, a sight that truly dazzled me. This room had not been buried as the others had. It was open. The walls were spectacular. Cupids riding sea monsters and dolphins were rendered in stucco, pulling an elegant green plaster drape, so life-like as to seem real. The motifs struck a chord in my memory. I ignored it. The figures were chalk white and the walls were an amazing sea blue green. Each character was rendered with exquisite preciseness, each face created with unique features. On the opposite wall was a mythological scene of more cupids. These ones played musical instruments, surrounding the god Dionysus and his grapes and flagons of wine.

There was more. A stack of jars, cups, and dishes sat on the floor. They formed a matching set of silver intended for a special event. On closer examination, as I flashed the light on the cache, I noticed that they all bore the same grape design. Most of the pieces were oxidized, hence their blackened and greenish appearance.

"Oh, wow." I heard the voice come from the gap in the wall. Marissa crawled out and thumped the dust from her clothing. "This is amazing."

I nodded. "I wonder if Luke knows about this."

"Yes. I wonder." Her voice took on a suspicious note. She reclaimed the flashlight from me. She spotlighted the silver.

"You still think Luke is a thief," I accused her.

She sent her light across the floor to play along the walls. "What I think does not change the facts. If he is, I will bring him down." She looked back at me and added, "And if you are his accomplice I will bring you down as well. He's a dangerous man, Lucy. Think well before you choose sides."

Her face took on a strange demeanor and I followed the direction of her light. "Look at that set of silver. It must be worth a fortune."

I turned and stared at her. In her official capacity of international police she was qualified to comment on how much an antiquity was worth. Archaeological objects were valued for their cultural and historical worth however, and not on how much they would bring on the black market. Her words repeated themselves in my head.

It must be worth a fortune.

She raised her brow, realizing what I was thinking. "Really, Lucy, you suspect me?"

A shiver rippled along my arms. It wasn't fear exactly. Marissa's face had changed and she spoke in her real voice. She was once again the officious Alessandra Piero.

She laughed. "Lucy. I am the *only* one you can trust. And must I remind you that your life may be in danger? Tommy was a friend of yours. He left the evidence with you when he should have left it with me…. Damn that boy for meddling. He would be alive right now had he not been poking around. And now he has put your life in jeopardy as well." She paused before continuing. "You realize of course that it was *he* who opened this chamber?"

"It's only silver, Marissa," I said. "It can't be worth that much."

"It is not the silver those devils are after."

"Then what are they after?"

"The gold."

What was she talking about? What gold? I was about to ask when I noticed her distraction. Her eyes were scouring the room. There did not appear to be any other openings. There was only one way out of here and that was through the gap where we had entered.

"You knew about this antechamber," I accused her.

The look she gave me was veiled. "Yes. I did suspect the existence of a secret antechamber beneath the church. But I was unaware of its exact location." Her voice had reverted to the Italian accent. I realized, as I watched her, that she was older than I had thought. My original estimate of her age had been mid thirties. Now I speculated she must be at least forty.

"We must find the man with the tattoo," she said. "I have no doubt that it was he who not only tripped Tommy Buchanan overboard when we were on the yacht, but he is also our killer."

It dawned on me, somewhat late and perhaps irrelevantly, that Tommy was the photographer that had snuck into Marco Ferri's home at the Torre Trasita last summer, and discovered the lost Black Madonna. Ironically that wasn't the reason he was killed.

"Tommy could identify him because of that tattoo," she continued. "But the attacker had a more urgent reason for wishing to eliminate him. Tommy Buchanan was the one who found this antechamber."

I was beginning to see that this mystery had deeper roots than I imagined. What was so special about the chamber, other than the wall paintings and the Roman silver? In dollars and cents it was hardly worth murder.

I stripped off the latex gloves; they were making my hands sweat and asked, "How could Tommy have known about this chamber?"

"He disappeared yesterday. He failed to return to the boat. Perhaps he was exploring just as you were, and found the gap in the wall. He could easily have stuck his head in here and snapped a picture of the evidence. Norman found him without his phone. You know how he always carries that thing around with him. My guess is, whoever killed the boy took care of that. His device is probably at the bottom of the sea by now, along with any incriminating photos. To the murderer he is no longer a problem."

"But why is this chamber so important?" I asked.

She paused. She still had the envelope with the photos in it. She removed the one of the tattoo. It was dark in here. I could see the general shape of the image as she flashed the light onto it. Then it hit me. The tattoo was of a cupid riding a sea serpent. It was the spitting image of the motif on this wall!

Was she about to give me a name? Who did she suspect? Sounds came from the outer chamber. She shoved the photo into the envelope and the envelope into her pocket. She put a finger to her lips and whispered, "We don't know who that is. It could be the killer returned to the scene of the crime."

She switched out the flashlight. The last thing I saw before the blackness descended was her drawing a gun from a shoulder holster concealed beneath her jacket. "Stay here. Don't make a sound. No one must know we have located this room."

I sealed my lips. I had no doubt she was a crack markswoman. I understood perfectly her reasons for absolute silence. If the wrong people found us here we were dead.

I listened. When all was quiet, I heard her creep out of the antechamber with the gun. I was alone.

I had a lot of time to think while she was gone. All of this treasure could be sold on the black market. The silver and the wall paintings could be removed in pieces and sold to unscrupulous dealers. But that wouldn't be all. These frescoes and bits of silver could not possibly be worth killing for. It was something bigger.

A light appeared through the gap. I was just awakening from my dark thoughts. I was about to follow the light when I heard the grinding movement of rocks and rubble. The dim light that had shone beyond the gap from the battery-powered lantern vanished. Blackness descended with a vengeance, burying the cupids and sea monsters and the god of wine with me. My eyelids blinked rapidly as though that would clear the blindness. I was going to be buried inside! I started to panic, my heart racing and my pulse hammering in my throat. I dropped to my knees and fumbled over the loose rubble on my side to find the gap. I heard a *ping* of metal and a clatter of wood as I realized I had kicked the trowel away in my desperation and haste.

After several tries I found the edges with fumbling fingers, but I was too late. A solid mass had entirely plugged the gap. I started to dig at the blockage with gusto. I reversed my position, and shoved with my feet, hands braced on the floor. It was no use. Someone had placed the planks from the scaffolding against the opening and then shoveled rubble and rocks and earth against it.

CHAPTER
20

My breath was shallow. My heart thudded against my chest. A cold sweat broke out on my forehead and my hands. A wave of vertigo struck me. I would have fainted, but then I realized that the air was not stuffy. It was cool, and it moved. That meant there was a draft coming from somewhere.

Marissa had taken the flashlight with her. I had my smartphone and I dug for it with anxious fingers inside my shoulder bag. Thank goodness I had charged it at Signor Ferri's house. It shone bright, as bright as a small flashlight. I quickly tapped Luke's number. No response. I glanced at the screen and saw a NO SERVICE message. Now what? The panic was escalating. My breath was coming in short, sharp gasps. *Stop it!* I ordered myself. Panic would not help. I illuminated my surroundings, highlighting the wall paintings and the silver on the floor.

Now that I was calmer, I could breathe. That meant there was fresh air coming in from somewhere. I went to the wall and felt the textured surface. For some reason the painting of the blue-green drape with the cupids astride their sea monster mounts caught my attention. I noticed that they appeared to be drawing the drape. If this were a drape of true fabric rather than a plaster one it would move.

It *did* move. To my shock and utter surprise the wall began to move.

I stepped back, once again every nerve in my body jangling.

A light shone into my eyes, and I didn't know whether to laugh or cry. A dark figure appeared. His face was a black blob against the infuriating light. When his hand reached out to seize my wrist, I almost screamed.

"Lucy? What are you doing here?" It was Norman's voice. I recognized the slight French lilt.

I said nothing.

His gaze took in the tight enclosure, noting the absence of an exit. "It's all right, you're safe now."

My voice refused to obey.

"Are you hurt?"

He had released me and lowered the light so that I could see into his face. Yes, it was Norman.

"It's okay." He spat a short curse in French while his flashlight traveled up and down the length of my body. He could see I was covered in dust and grit. "*Merde*, Lucy. What happened to you?"

"Norman." I managed his name. Why was he so angry? His sudden appearance had given me a shock. My heart was still hammering but beginning to subside. I now wished that I had never come to this idyllic paradise that was proving daily to be less than paradise.

"Luke is with me. He's down the tunnel." He turned. "Luke! I've found Lucy!"

Tunnel?

It was freezing in this place. I could hardly speak. Only now did I realize just how cold this subterranean chamber was. Norman noticed my failed attempts to hide my shivering and reached for my hand. I almost pulled back.

"*Mon Dieu*, your fingers feel like ice."

He cupped my hand with both of his and began rubbing. Then he lifted the other one and covered them both in his large palms. He drew me towards him. A twinge of fear mixed with excitement washed over me. He rubbed my arms. The heat of his body, so near to me, was doing all sorts of confusing things. I pushed him away.

He sent his eyes back to me when he realized I was afraid of him.

"I was not trying to fondle you. If you don't get warm you may develop hypothermia."

"I'm okay," I stuttered.

"No. You're not... Luke!" he shouted over his shoulder. It's Lucy. Where *are* you?" The tap of footfalls came from someone behind him. "I think she was locked inside this antechamber. As far as I can tell she's unhurt. Just scared."

A tall figure pushed his way past Norman and I was in his arms, lifted high and held tight to his hard, muscular chest. "Shit, Lucy," he said. "How did you get in here?"

I hugged him back, remorselessly. I had the awkward sense that Norman was observing every move we made. "Can we get out of here first? I'm freezing cold. And I'd like to get cleaned up."

Luke ripped off his shirt. He forced me to raise my arms. He tugged the garment over my head as though I were a child. He wore nothing under his t-shirt and I was alert enough to realize this. He rubbed my arms. "Jeez. You *are* cold. How long have you been down here?"

Too long, I thought. More than an hour. I was wearing a light cotton blouse, now smeared by dirt, with no jacket or sweater. The temperature in these underground caverns was at least ten degrees colder than ground level, and possibly twenty degrees colder than it was outdoors.

"There's a tunnel?" I managed to murmur.

"Yes. Come on. Let's get you out of here."

"Where does this lead to?" I asked.

"You'll never believe it."

Norman led the way. The tunnel was a long passageway dug into the earth beneath the town. The walls were of stone as was the floor. It was cold in here, too. After no longer than ten minutes we approached a wooden door. Norman opened this door and we emerged into what looked like a stone grotto. There was a sort of cave-like opening. Norman summoned us over. The dark, narrow cave led to another door, this one of metal and of a deep stone grey. In the dimness the door blended in with the rock walls just like the one in the cupid chamber. It opened into what turned out to be a wine cellar. We were behind some huge stacks of unused oak barrels. After we navigated our way through a maze of these barrels, and now a few crates, we rounded the corner to the space where the wine was actually stored. The smell was musky and woody with the piquancy of vinegar and fermented fruit. There was also the salt-sweet odor of the sea. Numerous iron racks were bolted to the stone and mortar walls, filled with corked bottles.

"Where are we?" I whispered.

Luke answered, "In the wine cellar of the Torre Trasita."

I was confused. I don't know if it was the cold, the fear, or Marissa's abandonment of me, but I could not determine who was friend or foe. "You mean, Signor Ferri's wine cellar? Marco's wine storage? Where is he?" I asked.

"He was called away on a business trip. Won't be back until the day after tomorrow. I offered to housesit. We have the place to ourselves."

I frowned. "So you decided to take it upon yourselves to go snooping? Or did you already know about that tunnel?"

"I have a lot to tell you, Lucy. Let's get inside and warm you up and then we'll talk. I need to know what you found out about Marissa."

Not as much as I learned about you.

I tried to keep my teeth from chattering. I realized that the wine cellar led through another passageway into a home gymnasium and then up some stairs to the kitchen. When we finally arrived on the upper floor, what a blessing and a relief it was to feel the sunshine flooding through the windows onto the quartz countertops of the immaculate kitchen. I involuntarily placed my hands on the warm stone. White cabinetry with silver hardware surrounded us.

"Come on upstairs, I'm going to draw you a bath," he said.

This was no time to quibble. I shivered, my knees barely able to hold me up. I followed his naked and very muscular back quite willingly up the stairs to our bedroom. I swallowed the lovely familiar blue and white décor as Luke went to the huge marble bathtub in the adjoining bathroom. He turned on the faucets. Hot steam rose, filling the ceiling and the enclosing walls. Luke reached over to the marble countertop where a bottle of blue bubble bath sat and poured in half of its contents until the water began to froth, before adjusting the temperature.

"Strip and get in," he said, flipping on the fan.

I hesitated.

"Get in. Unless you like wearing that cloak of dust. Your teeth are chattering. I want you to be warm. Then we need to talk."

I stripped down as he watched me. I caught snatches of my nakedness in the half-condensation on the mirrors. He kicked my clothes aside and took my elbow, brushing a hand over my breast, catching his finger on the tip. He lowered his head and kissed me on the side of the neck, then gently lowered me into the steaming bath.

As the hot water poured over me, engulfing my gooseflesh I heaved a sigh of ecstasy. I no longer cared that he was complicit in the concealment of a valuable artifact. Or that he might be involved in Tommy's murder. The latter I absolutely refused to believe. I leaned back and wiggled my toes with pleasure. The bubbles foamed and popped, sealing me in a blanket of fragrant suds.

Luke smiled and turned off the taps. He kissed me on the forehead. "Better?" he asked.

"Oh, *so* much better."

His very presence made it impossible for me to believe that he was bad. Somewhere in the back of my thoughts I hoped he would join me.

I was not to live out my fantasy. He picked up the shirt I

had dropped on the floor and pulled it over his head. I had forgotten that our trek through the cold stone tunnel had probably chilled him down too. He went over to the toilet and dropped the lid, then sat down on it to watch me. I sighed, and let the warm water do its trick. I shut my eyes in heavenly bliss. All I needed was a glass of brandy and this would be perfect.

My eyes blinked wide in astonishment as the fumes of an expensive cognac drifted to my nose. Norman was standing over me with a brandy snifter. My instinct was to clutch at my chest to cover my nakedness.

His voice came quietly as I shrank from his nearness. "It is nothing I have not seen before."

Did Luke hear that? I covered myself to my throat in thick suds.

Luke remained seated where he was, a brandy snifter in his hand. "Drink up, sweetheart. We have a lot to talk about."

There was nothing to do but take the glass.

"What were you doing in that antechamber?" Luke asked me.

The doubts returned.

"Is this an interrogation?" I was at a distinct disadvantage. After all I was naked in a bathtub and they were fully dressed. Norman leaned against the long sink counter while Luke perched on his spot on the covered toilet, sipping his brandy. Once again, Norman was not imbibing.

"Relax, *Chérie*," Norman said. "If we were going to hurt you we would have already done it. And we certainly would not go to all the trouble of making you a bubble bath."

Luke smiled. "I'm sorry, Lucy. Are we making you uncomfortable?"

I laid back. Then I laughed. "Well, thank you for rescuing me."

"How did you get stuck in that antechamber? How did you know it was there?"

"I didn't," I said. "It was Marissa who got us inside the church. Only her name isn't really Marissa."

"I told you," Norman said. He cursed softly in French, as he turned to Luke. "I knew she was an imposter. There was always something wrong about her. Is she a cop?"

"You might say so." I looked at Luke and then at Norman. They exchanged concerned glances. They were definitely worried that Marissa was on their trail. They were trying to hide their angst. What they failed to grasp was that she was Alessandra Piero.

How much did Luke trust Norman? From the appearance of things, especially this current situation, I realized he must be solidly in his confidence. My only question now was what side was Norman on? Was this a bluff and was he actually conspiring with the smugglers? Was this all an elaborate con? And if so, how did I play into it? Clearly, he was happy to find me or else he was a really good actor. Whether that was because he actually cared or because I had information he needed was the question.

There was also the matter of what I had witnessed last night. I looked across the room at Luke. He was keeping secrets from me. That was why I withheld Marissa's real name and profession. But I did provide him a version of the truth—how she had gone out to investigate sounds from the outer cave. When I tried to follow I was trapped.

They thought it was Marissa who trapped me. I let them think so.

I hid the part about the tattoo. Luke sported no decorations on his muscular arms and shoulders. What about Norman? I tried to think back to that infamous night on the beach. He had rescued me from myself. I woke up with a hangover to beat all hangovers. I was wearing Norman's shirt. Norman was bare-chested. Did he have any tattoos? I vaguely recalled a bluish patch on his arm near his shoulder.

"My poor Lucy," Luke said, rising and coming to me. "Come on, get out of that tub. Are you warm now?" His hand reached out to take my glass. Then he took my other hand to pull me up. I resisted. There was the matter of the third party in this bath scene.

"Norman, fetch her a towel."

I continued to resist until I realized something. Luke was ambivalent when it came to his bodyguard. Norman could see me naked or not. And for Norman's part, he already had.

I rose and the suds slid off my slippery skin. Norman handed Luke a towel. He wrapped it around me. Then he lifted me as though I were a child and carried me into the bedroom where he deposited me onto the bed. I could hear the suction of water as Norman unplugged the bathtub.

"There's a bathrobe behind the door," Luke called to his bodyguard.

Norman appeared in the doorway, surrounded by steam, and with both brandy snifters in his hands. He placed the glasses on the vanity and went to fetch me the robe. Meanwhile I took advantage of Norman's absence and rapidly toweled down. Just before he returned I draped the towel over me like a blanket.

"Norman, give us ten minutes," Luke said.

Norman gritted his teeth. "Sure boss."

He tossed the silk robe onto a chair to his left, walked out and closed the bedroom door. I glanced up at Luke nervously.

Oh, why was I so weak around him? What if everything he had told me was a lie. I was ready to spread my legs for him even though I knew he might be a criminal.

His hand went under the towel and stroked my thigh. I was warm now and still damp and completely aroused. I have to admit that having both Luke and Norman present while I was in the tub was a turn-on, and I hoped like the dickens that neither he nor Luke knew it. "Do you always walk around like this?" he asked, a finger stroking between my legs."

"Only when you're around," I whispered, nuzzling his neck.

"Then, I'll plan to be around a lot more."

He ripped the towel out from under him, leaving me naked. His fingers were busy. He moved his hand rhythmically, bringing me to near ecstasy. Then just before I came, he climbed on top of me. He rose, thrusting himself up above me with his hands until the only part of our bodies that touched was our sex. It was the single most titillating experience I had ever known. I had no idea that by isolating that part of the body you could climax almost instantly.

He collapsed on top of me, kissed me. I giggled and he planted his lips on the tip of my nose.

He turned his face to the door. "Norman are you out there."

"Sure," a voice replied.

"Get in here, we're done."

I looked up to see Norman in the half-opened doorway. Luke rose, leaving me exposed. I quickly brought my legs together and groped at the bed coverings. Naked, Luke fetched me my robe and then dressed himself.

You would almost think Luke was flaunting his sexual prowess over me in front of his bodyguard on purpose. I quickly recovered myself and slipped on the silk, as Luke buttoned his shirt.

CHAPTER
<u>21</u>

"Marco's okay," Luke said, staring at me from across the room. I adjusted the robe; the silk was so slippery. "We can trust him."

Fine, I thought, *but can I trust you?*

"What's the matter, Lucy?" He shook his head. "Oh come now. Don't tell me you still suspect me? After all I've told you?" He grinned. "And after what we just did?"

I refused to succumb to his charm. "You didn't tell me everything, Luke."

Of course he didn't, and he knew it.

"What did you learn that has put me in the hot seat?" he asked.

A person did not simply admit information to a potential criminal.

"You lied to me, Luke. You know the whereabouts of the Black Madonna."

His brow crinkled with worry. The line of his mouth tightened. I was aware that somehow I had made him angry. Then just as quickly the anger disappeared. A sneer broke across the frown. "Well... if I do, I'd like myself to tell me where it is. That would solve all my problems."

For some reason I felt calm. Even if it turned out that he

was the enemy. It was exactly as Norman had claimed. If they had meant me harm, they would have done it already. Besides, what did I know that could possibly incriminate them? Except that they were co-conspirators with Marco Ferri.

He laughed outright. Norman laughed too. I, on the other hand, found nothing amusing in his remark. He suddenly became serious when I refused to share in the joke. "Marco has the icon. He's hidden it. Says it's best if no one knows where it is until we can figure out how to return it to the church."

"Are you working for the smugglers?" I demanded. I knew I was taking a chance. If they were guilty I could be in big trouble. But I was done playing games. I needed to know. If my body was going to surrender to him every time he glanced my way, then I had better know what I was getting into.

"Am I... *What?*"

"Are you working for them? I overheard you and Marco talking last night. About the icon and... and about Tommy... I woke up and you were gone. I went downstairs to look for you and heard you two whispering. You obviously wanted privacy. But I overheard. I was eavesdropping on the staircase...." My last sentence trailed away rather lamely.

He was watching me, his eyes narrowed. "Tommy?"

"Yes." If it were anyone else I would have kept my mouth shut. Admitting to knowing about his midnight rendezvous might put me in danger. Somehow, deep down in my heart, I refused to believe that Luke would stoop to murder.

"Of course, I'm not working for them." His voice was thick and tinged with irritation. "What is all this rubbish about Tommy?"

Our eyes locked. He suddenly realized what I was thinking. He was mulling over his suspicious conversation with Marco. It was evident in his expression. "Ah. I see what has upset you so much. You overheard me say I would take care of the boy... Yes, taken out of context that would certainly sound incriminating—and if not incriminating, then ominous. But I didn't mean that I would murder him. I meant that I would talk to him and ask him to stop poking around. Good Lord, Lucy. You know me better than that."

Did I? I waited.

"And if that's what you think. What does that say about you? What kind of a woman has sex with a murderer?"

I felt myself flushing to the roots of my hair. Which, by the way, was still damp and leaving wet spots on the shoulders of my borrowed finery. To make things worse, the purple silk robe slipped. Both men's eyes moved instinctively.

I snagged the robe into double folds to cover myself. Involuntarily my eyelashes lowered. As I raised my eyes I found them wandering up to Norman. My face flushed. I was certain my whole body did. I was also certain that Norman had noticed.

I heard a low moan in Norman's direction. Luke growled. "*That?* That turns you on? Get used to it. You're my personal bodyguard. You're going to see a lot more of that."

Norman said nothing.

"Lot's of available ladies in this town," Luke said, sympathetically.

His bodyguard nodded.

"And certainly one particular lovely in closer proximity."

Norman seemed to know to whom he referred. I still felt left in the dark. And yet cringed at the knowledge of whom it might be.

I rose and spoke quietly. "Maybe you guys should leave so that I can get dressed."

"No. Wait Lucy. I'm sorry for that digression. And so is Norman. Aren't you, Norman?"

He shrugged.

I decided to take the situation into my own hands. The

last thing I had ever expected was to have Norman attracted to me. Odd thing was, now that I knew he found me physically desirable, it made him more attractive than ever. I had, however, no intention of acting on it. Sexual attraction was not the same as love. And with Luke, oh hell. With Luke I wasn't sure what it was....

"Sit down, Lucy," Luke said.

I sat.

"Do you want to know the rest of it?"

I nodded. I was one hot blush from head to toe. And I was taking too damned long to cool down.

He took the towel from where it had fallen on the floor. "Marco's going to kill me for getting his white bedding all stained."

He dropped the towel beside me and stared at me longingly. He had mistaken my reaction to his bodyguard for a reaction to himself.

"Actually, Norman. Why don't you take the rest of the day off? I think we could all use a break." He moved forward to kiss me on the throat.

"Wait, Luke," I whispered into his ear. "Are you sure you won't need him?" I was thinking of what had happened to Tommy and the fact that Marissa was now missing.

"Pretty sure."

I was already anticipating the ecstasy. I wasn't even aware anymore if Norman was still in the room.

                            ***

This time our lovemaking was rushed.

"Good God, Lucy. What you do to me. I can't control myself when I'm around you."

And vice versa, I thought. I kissed his ear and whispered. "Is that why you let Norman in the bathroom with us earlier?"

"That's his punishment for getting turned on by you."

"You knew? Since when?"

"Since he saw you in that black dress at the boutique

back in Toronto."

My holding my breath deliberately checked the gasp that was forcing its way out. When I could bear it no longer I exhaled. "Don't you think that will just make it worse?"

"Not if he wants to keep working for me."

"Sometimes you are just really cruel," I said, forcing a giggle. To be honest I really did think it was cruel.

"Sometimes I am," he agreed.

"Do you think he left, like you told him to?"

"Probably...." Luke turned his head to the door, where his bodyguard had stood twenty minutes before. "Norman, are you still here?"

No answer.

"Guess he's gone."

Would he, one day, double-cross Luke for treating him the way he did? The idea scared me. Norman would make a formidable enemy. I found myself wondering more about Norman.

"What's the matter, honey?"

"Nothing," I said. "I want to go clean myself up."

Some physical distance between Luke and myself wouldn't hurt either. I needed to get my head back in order and think properly.

When I got out of the bathroom Luke was gone. I dressed in a beautiful sundress, made of some gossamer filmy material that he had left on the bed for me. It was turquoise and white just like the room, and looked expensive. I knew it probably belonged to Isadora, Marco's wife. We were the same size. There was a pair of blue sandals to match of lightweight Italian leather.

***

Downstairs, I found him in the stylish living room, seated on the tasteful white furniture that looked as though no one had ever sat on it.

He was on the phone with Norman and he had tapped on the speakerphone. The device sat on the coffee table in front of him.

Those two were chained at the hip. Even when Luke gave Norman the afternoon off they stayed in touch. I smiled.

They were discussing the possible whereabouts of the church's stolen property. "Why are you helping Marco?" Norman was saying. "You don't want to be associated with the theft. Why not just tell the authorities that it's in his possession?"

"Because he didn't steal it, Norman. He bought it from a legitimate dealer. A few years ago it just showed up at an auction. An accusation of theft could destroy his family."

"If Interpol wants it that badly—"

"About Interpol," I said, walking into the room.

Luke looked up from where he had been staring at Norman's image on the phone's high-tech screen.

"I was trying to tell you earlier. Marissa Leone works for them. Her real name is Alessandra Piero." I nodded when Luke's eyes widened, and Norman made a guttural sound over the speaker. The realization finally struck home for both of them. Not only was she a cop that worked for the International Police—but she was also working undercover among us. "That's right. She wrote that letter. She works for Interpol. And... *and* I think she guessed who killed Tommy."

Luke stared. "Who?"

"I don't know. She disappeared before she could tell me."

He exchanged glances with Norman in the phone's small screen. "I'll call you back."

He ended the call with Norman and turned to me.

"That was rude," I said.

"He's used to it."

"You could treat him better. Then maybe he'd be nicer."

He smiled. "I hardly need a bodyguard who's nice."

Right. I'd forgotten. Norman's job was not to be a nice guy. Norman's job was to protect Luke's body and the precious artifacts he handled.

I sat down across from him on one of the pieces of white

furniture and said nothing.

"I think you better tell me what really happened in that antechamber."

Despite lingering misgivings, everything Marissa had told me suddenly spilled out. I included the evidence Tommy had left with me. I described also how she had disappeared into that gap leaving me in the dark. "I don't believe it was Marissa who blocked the entrance. She made me promise not to make a sound. I think she went after whoever was in the outer chamber. But his accomplice returned, and seeing the gap, blocked it so no one else would find it." It was the reason why I had not screamed for help. I had expected her to return for me. I wondered if she had. If she'd returned and found me gone, she too might have discovered the hidden doorway in the cupid painting.

"You think there's an accomplice?" he asked.

"Don't you? This job is too big to just involve a single person. And the amount of loot we found in there is proof of it. Unfortunately for Tommy, he was at the wrong place at the wrong time. He was close to learning the truth." Luke listened to every word I uttered without interrupting. "He was silenced. Marissa was worried the same thing might happen to me. In fact, you were her number one suspect—until I insisted you had no tattoos."

My mention of the tattoo caused me to think once more of Arianna.

Marissa had been prying around Luke's desk on the yacht to find evidence that he was involved in the church's stolen property or that he was somehow connected with the smuggling. Was Arianna involved? I decided to ask him. Or more correctly, tell him. I recounted the day I saw the man with the tattoo in her office. Was I certain the tattoo was the same? Not one hundred percent. But if it wasn't the same man, it was a freaky coincidence. "Do you know who he is?" I demanded.

Luke was disturbingly silent. He went a long time without speaking. I almost asked him again, but then he said,

"No. Are you sure you saw a tattoo on the man's arm?"

I nodded.

Silence again. "It makes no sense," Luke finally said. "Why would Arianna have someone like that in her office?"

"Well, he wasn't unattractive. From a distance, at first I thought he was you."

"You said he wore a baseball cap? Since when do I wear a baseball cap? Since when do I wear *any* kind of hat at all? No, it wasn't me. I have no tattoos."

I was quite aware of that. I wanted to ask him to phone her. It was the only way to know for sure. But if she had involved the museum in something shady, why would she tell him? And if it were only a fight with a new lover, how would that make Luke feel?

"Well one thing we do know. Marissa wasn't after the letter. Why would she want to see a letter that she'd written to you herself? Unless it was to hide any evidence that she had ever contacted you. She must have been searching for clues on your desktop and in her haste shoved it under those papers so we missed it—at first... Luke, how much do you trust Norman?"

"With my life."

"Where is he now?"

His eyes flicked up and over toward his phone. Which incidentally remained on the coffee table. "Emily and Norman recently became an item. Hadn't you noticed?"

Sort of. Was that where he was now? I felt a twinge of jealousy. It reminded me of that flirty Italian girl, the young waitress at the bistro on that disastrous night on the beach. He had not mentioned a word of the incident to Luke. I realized somewhat sheepishly that Norman was a man I should trust.

His sex life was not my business. With some effort, I dragged my thoughts away from him. "So, as far as Tommy is concerned, it seems he had some suspicions of you. He didn't trust anyone on your boat and wanted to learn the truth on his own. Why is that, Luke?"

His shoulders heaved. His eyes turned from a kind of icy wariness to a gentle warmth.

"What I'm about to tell you to the best of my ability is the truth. But there is one thing you have to believe, Lucy—I would *never* hurt you."

I wanted to believe him. I *so* wanted to trust him.

When I remained silent, he said, "Here's my theory. The night you and I spent here at the Torre, Tommy went back to the church. I'm assuming he was the first to discover the antechamber you were later trapped in, and the tunnel. He took pictures and posted them on WikiLoot. He discovered the ancient passage where the smugglers used to take the loot through the church to the beachfront. At low tide, it's just a few paces outside Marco's house."

"But doesn't that mean Marco *is* in on it? *Was* in on it from the beginning?"

"No. Marco didn't buy this place until five years ago. He gutted it and remodeled it. Before he and his family made it into their summer home."

"But the smuggling took place fifteen years ago, Luke."

"And the passageway is still there. I think it's been there for a very long time. It may have been there as long ago as the Saracen pirate attacks, and was used as a means of escape for the watchmen when the rogues stormed the tower."

"So the gang you worked for—all those years ago—used that passageway? But it leads to a church. Wouldn't someone at the church have noticed some suspicious activity?"

"Not when the smuggling took place at night. No one was there, and the church was left unlocked. Who would suspect a church to be a smuggler's lair?"

"But I thought the excavation under the church was recent?"

Luke shook his head. "Two decades ago, the Church of Santa Maria Assunta had just discovered ruins beneath its foundations. Preliminary work opened up passageways but the real excavation wasn't done until later. *Much* later. They had no funding so the original work came to a halt. Then I came along and took over. The reason I wanted to excavate these ruins was because I knew that the smugglers, when I was working for them, carried the loot from some secret corridor and stored it nearby. You see... I brought the boat to a small pier, which is no longer here. I knew it was in front of this tower. Fifteen years earlier this tower was still a throwback from the old pirate days. It wasn't a modern home; it was a crumbling old ruin.

"I'm trying to locate the Black Madonna, Lucy. And return it to the church with no one the wiser."

"And Marco has it?"

"Yes, but he won't tell me where he's hidden it. To protect me, he insists. If I don't know where it is, I can't be linked with the crime."

"Then why doesn't he just return it?"

He shrugged. "I'm going to tell you something. Something that only Norman knows."

"What is it?"

"Marco Ferri was the fisherman whom I met on the beach on that ill-fated holiday, and whose position I replaced in the smuggling racket. So returning it is not as easy as you might think. He mustn't get caught. Or there'll be hell to pay. He has a family, remember. All those convoluted explanations, tied up in court for years, and possible jail time if he's found guilty. He's trying to avoid that for the sake of Isadora and the boys."

"How do you know you can trust him?"

"The same reason I trust Norman." He looked at me. "The same reason I trust you."

I paused before responding. It always came back to the Black Madonna.

"Luke," I asked. "What makes that icon so valuable?"

"I don't know. Like I've said over and over, although no one would believe me, I have never seen it myself. All I've seen are police photographs and the pictures Tommy took and posted on WikiLoot."

"Tommy thought it was worth dying for."

"I don't know that he realized he'd be killed because of it, but yes, you're absolutely on the right track. There is something so valuable about it that the boy was willing to stick his neck out, risk the wrath of thugs and cops, and get himself killed."

"The legend," I said. My thoughts were taking a different track. "The legend claims that it had magical properties. That it caused a storm to rise and forced the pirates who had stolen it to return to shore. They left it at Positano."

"I don't think God himself had anything to do with it... Neptune maybe." He chuckled. "No. The real reason for its value is much more materialistic than that... But I know what you mean. It's almost like it has some sort of innate power— and it wants to go home."

"We have to find it. And return it to where it belongs. Didn't the original legend have the pirates leave the icon in a cave? I vaguely remember Tommy telling me something like that. So wouldn't that be the logical place to look?"

Luke frowned. "Maybe you've got something there. The Amalfi coastline is riddled with caves. There's the Emerald Grotto, the Grotto La Porta and the Blue Grotto, but those are all tourist haunts. Marco wouldn't have hidden it in plain sight. Not anywhere that a lot of people might visit. Besides, I think those caves are mostly underwater now. The sea spray would damage the artifact."

I nodded. "I think we should have another look at that tunnel."

CHAPTER

22

If we were going spelunking or just exploring subterranean tunnels I was going to dress the part. I borrowed a pair of skinny jeans, a t-shirt and a sweater from Isadora's wardrobe. Then I fastened my running shoes before rejoining Luke downstairs. He was waiting for me in the kitchen. We descended the steps into the gym, went through the wine cellar, past the bottles in their iron racks, and back through the metal door that was hidden behind the oak barrels and wooden crates.

It was not a long tunnel. I was beginning to suspect that maybe we were mistaken. Perhaps there was no offshoot leading to some hidden cavern.

I was wrong. Luke had brought a strong flashlight. He traced the beam slowly along the curved walls as we walked. We came to a spot where another metal door was just visible in the stone and mortar. Had we not been searching for it, we would have missed it. The color of the metal blended almost invisibly with the stone.

Like the other doorway into the church's subterranean chambers, this one was unlocked.

"I'll go first," Luke said.

He took my hand. He kissed my fingers, then dropped

them. I was not about to argue with him.

His tall form blocked my view of the new passage but it wouldn't have mattered anyway. It was dark as night inside and I followed meekly behind. The smell was different in here. It was salty and strong like the sea, with the distinct odor of fish. The air flowed rapidly and I knew it must open to the outside.

I could hear the rush of the ocean now, waves slapping on stone, and the hollow ringing tones like when you hold a seashell up to your ear.

We ducked under a low overhang of solid rock and found ourselves in a dimly lit grotto, sparkling green and blue as Luke waved his flashlight over the gently moving water.

"There's a reason why this tunnel leads out to these caves."

"Is any of this familiar to you?" I asked.

He shook his head. "You have to realize, Lucy. I was only a smuggler's lackey for one summer. They didn't entirely trust me. That's why no one showed his face around me. To this day, except for Marco, I have no idea what any of those people look like. Smart move on their part, because the next year I was caught."

"The gang abandoned you?"

"Of course they did. I took the fall. They knew my father would get me out of it, and he did."

"Luke," I said, turning him to face me. "The truth. Are you and Marco back in the trade?"

"No. I quit all of that, fifteen years ago. I swear. The only reason I'm here now is to get retribution. Those sealed government records say that I stole the thing. I did not. And I don't want that albatross hanging around my neck for the rest of my life. I want to—no—*need* to—find the icon and return it to the church. I will not sleep until I do."

***

The gently surging shadows cast by the flashlight rippled

across the deep blue-green water as though the water itself were a massive gemstone. We stood on a shallow shelf of sand and pebbles. All around us was enclosed by solid stone with gentle hollows carved out by centuries of the sea's motion. The hollows gave the ceiling and walls the impression of a giant Swiss cheese.

The play of light and shadow drenched the place with a surreal feeling. I found myself frozen in a kind of mesmerizing reverie.

The air was fresh and clean. The honeycomb of caves with its numerous hidden caverns was open to the sea in this spot. The opening was large enough to admit an oblong of daylight that brightened the cavern enough to see by, once the eyes adjusted. Deep shadow hid the true size of the space. With our modern devices we bounced cold light off the curved walls, ragged pillars and fangs of water-molded stone. My eyes returned to the opening. At high tide this aperture might be almost submerged. At low tide it would allow a small boat to pass. I could tell by the look on Luke's face that that was what he wished he had right now. A boat. Or a jet ski.

"Do you think Marco would have hidden the icon in here?" I asked. "Seems to me, the close proximity to the sea would damage it."

"That depends on what it's really made of. It hung on the church wall for centuries and no one ever took it down to clean it or test its chemical properties. Since its theft in the early millennium all sorts of rumors sprang up about why it was stolen. There are stories now that say the Black Madonna was sculpted out of everything from wood to plaster to metal. The original tale says it was made of painted wood, and I believe the gold was supposed to be gold leaf. One thing they all agree on is that the thing was as heavy as lead."

A gust of sea air drew our attention. We jerked out of our individual thoughts. I stole a look at his face and noted that he was as jumpy as I.

"Should we have a look around?" I asked.

Something caught my eye in the diffused lighting from Luke's flashlight. I had no light source myself, except for my smartphone. I switched it on and it lit up the corner of the dark cave. A dim flash startled me, and I bent down to pick up what looked like a slightly tarnished silver spoon. I recognized it to be Roman. I had seen enough Roman spoons to recognize the style. The motif on the handle was familiar. It was a cluster of grapes.

I had seen this motif before, and I knew exactly where. It was etched into the Roman silver in Shaun's lab. My heart threatened to stop. How exactly was he involved? Surely he had no idea the stuff was contraband?

"What have you got there?" Luke asked.

"A Roman spoon."

"Where there is one piece of silver there must be more."

I agreed. We began to search the entire cavern. There were so many nooks and crannies and holes that led to nowhere.

Our diligence paid off. The search actually took less time than it seemed. At the far corner, in a place we had scoured twice earlier, we found it. Like the room under the church with the gap in the wall it was unobtrusive. A large stalagmite camouflaged the opening. But behind it was a crevice large enough for us to squeeze through.

On the other side, Luke's flashlight illuminated a cache of small marble and bronze statues, pieces of intricately and brilliantly painted frescoes, and the rest of the silver dinnerware. There was also a huge pile of Roman coins and weaponry.

Luke stared at the hoard of rich treasures. He looked pleased, perhaps even relieved at the discovery. I found it troublesome. Was this really enough to kill for? Then his expression soured as something occurred to him.

"What's the matter, Luke?"

"I recognize some of this stuff. Actually, all of it. So... it's been sitting here, waiting to go on the black market, piece by piece, slowly, so that no one would become suspicious if the market was suddenly flooded with Roman artifacts."

"*You* smuggled this stuff here?"

He shook his head. "No. Sometimes I would pick it up from a cave. It's just that it was so long ago and all these grottos look alike." He darted his eyes cautiously about. "I didn't recognize this one when we first walked in. Still not sure that I do. There are numerous honeycombs like this all up and down the coastline. And the shape of them has changed over the years."

I stooped. I inspected the spoon I still held in my hand. I compared it to the silverware that was piled against the curved stone of the wall. The motif was the same, a grape cluster. "They were ferrying the silver from that hidden antechamber under the church through the tunnels to these caves. Are you sure Marco doesn't know anything about that?"

A thud came from the outer cavern. Luke swiftly doused the light. He fumbled in the dark for my hand and dragged me slowly in the opposite direction of the opening. I recalled that there were some stalagmites at the far wall. We carefully, although awkwardly, made our way backwards to these.

My back bumped into a hard pillar. I knew we had found some cover. Luke dropped my hand and I fumbled my way behind the comforting rock. Swiftly, he followed.

Just in the nick of time. A light flashed at the entrance to the cavern. It wobbled. Then waved back and forth searching for the stash. We couldn't see who it was because every time we ventured a glimpse the light would blind us.

We could hear the scrape of metal and multiple clinks as whoever it was gathered silver into their arms. If they hadn't been making so much noise, they would have heard my wretched breathing.

They made three trips before it was relatively quiet. Then there was the unmistakable but muffled sound of a motor.

"I'm going to have a peek," Luke whispered. "Stay put."

He was gone for what seemed an eternity; it was probably only ten minutes. My heart thudded uncomfortably in my chest, banging against my ribcage. It was getting so I had almost stopped breathing. Just as I was about to barge out there and check out the situation myself, he returned. Whatever he had witnessed was bad. His eyes were dark. His mouth was tight with anger.

"He's gone. I have to go after him. I don't want you with me in case things go south."

I raised my eyebrows, anxious and confused. He yanked out his gun from the ankle holster on his right leg. "It's Marco."

"No."

"Good news is, I found a boat hidden in a cranny. It must have been stashed there for emergencies. I'll have to leave now if I'm going to catch up with him. I can't believe he double-crossed me."

There was an urgency to his voice I'd never heard before. He was upset. I mustn't press him for further details.

His tone was taut, controlled as he explained his plan to me. "Can you find your way back through the tunnel? Go to the Torre. Marco won't be there. He wouldn't dare stash the stuff in his house. But don't stay in the tower in case he returns. Get outside and get somewhere safe. Somewhere public. Or better yet, go to the church. The church is safe. But stay out of the ruins. Go to the chapel. I'm going to text Norman to come here and watch the goods."

He tucked the revolver in his back pocket and contacted the bodyguard. When that was done, he led me back to the outer cave where the boat was hidden behind some outgrowths of stone.

"Go straight back through the tunnel," he warned. "I've got to go now, or I'll lose him."

I wanted to go with him, but I understood why I had to stay. There might be shooting and he needed me out of the line of fire.

"It's okay, Lucy," he said. "You'll be safer here. I can't risk you getting hurt if you come with me. And I won't be able to do what I have to do if I'm worrying about you."

CHAPTER

<u>23</u>

Something seemed wrong with this whole setup. Why would anyone kill for some wealthy Roman's household wares? Museums were full of the clutter. Although some private collectors (of questionable ethics) would pay for the treasure, most would recognize it as more or less commonplace. Even the statues were nothing special. They were unchipped and in pristine condition, but that was all I could say for most of them. I relocated the inner chamber where the silver and statues were stashed. I should have minded Luke and exited immediately through the opening to the tunnel.

But some instinct made me stay. Something in the air that didn't quite match with the sea and enclosed rock and sand smells.

Luke had left the flashlight with me to prevent my stumbling about in the dark. I swirled the light in a semi circle to get a wider view of the chamber. My light caught on a flash of red. I swung it back. I widened the beam and hurried across the floor.

***

They had not bothered to bury her. Only a bit of rubble

had been scattered over her body. There wasn't much here to bury her with. I recognized her red blouse.

Marissa lay in an awkward heap in the rubble and sand. Her head was turned at a strange angle. When I shone the light into her face, her eyes had a dull look to them. She was either unconscious or dead.

I was afraid to touch her. But I had to. I had to know for certain.

Cautiously my hand touched her throat. It felt cold.

Was she alive? There was no blood. So she hadn't been shot. My head jerked up at a sound. But it was only the echoing of the cave. It was whispering its sea songs. Who could have done this? Marco? It must have been. Luke had recognized his old friend leaving the cave with the stolen goods. Even so, I could not imagine the friendly Italian—whose hospitality I had so recently enjoyed—twisting the neck of the Interpol agent.

No point in debating the issue. She must be dead. This time when I heard the sounds I knew someone was coming. The sea songs in the whispering cave seemed to stop. The thud of heavy footsteps replaced the soft sighs. Then came voices.

I turned to escape. By swinging too abruptly around, however, I struck the flashlight against a stalactite and it went spinning out of my hand into the soft sand near Marissa's face. The bulb must have jarred loose because the light snapped out. I fumbled for the metal handle but in the darkness was totally blind. No time to search any longer. The footsteps were getting closer. They stopped as if the intruders paused to listen. There was a crevice nearby, a narrow one and I fit. My clothes caught on the crags before I broke free and fell further inward.

My first thought was to crawl into the rock as deep as I could go. Then it occurred to me that this nighttime spelunker might be Norman. But would he have brought a companion? I was about to venture out just a few inches when the beam of a flashlight blinded me. I froze. It hovered, and then moved on.

I let out a hiss of breath. They had not seen me.

I gripped the edge of sharp rock that was my shield between danger and safety. I wanted desperately to know their identities. They were two men, from the size and shapes of their builds. They seemed vaguely familiar and I knew instinctively that neither was Norman. One was tall and powerfully built. The other was smaller and thin. The tall one's clothing appeared to be some sort of uniform, although I wasn't able to see clearly. I only remember the flash of brass buttons. But one thing was obvious. He was in top physical shape. Like Norman he moved like a soldier.

The smaller man set the flashlight on a ledge of rock. He aimed the beam on the Roman weaponry. Just my luck. Who needed a gun when one could pilfer a sword? If only I had thought of taking a dagger with me. I was flabbergasted, even horrified, by my own thoughts. Mild mannered Lucy Racine—who was no danger even to a spider—was thinking of stabbing a man.

He stooped to lay his hands on the swords. He lifted one. He examined it as if for sharpness, then crowed. "Look at me, I'm a Ninja!"

He swung the sword like an actor in a fantasy film. The tall man yelled. "Drop it, you idiot. We're not here to play."

"Fuck," the thin man said. "It's *so* pretty."

Something about the way he said that sent a chill up my spine. It didn't take much to imagine the patchy beard, the dull grey eyes and the shaved scalp. I recognized who he was, and that meant I probably knew who his companion was too. He gave me the creeps, just as he had back then. Only the exact phrase then had been: '*You're* pretty.'

He lowered the sword with a clang. I fought a grimace. No time to be sanctimonious over how artifacts should be handled. The tall man said, "Start moving this stuff. *Now.*" The thin man gathered an armload of silver and left. It was too dark to see where he went. Now the tall man moved to the pile of coins and reached out to cup a handful. I glanced up. His head was in shadow. But I did not need to make out his face to know who he was.

It was Captain Spatz!

I was too nervous to think. He was so close to me I feared he could hear the rasps that served for my breathing.

A noise drew my attention. Spatz pulled some crumpled plastic bags out of his pockets and began to fill them with the coins. The sounds rang eerily loud. I was grateful. Any movement I made now would be shrouded by this clatter.

The creeping flesh he gave me just by his presence warned me to put as much distance between us as I could. I moved back further into the crevice, as far as I could go.

I was inching deeper and deeper into the crevice. Here it widened. Then suddenly I fell through. I would have fallen flat on my backside had I not grabbed at the rock wall and managed to snag my hand onto a rough knob of stone.

Here was another passage—or a cave? I listened to hear if Spatz had heard my stumble. I concentrated on the melodic sounds of metal on metal. Then silence. Before the metallic clinking began once more.

It was pitch black in here. All I had for a light was my phone and nothing could convince me to press it on just yet. Perhaps if I blocked the opening with my body, I could flash it on just for an instant to get my bearings. I fumbled for the edges of the entrance and turned my back on it. I pressed on my phone. It illuminated the first meter of the cave. I turned to examine my surroundings. My eye caught a glint of something brilliant—gold—before I lost my nerve and turned out the light.

What was that I had seen? Was it really gold? Was this the gold Marissa had mentioned? Was this why she was killed?

I was standing on a sandy floor in approximately the place I had glimpsed the gold. I shaded my phone with my other hand and pressed it on. The light caught the corner of the object, which was about a half meter away from my feet. I moved closer. I let the illumination swim over its surface.

Yes, it was an artifact. But not just *any* artifact.

It was the Black Madonna.

I would recognize her anywhere even though I had never seen her before.

She was beautiful. Her face and body looked solidly black in the ghostly light of my phone. Her clothing and the backdrop, and the frame, were gleaming gold.

I don't know what made me do this. I placed my phone on the ground and tried to lift her. She weighed a ton. Literally a ton. Well, maybe not literally. But why was she so heavy? I couldn't even budge her. It would take a tremendously strong man to lift her by himself.

Then I saw what I had not understood at first. The reason she was so heavy was because she was actually *made* of gold. Ebony and gold.

It was at that moment I noticed it was dead quiet in the outer cave. I doused my light and waited. I needed to tell Luke what I had found. Silence. More silence. Was it safe? Should I text?

I decided I should.

I have tickets to the concert.
And I know where she lives.

The message was in code and I hoped he would understand the concert I was referring to. Texts just like emails could be intercepted. It was safer to say it like this.

He might not receive this text for a while if he was in the middle of confronting Marco. I had to escape this place and locate Norman. Norman could help me remove the icon from here. Drat. I didn't have his number. That meant no phone call, no text. I was out of options. But wasn't he already on the way? Before leaving, Luke had contacted him to return to guard the stash. I would be waiting for him.

Then it dawned on me that the two smugglers out there might know where the icon was, too. I wasn't out of danger yet. And I had to leave this place as soon as possible.

Captain Spatz and Freddie Spelnick had not arrived via the tunnel. They had come through the outer cave, the one that opened out to the spacious Swiss cheese grotto and to the sea. They were moving some of the stolen objects, but to where? I had to follow them. There were no noises in the outer cavern, but just as I concluded the thought I heard the roar of an engine. Those thieves had a boat. They were taking the silver and weaponry to some other hiding place—or to its final means of transport. Where or what would that be? A boat? Most likely a very large boat. And to what destination would that boat be headed? My busy mind returned to Shaun and the letter from Interpol. Was my museum involved? How much of it was real, and how much had Marissa invented to use as a cover? No matter now, she was dead.

They were gone. Outside my hideout everything was silent. I was desperate to escape the claustrophobia and inform someone of my findings. I exited through the tunnel. I decided to forgo the chance that the gap in the antechamber beneath the church had been reopened. If it had not I would be stuck. I went straight through the branching stone passageway to the Torre, through the grotto and the wine cellar, and past the gym before I stopped to catch my breath. I listened. If anyone was in the house it was imperative I evade them. Although, in a pinch, I could always bluff my way. Luke had informed me of Marco's offer of the house while he was allegedly away.

I heard no activity. Only silence. I opened the door. I walked into the kitchen like I was coming in from a workout at the gym. I was sweating enough.

***

Luke had been astute when he surmised that Marco would not be home. The sun was almost gone and I could see it fading red and orange on the sea outside the window.

The church was being invaded and their occupants deserved to know that it was currently used as a smuggler's route. I must return to the church and obtain help from one of the priests. I turned away and went upstairs.

Quickly, I changed my clothing. I was filthy dirty from that escapade inside the tunnels connecting the Torre, the church and the grotto where the stash of stolen artifacts and the Black Madonna were hidden. I washed my hands and face. I put on the blue and white sundress, a white sweater to cover my shoulders, and the blue sandals. I looked presentable enough to return to the church.

Just as I was about to leave I heard voices. Oh no. If Marco had returned what would I say to him? He was a thief. He was in possession of the most coveted artifact of the 21st century. If the weight of that icon was anything to measure by, it was worth millions.

But worse—he was a murderer.

I slipped out the side glass door into the shade of the cypress. The curtain of hanging wisteria on the small balcony shielded me should anyone on the ground look up. It gave me a false sense of security. At garden level a door opened. I saw Norman and Emily leaving along the path lined with lawn torches. From Emily's stiff, angry posture I could safely assume the two had experienced their first lover's spat. No time for this. I tore the vine aside to call to Norman.

Before a sound emerged from my lips, he spun around and went indoors. Emily stormed off up the street. The lampposts began to light up one by one.

The scene disturbed me. Why hadn't Norman responded to Luke's text to go to the grotto and guard the artifacts? If Marco's men managed to remove all of the illicit goods tonight—especially the Black Madonna—we will have lost our proof.

Was Norman Luke's man? Or was he a traitor? Marco had turned out to be a traitor. And so had some of Luke's crew. I decided to go to the rooftop patio to think. Norman would not find me there until I was ready to confront him.

The sun perched like the orange yolk of an egg on the edge of the grey horizon. Soon it would be dark. I had to act.

I despised this constant indecision. I paced the lovely

blue and white tiles, my thoughts spinning in circles. I went as near to the rails as I dared, and studied the fiery sea. I was beginning to feel breathless and stepped back.

A quick glance at my phone showed no response from Luke. I had texted him in code, so he might not have understood it. My mind was deliriously spinning. Who in this tiny town could I trust?

Just as I made up my mind that I would have to double back to the grotto to protect the precious icon myself, I heard a deep voice clear his throat. I panicked and turned.

"That's a nice outfit," he said. The voice was lazy, appreciative, and rumbled with a slight accent. Norman seemed always to notice what I wore. "I like the sandals."

My eyes lowered to the borrowed, pretty blue shoes.

Somehow he had come upstairs onto the rooftop patio without my hearing him.

"Where's the boss, Lucy?"

The answer was caught in my throat.

He came to me and took my hand. I reacted instinctively, jerking it back. His grip was strong. No matter how I tried, his will was stronger than my physical strength, and I failed to free myself. Behind him the sky darkened. A few clouds bunched on the horizon leaving thin cracks, allowing the last pink rays of the sun to reflect in the oily sea. "Why don't you trust me?"

Nothing came out of my mouth. I wanted to trust him. Believe me I wanted to. But just how many of Luke's employees were involved?

He exhaled and a curse followed in French.

"Norman," I said. "Look, I'm sorry." I was on the verge of tears. I sorely wanted to believe in him. But so far, all anyone had told me was lies.

He nodded as though he had read my thoughts. "Yes, I see. You have every reason to suspect me... But I'm telling you I have nothing but Luke's best interests at heart. To me he's a brother. Do you understand? We have been through hell and high water. And yes, if you must know, I was with

him back in the day, when he and I were so stupid as to get
tangled up in that smuggling racket that ended in the loss of
the Black Madonna. But I did not steal her, nor did Luke. She
has haunted us for a decade and a half. We want to find her
and return her to her rightful place."

At first I said nothing. I could not respond. I wanted so
much for his words to be true. Something in his eyes was
beginning to crack me. "Please. Give me something that can
make me believe you. *Please,* give me something that will
allow me to trust you."

He sighed. "Didn't I just confess to being part of that
smuggling racket?"

"Yes, but you might just be saying that so I'll tell you
where she is."

Norman's eyebrows arched. I slapped a hand across my
mouth. Oh Lord, what had I done?

He jumped on it immediately. "You know where she
is?"

I said nothing.

"Lucy, if you know where the Black Madonna is, you
have to tell me."

"How *can* I, Norman? How do I know you're not just
like Marco? How do I know you're not a traitor? A
backstabber!"

"Marco? Marco Ferri is behind this?"

Norman still had a grip on my arm. He was hurting me.
Now I was really scared. Suddenly, he realized what he was
doing and released me. He began to stroke the reddened skin
where it had chaffed with his knuckles. He took my face into
his hands and looked me clear in the eyes. His own were
deep and pleading, and filled with something else.

Involuntarily, I felt my body respond. No. What was
wrong with me!

"Lucy," he said hoarsely. I knew what I wanted him to
say. How much I wanted him to say it. Every fiber of my
being desired his confession.

He didn't say it. He knew how I felt. But he still didn't

say it.

The sexy accent was stemmed. "I *don't* have feelings for you, Lucy." The statement was firm, adamant. But without conviction. He paused to see if I understood. His eyes had a hard, haunted expression that touched me. "I may have seen you first. But Luke decided he wanted you."

That day in Arianna's office returned to me in a flash. I had felt a warmth in his gaze, which I later decided I'd imagined. I had gone and doodled those drawings of his muscles. I looked down, no longer confused. Things were never clearer than they were at that moment.

I always wondered why he was so difficult every time he saw me.

I had thought he didn't like me.

"*Merde*, Lucy." I looked up. "You are Luke's girl. That's all that matters."

They say that when two people are meant for each other they can read each other's minds.

"You have that much loyalty to Luke?" I asked.

He shrugged, a multitude of twisted emotions struggling to escape.

What could possibly account for that kind of loyalty? I peeked quickly at Norman's handsome face, the kindness that had always been there but I had failed to see. What kind of man put aside his needs for those of others? A rare one for sure.

"Whatever it is you think you feel for me, squash it," he said. "It can't happen. And Luke—he must *never* know."

Perhaps, he already did. The thought popped into my head before I could crush it. I swallowed and hoped my feelings were not evident in my face. He interpreted my nervousness for fear rather than what it actually was—an uneasy realization of where my affections truly lay.

"You still don't trust me—" He scowled, threw up his hands. "I don't know what else to do.

I was quiet but not for too long. I licked my dry lips, touched Norman's shoulder lightly to get his attention. He

looked at me and I could see that his defenses had come
down. He was a man after all, and a person of passionate
emotion. I could have laughed at myself for thinking only a
few weeks ago how I had convinced myself that I was—how
had I put it—currently unattached? And content to be so.
And now… at this moment… I had two men in my life—

I sighed. Maybe if I had met him first….

Norman laughed. It rang not with amusement but more
of melancholy. He seemed to know what I was thinking.
Because the truth was, I *did* meet him first. And if I had gone
out with him first, and then he had introduced me to Luke
what would have happened? Norman's laughter shattered the
speculation. He was following my line of thought and the
amusement was sardonic. He scoffed, "He is a billionaire
after all."

I smiled, a tight-lipped smile. There was nothing
remotely amusing about this situation. But this was neither
the time nor place for true confessions. The clock was
ticking, and Luke could be in trouble. "There's just one thing
I need you to do, and then I can trust you," I promised.

He nodded. Became serious. "If I can, I will do it."

"Take off your shirt."

His look was half surprised, half pleased. He lifted my
head by the chin and let his thumb smooth over my lips.
"Lucy, *mia*," he said softly. Then he dropped the hand.

I don't know why I didn't jerk away immediately. I
guess I wanted to be reminded of his touch. But it was he
who pulled away first. "No."

"No? Norman, I'm not asking you to do anything wrong.
I need to see your arms and shoulders."

"Why?"

"Please don't ask me. Just take your shirt off. Then I'll
explain."

He shrugged. He was wearing a long sleeved t-shirt that
clung to his powerful physique. He raised his arms and
removed the garment. I saw instantly what I had hoped to
see. He had no tattoos on his arms or anywhere else. Only a

faded bruise on his left shoulder. I could not ask him to drop his pants.

The bell on the church struck the hour. We were still outside atop the rooftop patio. Dark had descended. The sea whispered high into the tower. And I realized we had to act fast.

"Marissa, the Interpol cop, is dead. I found her body near the Roman silver."

I had dropped a bomb. It might as well have been a real bomb for the effect was the same. He turned to me, stymied. "Interpol? Marissa? You found her... *body?*"

I nodded.

"My poor Lucy." He reached out a hand to comfort me. Then just as quickly let it fall.

My mind was whirling a mile a minute. We had to move fast if we were to stop these horrible people. "There's nothing we can do for her now. But we *can* save the icon from those criminals. The tunnel from the Torre leads to a grotto. That is where the loot is hidden, and it's also where the Black Madonna is stashed. Norman, you must go to the police and convince them to follow you there. Before it's all gone. Already Marco's lackeys are moving the artifacts."

Norman hesitated at first. I knew what he was thinking—that the police might think Luke was part of the gang. He wanted to protect Luke, but Norman was the only one of us whose Italian was fluent. He'd have less trouble convincing them than me.

He had forgotten to ask why I had demanded he remove his shirt. He drew it back on. I held back any explanation. There was no time. All he had wanted was for me to trust him and I did.

He seemed to recognize that time was short, and that the matter of the Black Madonna had come to a critical juncture. "Okay," he said. "I will fetch the police. Does Luke know?"

"He went after Marco. I texted him but I don't know if he read it... Norman, did you get Luke's text? He contacted you to go to the grotto to watch the artifacts."

"That must have been when I was with Emily. So, no I didn't see it." His mention of Emily gave me a strange feeling in the pit of my stomach. It reminded me of that sexy young, Italian waitress at the beach restaurant. He fetched his phone now and read the message. It took all of five seconds before he looked up. It suddenly dawned on him that Luke's friend Marco was the culprit. He swore; then apologized.

We subconsciously agreed that one of us had to phone Luke. Since Norman already had his phone out, he tapped the contact. There was no answer.

He hung up and looked at me. "Keep trying," he said. "I'll go and get the police."

His phone suddenly chimed. He glanced down. I could tell by the look on his face that it wasn't from Luke. It was from Emily. "She's a nice girl, Norman," I said through locked teeth.

The phone disappeared into his pocket without his responding to the text. His shoulders heaved. His next words were muttered into the wind. "But she's not you."

He turned back to say something else, didn't, and we stared at each other for a long moment. He was the first to break it off. He started for the exit and I followed. He spun abruptly when he realized I was right behind him. "I want you to go back to the yacht where it's safe," he ordered.

"I promised Luke I would wait for him at the church. If I'm not there when he comes back—" I gripped Norman's arm before realizing that I had. I let go and said, "Be careful."

Norman, who was about to place a foot onto the top step leading down from the rooftop patio, stopped. He gave me a reassuring smile, then grabbed the handrail, and dropped down the steep staircase barely allowing his feet to touch the steps and vanished into the darkness below.

I leaped forward with a start. In my fluster and confusion over discovering Marissa's body and the hidden Black Madonna I had neglected to mention one critical fact.

Luke's captain was Marco Ferri's accomplice.

CHAPTER
<u>24</u>

He was gone. Back downstairs into the wine cellar and through the subterranean passages, the underground route to the grotto. His plan was to call the police and have them meet him there. Hopefully they would believe him and he wouldn't have to go to the station in person. Appearing by tunnel would give Norman the advantage. The smugglers seemed to prefer arriving by water. Besides they needed their boats to transfer the stolen objects.

Me, I did the overland route along the beach, avoiding clots of tourists before climbing the boutique-lined cobblestone staircase. The steps met the piazza in front of the church. Over my head the mustard façade and bell tower faded into shadow. The dome with its blue, yellow, and green tiles reflected the night sky, the watchful citrus groves and the sleeping sea.

Above was the walkway tangled with bougainvillea and the noise of artists selling their wares beneath the lampposts. I was about a quarter of the way up the hillside. This time I had no patience to focus on the cultural, religious and architectural treats of Positano. Police tape barred the front doors, but I knew someone was still inside. The windows were lit, and I was hoping it was the authorities so that I could tell them what was happening, and that another body had been found. The officers had all gone home. The police cruisers on the street below were absent from the scene.

I ducked under the tape and rushed to the main door. No one saw me. I slipped into the open coolness, tall ceilings hovering over me, and wide-open floors. My pulse jumped as once again I drank in the gold and white interior, at night illuminated by wall sconces and candles.

I wandered along the central nave to the front where the conspicuous blank space, overhead, glared on the wall. The ghost of the stolen Black Madonna haunted that spot.

A voice spoke from behind me. I jumped. "The church is closed until tomorrow."

I turned around. "I'm sorry, Father."

Recognition dawned on me. It was the kindly old priest from before. His English was better than my Italian so we continued the conversation in my language. "I don't mean to intrude." I paused to gather my thoughts. "Do you remember me, Father? My name is Lucy Racine."

He nodded. "Of course, I remember you. Lucy. And I am Father Carmine. Come. Come and sit down. What has happened that has rendered you so breathless and distraught."

I was paralyzed from overwrought nerves. Where or how to start?

"You have done something you feel is wrong? It is all right; you can speak here. No one but myself is in the church tonight. Only I and God."

"No. That's not it." Although he had touched on a kernel of truth. A woman could not love two men.

Nothing I had done would bring on the wrath or even the disapproval of God, would it? He watched me hesitate. No, I decided. It would not. "Please. This isn't personal. It has nothing to do with me. This has to do with the church, and—" I glanced up over the altar, "—and *her*."

"Her?" He looked at me quizzically. "You mean the missing icon. The Virgin and Child."

"Yes. I believe I've found it. Norman, you remember

Norman Depardieu? He's part of the archaeology team. He has gone to fetch the police. It's here, Father. Not here inside the church, but here in Positano. Not far away, in a cave. By the sea."

Father Carmine was shocked at the news. He muttered something in Italian; I was at a loss to translate. I did get the distinct impression that he was concerned and very interested as to how I had stumbled across it. I had no time or need to explain. When he saw me staring blankly at him he reverted to English. "You found it in a cave?"

"Yes, me and the archaeologist, Luke Trevanian."

Now that I thought about it I realized that Luke had left to go after Marco Ferri before I ever discovered the priceless icon. So what I had just related to the priest was a total inaccuracy. Luke had no idea I had located the hiding place of the Black Madonna. Not unless he had read and deciphered my code.

"I promised to meet Luke here. Have you seen him?" I asked suddenly.

The priest shook his head. "No one has come in this evening other than you. There is the police tape, after all."

It was two hours since I had left Luke. What had happened? I double-checked the time on my phone.

"I must go, Father. If Signor Trevanian comes, will you tell him I've returned to the grotto?"

"Be careful, child."

I nodded, suddenly impatient to escape. I ran out of there, and made my way back down the rocky steps, along the dark street to the Torre Trasita.

Both Luke and Norman had warned me to stay away from the Torre in case Marco returned. There were no lights on and I had left the door unlocked. I went inside, shut the door behind me, and paused for only a second before I headed straight downstairs to the wine cellar, and made my way through the dark tunnel with only my cellphone for light. Norman would be there. And, perhaps, Luke. I was safe.

The smell, salty and strong like the sea, with the distinct odor of fish reached my nostrils as I continued on my mission. The air flowed freely. I was almost at the opening.

The rush of the ocean reached me, waves slapping on stone, and the hollow ringing tones of a seashell held to the ear.

I ducked under a low overhang of solid rock, and entered the cave. In the raised light of my phone I saw the dark, sparkling green of quietly moving water.

Had I carried a flashlight I would have noticed the boat at the far curve of the wall, but my cellphone only lit up the first meter or so.

The gently wallowing shadows cast by the dim light rippled across the deep water. I was standing on the shallow ledge of sand and pebbles enclosed by solid stone, with the hollows carved out by centuries of the sea's motion, making me feel once more like I stood at the center of a giant Swiss cheese.

In what direction was the entrance to the treasure hoard? At night, without the sunshine leaning in through the opening to the sea, the play of light and shadow was even more surreal and disorienting.

I searched for the large stalagmite that had hidden the crevice. As I bobbed my light around I heard a noise from behind me.

A flashlight shone into my face as I turned. I was expecting to see Norman but instead I heard the voice of the yacht's captain.

"Ms. Racine. Is that you?"

A chill threatened to topple me. I was not a good liar but I was going to have to do my best to sound convincing. I answered. "Captain Spatz. It's me, Lucy. Please, can you lower that light, it's blinding me."

He lowered his arm and opened the flashlight to wide beam so that the portion of the cave where we were standing was fully lit. He propped it on a shelf of stone and turned back to me, his gaze severe and mistrusting. "What are you doing here?"

"Is Norman around?" My heart was hammering but I made a concerted effort to hide it.

"No, why?"

"We found the tunnel that leads from the Torre Trasita to this cave. Did Luke send you?" I was cautious with the questions I asked, making every attempt to sound innocent. Nothing could make me trust him, but I had to convince him that I did.

"Yes." His answer came after a slight second's hesitation.

Every fiber of my being warned me to caution. That was an out and out lie. He was the one—I was sure of it now—that was here earlier transporting the treasure. I mustn't let him know, under any circumstances what I suspected.

"You shouldn't be here," he said. "It's dark and dangerous."

Was this a veiled threat? I had to let him know I wasn't alone. "Norman is coming with the police."

He stiffened at that. "So… Luke told you about the stash of artifacts?"

"Actually, we found the hoard together." There was no point in lying about this. The treasure was all around us. I had to continue with the charade at all costs. He must not know that I was on to him.

"I see." He mulled something over in his mind before he said: "I think I should take you back to the yacht. It's getting late. Luke and I will take care of things."

"But Norman will be here any minute with the police."

"All the more reason you should leave."

His agitation increased my discomfort. His fake politeness was *too* faked. He seemed in an awful hurry to get rid of me.

He was insistent. He reached out as though physical contact would compel me to submit to his will. It was at this moment his sleeve rose, slid up to his shoulder, and exposed the bottom of a dark, curving tattoo. His next movement placed the tattoo straight in the light. It was directly in my line of view, near enough to discern the pattern.

A cupid riding a sea serpent! I was right. He was the man in the director's office. He was the one I had seen arguing with Arianna Chase at the museum!

He saw me flinch and I knew I had betrayed myself. I had recognized the unusual tattoo. We had both seen its photo on Tommy's phone. One thing was certain. It was because Tommy had photographed the tattoo and knew the identity of the owner that he had died.

"I think you should get into the boat."

All the kindness disappeared. His voice changed. The command was cold. I had to think fast. I had to keep him talking. My eyes scoured the cavern for a weapon. What was nearby that I could hit him with?

"In the boat!" he repeated.

Oh, if only I still had my flashlight. I could hit him with that. All I could see were rocks on the floor of the cave. If I could just bend down without his suspecting... and grab a nice solid stone.... Perhaps I was wrong? Perhaps he wasn't aware that I had caught on? I could still save myself. All I had to do was pretend I hadn't noticed the tattoo.

He went to grab me. His meaty hands came at my throat. He meant to strangle me and I dropped to the ground in the direction of a large cobble. I raised it and struck him in the face but he saw it coming and feinted, so that I only managed to scrape his cheek before the weapon tumbled helplessly out of my grip.

"You shouldn't have come here, Lucy Racine."

He had me by the arm. I scratched at him with my nails, succeeded in tearing off two of his buttons. The metal bit into my flesh as I struck him with my fists.

He cursed. He slapped me across the face. He grabbed both my arms and twisted them up behind my back, but not before I could drop what I had in the ball of one of my fists inside my pocket. I tried to free myself. But that merely served to send me stumbling and losing one of my sandals. In my desperation to break loose I kicked the sandal further out of my reach. In the end I stopped struggling. I knew he could break my bones.

It looked like he wasn't going to kill me here. He nudged me toward the boat in the dark corner. It was moored beneath an overhang by the far wall. I could hear the sloshing of the waves. He was going to take me out on the sea and drown me.

I had to buy a little time and work out a plan. I must leave Luke and Norman some kind of clue to find me.

My eye landed on the discarded sandal, blue against the stone of the cave in the dusky light. "Get in the boat," he ordered.

This time I did as I was told.

I sat in the bow facing him while he manned the tiller at the stern. I noted that we were seated in one of the yacht's inflatable Zodiacs. That was good. That meant if he were armed he would not risk firing his gun while we were in the boat. It could sink us both.

From where I sat I could see the lights of the yacht in the distance. Was Luke there? Was he confronting Marco Ferri? Because now I suspected they must have been planning to use the yacht to make their escape. Spatz kept the engine low as he backed the boat out onto the open sea.

How was he planning to kill me? By now he must have located my flashlight next to Marissa's body. He knew I had found her. He knew I had guessed that he had killed both her and Tommy. He leveled his sight on me even as he tacked to swing the bow forward.

I swallowed, watching his face.

How had Norman planned to bring the police? Underground by the tunnel from the Torre or by sea in a police boat? Either way he wouldn't get here in time. There was only one thing I could do.

I had no weapon. Only hope.

I threw myself over the side.

The cold water engulfed me. I let myself sink as deep as

I could go. I was a good swimmer. The salinity of the gulf was especially buoyant, and if I could stay alive, I could make it to shore. I kicked off my remaining sandal and began to swim.

Two bullets shot past me through the water. Panicked, I started to flail, struggling against the drag of the water as though it were tar. I knew if I failed to move out of his range, I'd be dead. Another projectile plunged near my cheek. My panic had attracted his attention, sending ripples to the surface. I had to be cautious. I stopped flailing my arms and legs and let them sink with the pull of the sea.

I let the current take me. I dared not allow myself to rise for air. The evening tide was sweeping me towards the cliffs. I hoped that he thought he had hit me.

When I finally had to risk coming up to breathe, I saw a light in the distance. He had no idea which direction I had drifted. He was tacking now. Circling around, searching for me. He reached down, lifted something from the water. In the moonlight I could see what it was. It was my other sandal.

He stared across the open ocean at the moving waves. He turned his head. Had he seen me? The water was too dark. And he was looking in the wrong direction.

Beneath the cliffs was a myriad of sea caves. Luke had told me so. I would be safe there. Unencumbered by my shoes, I dunked my head under the heaving rollers. I was too scared to cry. And the saltwater would only mock my tears. I started stroking.

CHAPTER
<u>25</u>

Fortunately for me we had come to Italy at the height of summer. The evenings were warm, but not when one was soaking wet. This part of the honeycomb had no opening high enough for a boat to enter. I could wait here a few minutes. Then I must get out of the water or I would freeze.

It was quiet except for the echoes of the waves gently splashing against the stone. It was pitch dark. I breathed in the cool cavernous air. I dared not swim too far into the honeycomb for fear that I would become disoriented and drown, or simply trapped by the rising tide. Perhaps that was what Spatz was hoping for. It would be easy to do. Either way—disorientation or tide—I would drown. That would solve all of his problems.

The only reason I knew which direction was up and out was because of the full moon. The moon outside my hiding place sent silvery light onto the liquid surface. As I turned my head, glassy light reflected through the low opening in the cavern. How long had I been in the undersea grotto? I had no idea of the time. Was anyone searching for me? I only knew I had been in the water for a lengthy duration. *Too* long. I was shivering.

The clock was ticking. It was only a matter of minutes

before the tide would bring the sloshing waves into my refuge, and then my escape hatch would be closed. Already the breakers were forming in long rolling tubes of water slamming against the outer rock of the caves.

I took a deep breath. I felt the spray shoot through the cave opening and spatter on my face. I dived deep, then back up and out from beneath the overhang of rock, which now gave me barely a foot clearance. I raised my head. Drops rained off my face and hair. I blinked them out of my eyes. I blew the spray from my lips and wiped the back of my hand across my brow.

The Zodiac was nowhere in sight. I scanned the vista from one end to the other. Black water, moonlight, tiny objects settled on the surface of the sea, away off in the distance, and no boats moving. The Zodiac was no longer there. Captain Spatz must have thought he had killed me. He had no reason to believe that I could swim this far.

Where had he gone?

If he had backtracked to the treasure hoard, Norman and the police would be waiting to greet him.

I wiped the sting of salt from my lips. I swam around the steep side of the cliff to where a stack of fallen rocks gave me a handhold to climb. I dragged myself out of the water, struggling against the tug of the breakers, and collapsed onto dry rock. Exhausted, I gasped for air. My skin was a mass of wet goose pimples, my fingers drained of color, clinging for life like some feckless bird's claws. The stone was still warm from the evening sun. My wet clothing sent rivulets pouring over the arid surface. The sun had barely set and left the moon to guide my way. I hugged my body to the rock hoping to absorb some of its rapidly cooling heat and through dripping lashes, watched the evidence of my near mishap trickle away down the hard stone to the pounding surf.

After a few minutes I felt strong enough to rise. I squeezed the seawater out of my hair and stripped the ruined white sweater from my shoulders. I wrung out the dress by the hem. Fortunately the garment was made of some light filmy material that dried as quickly as nylon. Then I stood up, barefoot, having lost both of my sandals. White streaks of brine stained my skin. I could taste it on my lips. My eyes burned and I had to wait for natural tears to wash away the salt-sting.

I took a tentative step forward, dried salt and sand grating against my legs and the bottoms of my feet. Should I go to the church for help? I climbed around the rocks until I could see my location. The town was roughly divided in half by the cliff where the Torre Trasita was built. I was on the western side of the tower on the Spiaggia del Fornillo beach. I would have to go past it if I was to reach the other side to the Spiaggia Grande, and the town center and the church.

My phone was gone. Lost in the tussle, that option closed to me. Luke would be frantic wondering where I was. So would Norman. Did Norman manage to convince the police to visit the grotto with him? Had Luke cornered Marco?

I envisioned the gun in Luke's hand when he left me in the black grotto. I was no longer afraid. I climbed over the rocks and down to the beach. There, hauled high onto the sand was a dark grey Zodiac. I shivered, this time from excitement. Inside the boat was my blue sandal.

***

I retrieved the sandal from Spatz's boat. Walking with one unshod foot was no easier than totally barefoot. It had taken me longer than it would have had I worn shoes on both feet. The sand on the beach was a blessing. Crossing the cobblestone path however was an exercise in caution. I could not risk crying out on the off chance I stepped on a pebble.

I glanced up. I saw what I had hoped to see. The interior of the Torre was dark on my approach. On the street a police cruiser was parked. Upstairs, on the rooftop patio there were lights; Marco was home. That meant Luke was with him. I knew I should go directly past and run for the sanctuary of the church. Something made me freeze. Every cell in my body shrank from the idea of climbing up there.

Luke didn't know his captain was a murderer; that was one piece of information I had neglected to pass on to Norman. I had to go up there and warn them.

It was so damned high.

One thing that helped was the darkness; the other thing was my total preoccupation with Spatz's treachery.

My heart was pounding, my pulse galloped. The wind finally felt warm on my cold skin. The race across the beach had helped the blood to circulate. I was no longer shivering. I removed my one sandal, and dangling it by the strap, took a deep breath. Oh my God it was so high. *Just don't look down.* All the other times I had climbed to this rooftop patio had been via stairs indoors. The only outdoor stretch had been a short climb from the top floor to the roof. Now I had to make the entire climb from the outside. That was a lot of stairs.

I reached out an aching, trembling arm. I seized the cold metal of the handrail. I pulled my swim-weary legs up from behind me, and grabbed another breath. *Do not look down.* I scaled the steep staircase, resting at alternate levels where a small balcony opened to each of the bedrooms, not once sending my gaze to the ground. I was almost too weary to be afraid. My breathing was short and labored, but not from fear or exertion. It was anticipation.

Another intake of air. I plunged on. No lights on in any of the rooms, so whatever was happening was happening at the top of the tower.

Voices drifted down to me. I waited on the balcony just below the level of the patio. The furry shadow of the cypress leaned in to cover me in darkness. The vine of hanging wisteria made a veil to hide my face, and gave me a feeling of safety. I started once more to climb. Directly in front of me was a potted fig tree. There I stopped.

Six men were arguing on the patio. I recognized all of them except for the two constables.

Marco and Luke were at the far side of the floor, Marco

seated in a lounge chair and Luke pacing in front of him. Two constables leaned against the balustrade, one with his hand gripping the iron rail as though he suffered from vertigo.

Captain Spatz stood on the other side of Marco Ferri. No one had noticed the scrape on his face where my stone had glanced off his cheek in our struggle. He had on the uniform cap that he wore when the yacht was under way. It placed his features in shadow. Since it was already well past sundown everyone else was in shadow too. The soft lamps on the patio did little to illuminate the scene, and moonlight distorted everyone's faces. Two buttons were missing on Spatz's shirt. No one noticed that either.

Norman was the nearest to me. He stood just off to the side of the entrance to the steps where I was hiding behind the ornamental greenery. If he looked down, it was likely he would see me crouched behind the fig tree like a cat.

They were quarrelling about some hidden treasure. Marco was denying any knowledge of Roman silver or statues and he certainly knew nothing of the body of an Interpol officer.

"Lucy said she found a body," Norman insisted.

Captain Spatz objected. He had just seen her. This was certainly true. I was positive that he was the one who had left the agent's body in the cave.

He showed them a text he had received from Marissa's phone, not twenty minutes ago. The claim was a lie unless he had stolen her phone and typed the text himself.

His cool act, as though he had not just recently tried to murder me, increased my agitation. I was about to show myself to them and throw his alibi to the wind when Norman growled. He tried to speak. The constable cut him off. "You did not see a body, then?"

"I told you..." Norman's frustration was obvious by the grimace on his face. "When you refused to go to the grotto with me I returned there. And found this!"

He swung my other blue sandal by the strap. "This

belongs to Lucy. When I couldn't find her and saw signs of a struggle I knew I had to act fast. If he'd taken her by boat I needed your help to find him. Lucy told me that Luke had gone after Marco, and I wondered if Marco hadn't somehow given Luke the slip and returned to his cache. When no one showed up, I didn't hang around but came straight back through the tunnel and found you all here. Where *is* she?"

The accusation was flung at Marco. No one suspected Captain Spatz.

"Did you find a body?" The question came from the constable.

"No, I looked around quickly to see if I could find Lucy. There appeared to be a scuffle by the marks on the cave floor. They led to the aperture to the sea. I was worried the bastard had forcibly dragged her onto a boat and taken her somewhere by water, so I didn't look for the body. At the time I was more concerned about the living than the dead. As I said, I saw marks on the floor *clearly* indicating that someone boarded a boat."

Luke looked like he was going to shoot somebody. The constable asked everyone to calm down. "Why do you believe the girl is missing?"

"I just told you! Why would she leave one of her sandals?"

"Where is she, Marco?" Luke demanded.

"How would *I* know?"

"I've been searching for you all afternoon. I lost sight of your boat, and I *know* you had a boat. I saw you leave the grotto with it. But after you shook me off, I backtracked to the Torre three hours later, and found you here. You had plenty of time to return to the grotto and do your dirty work."

"I was in Salerno on business. You can ask anyone. They will tell you."

Signor Ferri was a well-respected man in Positano. He had several companies, one of which was his shipyard in Salerno. He may once have been a local fisherman, but he was now a multi-millionaire with his fingers in numerous businesses. He had made many contributions to the success of the town. If the police were going to believe anyone it would be Marco Ferri and not some foreigner who had come to mine their community for its treasures.

"Arrest him," Luke ordered. "He's the one who stole the Black Madonna and he has it hidden in the grotto."

"That's absurd," Marco said. "You have no proof."

"But I do. Not only did you openly admit to me that you have stashed it in a secret place, but I have this—" Luke took out his phone and showed them my text.

"What the hell does that mean?"

The constable looked from the millionaire to the text. "My English, maybe it is not so good." He read it out loud. "*I have tickets... to the concert? And I know... where she lives....*" He paused for a second then said, "I'm sorry, Signor Trevanian. I do not understand. What does that mean?"

Luke was quick to pick up on riddles. I knew he would be. He answered swiftly and with confidence. "She was referring to the Black Madonna. That's what 'ticket to the concert' means. It's a reference to the pop star Madonna. And Lucy obviously found the icon in the cave where I left her. Now tell us where she is!" He turned his frustration on Marco. "If you've hurt her, I will kill you—"

"Signor Trevanian—" The constable raised his hands to block Luke from attacking Marco. "That is enough. There will be no killing."

Marco was irritatingly calm. "I don't know where the signorina is. The last time I saw her was this morning when you two left for the church."

I was getting anxious. I should make my entrance soon. I knew Captain Spatz would not be expecting to see me. He was acting like an innocent bystander. Neither Luke nor Norman had an inkling as to the depths he had sunk. Was Marco Ferri his boss or was it someone else? I had to know.

"We're wasting time, constable." Luke fisted his hands. "Lucy could be in trouble. She was supposed to meet me at the church. She isn't there."

"You've been to the church?" the constable asked.

"I phoned them just before you arrived. Father Carmine said she left him two hours ago. Said she was returning to the grotto."

"I'm going back there," Norman said. "I'll find out what happened to her."

The constable scowled. "Let me get your stories straight. Then we will *all* go to the grotto and see who is telling the truth."

It was at that second Norman caught my eye. His eyes widened with disbelief and then pleasure. His lips parted to speak. I placed a finger hurriedly to my lips. He nodded. Everyone else was occupied with defending their comings and goings of the evening, and failed to notice our subtle interaction.

Norman acquiesced, said nothing, and moved toward me. I began a backward crawl to the stairs. I went silently down in my bare feet until I reached the balcony one level below the patio. Norman followed.

"Lucy!" he whispered huskily, as he landed quietly beside me. "Thank God, you're all right." He engulfed me in an enormous hug. Involuntarily my arms curled around his neck. His hands slid down my spine to my lower back.

I inhaled the sweet masculine smell of him and shut my eyes.

He kept his voice low as his lips brushed the top of my head. He released me. The intimacy of our touch would have been palpable if our minds weren't preoccupied by the lies being told on the patio. "Your clothes are damp. Are you sure you're okay?"

"I had a bit of an unexpected swim."

He observed that I was clutching the one blue sandal I had retrieved from Spatz's boat. He handed me the other. I quickly snapped them on. They were a little soggy still, and gritty with sand. "Quickly, what happened?"

"Do you have a gun, Norman?" My voice was as quiet

as his. "Captain Spatz tried to kill me. I had to dive overboard from his Zodiac and he shot at me. He was trying to murder me."

I could not see his face well, but I could feel his rage. He really did care. "Bastard. They didn't believe me when I told them you were in danger." He yanked out his gun. "Come with me. We will show them what he did to you."

"Wait! You have to go back to the grotto and make sure the icon is still there."

"Don't worry, Lucy. No one has been back there since I left it."

It was important he obey me. I had to convince him to leave, that I would be all right. Someone other than myself had to witness the discovery. Just in case something should happen to me. I answered him carefully, "We don't know that. He has others working for him."

I gave him quick directions, as well as I could remember, so he could locate the church's stolen treasure. "It's what you and Luke have devoted your entire adult lives to finding. It will clear Luke's name. Please, Norman. You must go and keep an eye on the icon."

"What about Spatz?" he demanded. "Can you prove he tried to shoot you?"

"No, but I can prove he tried to hurt me."

I shoved a fist into my pocket. My fingers closed around the small bits of brass. They were still there. My quick thinking after Spatz grabbed me had kept the evidence from vanishing into the sea.

"Go now. Once I've convinced them that those two up there are up to no good—that they are in fact murderers and thieves—we'll be right behind you."

He turned to leave. Compulsively I darted in front of him before he could start down the iron staircase. He glanced at me with a puzzled expression. I did not explain. I kissed him full on the lips. I glanced up at his startled face and then turned to climb upstairs to the rooftop.

CHAPTER
<u>26</u>

"Lucy!" Luke came towards me arms outstretched. I ran to him and he held me, relieved. He noticed my disheveled state and demanded, "Where have you been? Norman was convinced that Marco had done something with you."

"You see?" Marco said. "The girl is safe."

I was somewhat bedraggled after my dip in the sea, but the filmy dress was reasonably dry and my hair, too, albeit a tangled mess. No one had noticed that Norman was gone.

The shock on Spatz's face almost gave him away—if it wasn't for the fact that no one was looking. Everyone's attention was on me.

One of the police officers, a slightly portly fellow with shiny, olive skin and dark features, walked up to me and said, "I am Constable Constantine. You, I presume, are the missing woman, Lucy Racine?"

"Yes."

"Would you mind telling us where you have been for the past two hours?"

"I was trying to get away from him!" I pointed an accusing finger at Captain Spatz.

Luke looked over at his captain in surprise. "What? What did he do?"

Captain Spatz remained unruffled. He raised his eyes in equally shocked innocence. "I have no idea what she's talking about."

"I went back to the grotto, Luke. And he was there."

"What were you doing in the grotto?"

Spatz scowled. Luke suddenly noticed the black, bloody mark under his eye and clawed at the man's cap. The captain swung his head away but that only served to help Luke remove it faster. He had a firm grip on the visor. The proof of our altercation was all over Spatz's face. "What happened to your cheekbone there?"

The blood had dried. He had cleaned it up somewhat but the stone I struck him with had left some ugly marks. "*I* did that... when he tried to strangle me... And then he tried to drown me," I spat.

Luke's face spoke murder. The constables came between the two men and ordered them to separate. "Now explain what happened to your face," Constable Constantine commanded.

Spatz knew he was caught. Whatever lie he came up with would have to be good if anyone was to believe him. "Okay. I admit I was in the grotto. I found it the same way these two did." He gestured to Luke and myself.

Liar. How could he have found the grotto by accident? If any of what he said were true, how did he stumble upon it? The tunnel connected through the outside via the church and the Torre Trasita. What reason would he have to be in the wine cellar of the tower? And the cliffside was riddled with caves. How could he have zeroed in on the exact cave where the artifacts were stashed? The odds were against it. No. He had found it because of Marco. Marco was his boss. He had to be.

Marco was watching him closely.

"I found some things. Some artifacts. I slipped and scraped my cheek on the stone. The walls are uneven and low in the caves. I saw the girl there, but I never hurt her. In fact, I was trying to get her to safety. She resisted, so maybe I

used a little more force than I should have. Really, boss,"—
he was practically groveling at Luke's feet now—"Why
would I hurt her?"

"And the accusation that you tried to drown her?"

He shook his head at the constable. "A
misunderstanding."

A misunderstanding, indeed! "Then explain this." I
shoved one fist in my pocket. I removed the pair of brass
buttons that I had torn off his uniform in our struggle. "Why
would I tear off your buttons if you weren't attacking me?"

Constable Constantine took them from me and examined
them against the missing buttons from Spatz's shirt. "Even if
it is a match, it only suggests that they came from his shirt."

"Yes—" I turned to glare at Leo Spatz. "—And it's
what's *under* his shirt that will prove that he's a killer."

The constable stared at me. "Explain."

I waited to catch my breath. There were police officers
here. And Luke. I was free to reveal the truth. "The Interpol
agent, Marissa Leone—"

"Wait a moment. You knew Marissa Leone was an
Interpol agent?"

"Yes, but her real name is Alessandra Piero."

Constantine nodded. "I am acquainted with her. She was
sent undercover by Interpol. This afternoon she revealed her
identity to me. She confided something of her suspicions. But
there was nothing in her explanations that could possibly be a
motive for murder." He paused. "Or perhaps there was....
Tell me what happened. Are you saying that she is dead?
That *he* killed her?" His eyes flickered incredulously towards
the captain.

"Yes. That is exactly what I am saying. Isn't it obvious?
So why aren't we all rushing down to the grotto? Her body is
there, along with the stolen icon—the Black Madonna!"

There was a short silence as everyone absorbed my
words "If things are as you say and these two are the culprits,
there is no hurry," the constable said.

Constantine had a point. Marissa would still be dead and

the treasure still hidden.

"Please continue."

"Marissa—I mean Agent Piero—guessed who Tommy Buchanan's killer was. That's why she, too, was murdered."

He briefly mused over my statement. His eyes roved hesitatingly over the faces of the assembled men. None showed much emotion. Spatz wore a skeptical sneer, Marco Ferri displayed an air of boredom, and Luke showed stark impatience. The other policeman exhibited keen interest. He seemed confident that his partner had the situation under control. Constantine turned back to me. "She told me she suspected the killer possessed a tattoo on his left arm, near his shoulder."

"It's him." I pointed to Spatz. "He has a tattoo. Cupid riding a sea serpent. Ask him to show you if you don't believe me!"

No way was Spatz allowing anyone to rip off his shirt to learn the truth. He drew out his weapon and aimed it at me. "Why couldn't you just shut up? Why couldn't you just drown? The deed was done."

Luke had stayed silent for most of this conversation. Now he sprang to life. "Who else is in on this? Is it *him?* Is it Marco Ferri?"

Marco sat spine-stiff in his chair. "Not another word, Captain Spatz. You are entitled to legal council."

"Oh shut up." Spatz turned and glared at Luke. His gun was aimed at the billionaire. "You rich people are all alike. Why should you get to have it all? Some of that should have been *mine*." He punched his free fist to his chest.

It occurred to me just then. Did Captain Spatz even know the hiding place of the Black Madonna? Marco Ferri did. The eyes never lie. And I realized the Italian millionaire knew exactly where it was hidden.

"Not another word," Marco warned.

Spatz switched the gun back on me as Luke made to jump him. "I wouldn't do that if I were you—*boss*." The word ended with a hiss. "Maybe you don't care if I shoot you. Will you care if I shoot *her*—?"

I should have been more frightened. But the hour in the water and the breathless climb up the exterior of the tower had exhausted—numbed me—and left something in its wake. Rage.

The police had frozen when Spatz withdrew his gun. He placed his finger on the trigger. I know nothing about guns. But this was one big-ass revolver, similar to the one Luke owned. There was no doubt it could create a staggering amount of damage. "Hands where I can see them. If you move for your weapons I will shoot her."

Constantine said, "Give me the gun, Captain Spatz. It is over. You are doing yourself more harm by threatening to kill another person."

"It *isn't* over. That Black Madonna is worth a fortune. And I am not letting *him* have any of it."

So, I was wrong. He *did* know where it was. And he knew its potential worth.

"It is only a religious artifact. Its only value is to the church."

"Are you kidding me? Just ask *him*—" Spatz kept his gun aimed in my direction but he pointed to Marco Ferri with his finger.

I had never seen Luke so tense or so furious. The muscles in his jaw twitched and his fists were clenched. He had no fear of the gun and he was ready to pounce at the right provocation. It was taking everything he had to control this impulse. "You're going to jail, Marco. So you might as well come clean."

His words were not wasted. The Italian millionaire stood up. It was as though at that moment time stood still.

That must be why they use slow motion in films when something happens unexpectedly and quickly. It was like that now. None of us could have predicted what took place next. I swear all movement ground to a halt. All eyes were on Marco Ferri. We thought this was his moment of confession. I, who prided myself on being a good judge of character, of having extra sharp intuition, could not read his thoughts. What he did next took us all unawares. He ran to the rail and leaped over it.

The stop-action effect lingered a second longer than it should have. We were stunned into inaction. Then all hell broke lose. The constables, Luke, and even I ran to the rail.

We had all forgotten about Leo Spatz's gun. Spatz took advantage of the distraction. At the unexpected suicide of his boss, he took the opportunity to dash for the staircase.

"He's getting away," Luke shouted, turning.

The police raced after him.

Spatz leaped the steps four at a time, clinging and swinging from the handrails like a monkey. The constables fired their guns. It had no effect. Spatz was already on the ground making a run for it.

Luke was halfway across the patio. He shouted to me over his shoulder. "Stay here, Lucy."

I ignored his command and raced after him. He was kidding himself if he thought I was missing out on this. I grabbed Luke's arm as he started down the staircase. "It's okay, Luke. I sent Norman back to the grotto. Spatz won't get the Black Madonna."

CHAPTER
27

On the ground, one of the police officers examined Marco Ferri's body. Could there be any doubt he was dead? The other, Constable Constantine, bolted after Spatz.

"I thought he was my friend," Luke said. "Poor old Marco. I warned him when he told me he was in possession of it. I begged him to tell me its location so I could return it. I promised to take all the flack, and leave him out of it. I tried to protect him and his family, but the temptation was just too much for him."

I looked up at that. So Luke *did* know the Black Madonna was made of solid gold. I never told him. Why else would he have made such a comment? If he thought the Madonna was only a valued religious icon why would he say: '*The temptation was just too much for him.*' Something composed of that much gold was worth a fortune.

This was one more secret Luke had kept from me. Why was I feeling so desperately uneasy?

He sighed. "If only Marco had listened."

I exhaled, unable to look at the broken body bloodying the cobblestones on the side of the tower. I was silent. Nothing I said could possibly make Luke feel better.

"How am I going to tell his wife and kids?" He was

honestly concerned.

I replied, "Is it your job to do so?"

He shrugged. "Better to come from me than from the police."

"There's nothing we can do here, Luke." The constable was talking on his phone, calling for backup and an ambulance. "Captain Spatz is headed for the grotto. I know he is."

Luke nodded, hauled his eyes away from the horrible sight, a sight I had steered clear of after the first gruesome glimpse. "We'll take the short cut."

"What about him?" I shoved a finger in the direction where Constantine had barged down the beach.

"He'll get a boat and follow Spatz if it's the sea he was headed for."

"It was. I saw his Zodiac on the sand."

"Then we'll cut him off at the cave. Let's go."

There was no argument from me. He grabbed my hand and we ran the remaining distance in the dark, under the softly lit lampposts, until we reached the south entrance to the Torre. Luke jiggled the door lever. The door was open. We shot in through the unlocked door, down the stairs to the wine cellar and through the portal to the tunnel.

"Hadn't we better warn, Norman?" I asked, gasping for breath.

He stopped and raised his phone. His thumb scrolled down through his contacts. He tapped Norman's number and warned him to watch for Spatz.

When we reached the grotto Spatz was not there. Norman was waiting with the treasure. But the Interpol agent's body was nowhere to be found. "I looked everywhere. Even tried to dig around to see if they had buried her…. Nothing. Are you sure you saw a body, Lucy?" Norman asked.

I nodded. How could I mistake a dead body for anything else? Especially the corpse of someone I recognized. I returned to the spot under the ledge of rock where I recalled

Spatz abandoning his flashlight to attack me. The light had shone directly at us, placing the body beneath it in total darkness. He had positioned the flashlight there on purpose while he decided whether or not I knew about her.

The spot where she originally lay was stirred up, but so was the sand and pebbles everywhere in this cavern. Too many people had visited the grotto and the evidence was disturbed.

Luke poked a toe into the piled up silver and marble. "At least, some of the loot's still here. No time to move it all I'm guessing."

"None of this is important without the Black Madonna," I said.

All this time the men were poking around in various dark corners and crevices.

"Where is the cavern?" Norman asked. "Now that you're here, Lucy, maybe you can show us."

I led them to the wall and to the stalactite where I had lost the flashlight after my scare of earlier that day. I ducked behind the stone formation and found the crevice. It was a tight squeeze for the men. I remembered to turn my body sideways for an easy glide as smooth as a knife through butter, and signaled for them to do likewise. For them the effort was more like stuck toast. I had a brief stab of alarm as it took them a moment or two to get unstuck.

It was dark at the end of the craggy passage. And even with the light of Norman's flashlight—plus the one I had recovered from the floor that I had lost earlier—there was no sign of the precious Madonna.

"How could it have disappeared in so short a time?" I was distraught to the point of tears.

Norman wanted to comfort me but it was Luke who came to my side. "Obviously someone moved it, and it had to be Spatz."

"Do you suppose he could have done it earlier?" Norman asked.

"There's always that possibility. But where did he take

it?"

Like Norman, Spatz was trained in the military. He was one tough dude. If anyone could move that heavy object, Leo Spatz could. I knew firsthand how strong he was. Besides he had help. That creepy little man with the shorn head and the earring was his accomplice.

As we discussed the options, the sound of a motorboat came from the sea just outside the cave entrance. We returned to the outer cavern. It was Constable Constantine and he wore a stern look on his face. "I need the three of you to come with me."

Frustrated and tired, we obeyed and climbed into the police boat.

"The Black Madonna is gone," Luke said.

Constantine had expected this. Weary, he was ready to wrap up the crime scene.

"Did you get that rat of a captain?" Norman demanded.

The police constable slowed the boat and turned to Luke. "Unfortunately he was trying to make off with your yacht, Signor Trevanian. We had no choice but to shoot him."

"He's dead?" Luke asked.

"He is dead."

"So all of the criminals involved in this case are dead."

Constantine studied Luke at length. "I am hoping that that is not the case... If it is... we have no way to track them."

"There is one other person that I know of who is involved." Everyone seated in the police marine cruiser turned eyes my way. My own gaze landed on Luke. He was going to hate this. Not only was his captain a traitor and a crook, but so was one of his yacht crew. "It's that skinny guy with the earring, on your boat. The one with the shaved head. I saw him conspiring with Spatz. He was helping to move the loot."

Norman's eyes widened. He knew the man. "I never trusted the little skunk."

"What's his name?" Luke demanded.

"Freddie Spelnick." Norman and I had spoken simultaneously. We exchanged knowing glances as the name hung in the air between us. He was the very unpleasant sailor who had hit on me at the start of the voyage.

Luke rubbed his forehead. "Why don't I recognize the name?"

"Spatz hired him last minute when one of the crew bailed. Now that we understand the extent of his involvement, it makes sense he wouldn't have wanted you to know him personally." It was Norman that had answered.

Almost midnight now. Constantine revved the engine and took us to shore, and then to the station to make our depositions.

"It is too late to do anything tonight," he said. "We will search for this Freddie Spelnick tomorrow. And I will also speak to all of you, again, in the morning."

He returned us by marine cruiser to the yacht. I was so exhausted all I wanted to do was sleep. Luke recognized this and left me at my room. Norman glanced at me, and said, "Goodnight, Lucy."

***

On reflection I wished Luke had stayed with me that night. I went to bed exhausted. I was thinking the worst was over when I heard a sound at my door. Sometimes over-exhaustion makes it impossible to sleep. I was wide-awake, listening to the sound of the waves outside my opened deck door. I think I mentioned that my stateroom opens out to a private sundeck. I had no reason to think it was dangerous to leave the doors wide for the fresh sea air.

I was *so* wrong.

He was very quiet. At first there were no noises, and I closed my eyes on the verge of drifting off to sleep. Suddenly, I felt a hand on my mouth. I jerked up in terror, bit down and caused my assailant to shriek. I rolled to the other side of the bed, scrambled off and onto my feet in my thin, filmy nightgown.

There were no lights on. Lights were unnecessary for me to guess his identity. The glint of gold in his right earlobe was enough to give him away. I should have insisted the police go after Spatz's accomplice tonight. But no one thought he'd have the guts to return to the yacht.

He came at me with what looked like a knife. "You scream and this goes into your chest, bitch."

"What do you want?" I demanded.

"You saw me, didn't you? You saw me in the cave with Spatz."

"No. No I didn't."

He laughed. "I don't believe you. The minute I'm gone, you'll go running to your billionaire boyfriend. You know. You are nothing. You think you're the first woman that pretty boy has fucked on this boat?"

He was deliberately trying to offend me with his language. I refused to let him cow me. "Why did you do it? Why did you help those murderers?"

"Why do you think? For the dough, what else? You screwed everything up for me. I was going to get half a million bucks for this job."

Half a million? Was that all? Well, I guess he was only a lackey after all.

"Where is she?" I demanded.

"Where is who?"

"You know what I'm talking about. Where is the Black Madonna? I know you're an accessory to murder and grand larceny. Don't add assault to it."

"Assault." He snorted. "Is that what you think I'm going to do to you? Baby, you have no idea—" He made a smacking noise with his lips. "It will give me great pleasure to hurt you very much."

Terror prickled up my arms. Had I known how crazy this individual could be, I would have treated him with kid gloves. I backed away.

"You be a good girl, be nice and quiet and I'll make it fast."

I needed a weapon; I needed at least something I could use as a shield if he threw that knife. I knew he meant business. He would spear me with it if I screamed. All that was between him and me was the bed. Thank God it was a King. My eyes shifted left to right ever so slightly. There was a book on my nightstand. A hardcover. Maybe I could use that.

A movement caught my eye behind the intruder as the wind lifted the sheers and left them flapping. Someone was there! I drew my eyes away to distract my attacker and snatched up the book. He made a spasmodic motion, as though to throw the knife. Then hesitated.

"Freddie," I said, holding the book to my chest like a shield. I jerked my eyes from the curtains so that he continued to focus on me. "That *is* your name, isn't it? I'm sorry I insulted you. I didn't mean to. I was rude and I apologize."

"You think I'm not good enough for you." He threw the words at me as though they were the knife.

I swallowed, watched his weapon hand tremble. Caught the movement again behind him.

"I never thought that," I continued, tremulously. "It's just that I'm... I'm with Luke."

"Yeah, stinkin' billionaire. You know what he's gonna do when he's done with you, don't ya? Dump you."

"Probably," I said. I kept my voice small and my eyes on his.

His narrow, shorn head wagged from side to side. I caught a flash of the gold earring beyond the shadow of his patchy beard. "If I go down, I'm taking you with me."

I put my hands out in a defensive gesture. I was still clutching the book. "If you run now, you won't have to go down. You *know* where the Black Madonna is, don't you? You can escape, and take it with you. You'll be a millionaire." He hesitated and I knew he was seriously giving it some thought. Except for the fact that a man his size would need help to move it. But if I could get him to admit he knew its location—

It was then that the shadow behind the curtain crashed down on Freddie Spelnick. His wiry form collapsed onto the floor unconscious as Norman's massive physique buried him.

There was no struggle. The bodyguard's blow must have knocked the man senseless.

Something moved—Norman—he rose and rubbed his elbow, and I ran to the other side of the bed to join him.

I almost fell into his arms except that he wasn't holding them out to me. I stopped myself short and stood above him where he crouched on the floor by the intruder.

"Turn on the light," he said.

I reached over his head and did. Like an idiot I still clutched the book in my hand, trembling.

"What were you going to do with that?" he asked, a smirk on his lips. "Bore him to death with a public reading?"

It was typical Norman to distract me so that I would forget the true danger facing me just a few seconds ago. It worked. I scowled. "This is *Pride and Prejudice*."

He answered, jeeringly. "Jane Austen, I know. *Bo*-ring."

"She is *not* boring. And if you must know, that creep threatened to use me for a dartboard. I thought I could block the knife with it."

"Smart thinking."

"Yeah, well. I'm not completely helpless."

He smiled. "Nobody said you were."

I felt my hackles rise. My defenses were up. "We can't *all* afford bodyguards," I snapped. And *that* was a deliberate jab, except I now realized I was jabbing the wrong person.

His tone softened. "You don't need to."

What was that remark supposed to mean? I squeezed the book in frustration and glared at him. His next words came with haunted eyes. "You'll always have your own personal bodyguard, Lucy."

I stared at him but he had looked away. His sight was drawn to the bed legs. He still hadn't risen up off the floor and was on his knees searching for something.

I felt my heart go out to him, despite how his jibes made me feel. "How did you know I was in trouble?" I asked.

"I always leave my doors open. And I sleep like a junkyard dog. Nothing slips past me. Besides, that dude yelps like a girl."

I sneered at him. He resumed his search.

The knife had slid under the bed and Norman retrieved it by reaching forward and ejecting one of my pillows from its case, and using it like a glove. He was not taking any chances on leaving his own prints on the weapon.

While he was busy with that I examined the intruder. It was Freddie Spelnick all right. And he looked like he was dead. I clapped a hand to my mouth in horror.

"He's not dead," Norman said, placing two fingers on the man's throat. "But he's going to have a whopper of a headache when he wakes up." He looked up at me as the breeze blew in and flapped my flimsy nightgown around my torso. He watched me wrestle with it, and his face turned serious. "Are you okay, Lucy?"

"Yes, thanks," I said, grabbing the hem to hold it down. *No. Not really.* I wanted him to hold me. I wanted to feel his strong muscular arms around my shoulders and his hands on—wherever he wished to put them.

He did not come to me or touch me, only looked at me with that soft concern in his eyes. "Let me just take care of this ass…. jerk and I'll be right back. I've already called the police. I can see the cruiser now. I contacted them the minute I heard that shriek. What did you do to him by the way? Sounded like a cat screaming."

I smiled. "I bit him."

"Good girl." A pause. "Do you want me to go and get Luke?"

"No, no. Please don't wake him up. I'm okay."

"I'll have to tell him you were attacked."

"I know. But you don't have to tell him tonight. Please. It can wait until tomorrow." I hesitated. "He's the last of the smugglers, isn't he?"

He looked down at the lump of human flesh on the floor. "Hope so. I'll be back in a few minutes after I deliver this piece of crap to the authorities."

He left, hoisting Freddie's limp body over his shoulder, and the pillowcase with the knife clutched in one hand.

He returned in half an hour knocking lightly at my door. I opened it and let him in. We stood staring at each other for a long moment. I never doubted that he'd return. "Are you going to be able to sleep?" he asked.

"No," I said.

"Sure you don't want me to wake Luke?"

"No—I mean yes. Yes, I'm sure. Please don't wake him up. He'll make a fuss. And there's nothing for him to do."

"He can keep you company."

I want you *to keep me company.*

"I'll be fine." I went up to him and patted him on the arm. I drew my hand quickly away. If only I could hug him to thank him for rescuing me. I wanted to throw myself bodily at him, and kiss him with fervent gratitude, but knowing his conviction, what was the point? "Go back to bed, Norman. I'm okay."

He shrugged. He went to the glass doors and closed them and locked them. "Better like this, until the police wrap up the case."

I wanted to object, and had I been more prudent earlier Freddie Spelnick would be on his way to jail instead of a hospital. And my nerves would have been spared. Norman left. I listened for the sounds of his footsteps. Deathly quiet. I went to my nightstand and switched off the lights. The glass doors to the sundeck allowed in a river of moonlight, the thin sheers resting quietly pushed to the sides. I lay down on my bed. I continued to listen.

No use. Sleep was impossible. I switched on the light, lifted my book, and tried to read a few pages of Jane Austen. No good. My concentration was shattered. I reached for the light-switch, returned the room to blackness and rose. I stood in the middle of the floor.

I went to the door, unafraid. I opened it.

Norman looked up as I appeared in the gap.

He was seated on the floor, his back resting against the wall. "Hey," I said, shutting the door and sliding my spine down the wall to land on my backside beside him.

"There's nothing to be afraid of, Lucy. I'm here."

"I know," I said. "I'm not afraid."

"Then go back to bed."

I was pressed to his side, my arm against his, my knees bent so that my nightgown slid down to the tops of my thighs. Norman's eyes had followed the movement of the thin fabric. He glanced up until our eyes locked. "Are you flirting with me, Lucy?"

"Isn't it obvious?"

"Well, stop it. I know you feel grateful to me for clobbering that creep that got into your bedroom. It's okay. You are welcome. It's all part of the job."

I sighed. "Since when did you become my personal bodyguard?"

"Since you became Luke's girl."

Luke's girl? The last thing I felt like was Luke's girl. We were friends with benefits. That's what it felt like to me. Where was Luke all those times I was in trouble? Where was he now? Safely ensconced in dream world while I—I tried to shake off the negative thoughts. None of this was Luke's fault. How could he help me when he didn't know I was in trouble? And why was it that Norman *always* knew?

His gaze returned to my bare legs. He broke into my thoughts by saying coldly, "You can cover those up. That's not an option."

It was happening again. Just like that time on the beach. How many more times was I going to allow myself to be rejected by this man?

I lowered my chin. Why bother to cover up my legs? They were having no effect on him anyway.

Maybe it was only the residual terror of being attacked in my bed, and threatened with a knife, and spending the whole night trying to save myself from drowning and being shot by a maniac, but I was spent. I felt like collapsing into tears. All I wanted was someone to comfort me. Some human contact. For the first time in months I desperately missed Colleen and Shaun.

I made to get up before the tears could spill. But it was too late. Drops landed on his shirt as I tried to wriggle to my feet. He grabbed my hand and pulled me down beside him. It felt amazing to hold his large hand in mine. He squeezed it tight, pressing our elbows together. His hard muscles hurt and thrilled me. The tears were falling fast. I struggled to get out of his grip. He let go and draped his arm around my shoulders. His hand drew my head to his chest and I wept until his shirt was soaked. I felt his lips brush my hair and I dared not look up.

His other arm came around my chest until he had me in a bear hug. Words were pointless. He knew that.

When my sobbing finally subsided, he stroked my hair and then lifted my chin to his face. He kissed me on the forehead. "Come on," he said, pulling me to my feet. "You need to sleep."

He took me inside my room, brought some tissues from the bathroom and waited until I had blown my nose and mopped up the residual tears. He squeezed my wrist and told me to get into bed. He drew the covers up over me and sat down on the bed. "You're suffering from shock," he said. "You'll be okay after some sleep."

He left then and shut the door, leaving me in darkness.

I closed my eyes and fell asleep.

Somehow I knew he never returned to his room, but stood guard outside my door all night.

***

The sun sloped cheerily through the sheers and splashed along the bedcovers in dappled patterns of shadow and light. I got up. I felt much better having acquired some solid sleep. Norman knew sleep was impossible unless I felt safe, and he had made certain that I was safe. I felt guilty for making him stay awake all night, but at the same time I was truly grateful.

I went to have a shower, washed my hair and all the salt from last night's tears, plus that horrible dip in the sea, and came out feeling scrubbed clean and refreshed. I brushed my hair dry, and then I wrapped my white terry robe around me, tightened the sash and went to the door. I opened it and saw Norman seated on the floor at the doorway. He was awake.

"Don't tell me you've been here all night." I was ashamed of how I had crumbled last night and made a supreme effort to sound light. Did I sound convincingly surprised?

He smiled, noted that I was in my bathrobe, and said, "The least you can do is get dressed so that I can get some breakfast."

I pretended to suppress a grin, and raised my brow. "What's going to happen to Freddie?"

"He'll be charged and asked to reveal the location of the Black Madonna. If he refuses he'll go to prison. Otherwise they might swing a deal."

"Did you tell Luke?"

He shook his head and started to rise from the floor. I reached out a hand to help him up. He looked at me with that gentle twinkle in his yes. "You know what happens if I take your hand? You come down on the floor with me."

At the moment there was nothing I would like more. I crushed the thought and withdrew my arm with a smile.

"So you didn't tell him about Freddie? Thanks. I—I'd rather tell him myself."

I was grateful he was mute on my emotional collapse of last night. He was taking his cues from me. And oh man, what I wouldn't do to forget my embarrassing meltdown! He rambled on as though we were two detectives discussing the outcome of a case. "At least the dirtbag's in custody," he said. "That's one more person associated with the crime put away. Luke will only feel satisfied when he knows every last individual involved with the theft of the Black Madonna is brought to justice."

But we still needed to locate the icon. "Did Constable Constantine get anything out of Spatz before he shot him?" I asked.

"All I know is that when Constantine went after him, he was headed back here to the yacht. No one knows why, except maybe he thought he could steal it and get away to the open ocean. Then he would be out of the Italian authorities jurisdiction. Constantine ordered him to stop. He reached the launching platform and leaped up and started up the companionway. Constantine fired a warning shot but the man continued to climb. He had no choice but to shoot him in the back. By that time his partner had called for backup, such as it is in a tiny town. They took the body away, but by the time they conveyed him to shore and to the hospital he was dead."

The sexy French rumble in his voice drove me crazy! He only ever talked that way around me. Most other times he sounded much more American. Could I possibly learn to ignore it? I would have to if I wanted to retain my sanity. "So they never got it out of him. He didn't live long enough to reveal where he hid the church's icon?"

Norman shook his head. I fell silent, trying to figure out how this nightmare could finally end, so that we could return to the reason we were in Positano in the first place. "Well, maybe they'll get it out of Freddie."

Norman nodded. "You gonna get dressed? Luke will be waiting for us."

I clutched my robe around me, suddenly aware that I was naked underneath it. "Yeah, sure. Come in, I won't be a second."

Norman hesitated. A smile tugged at my lips but somehow Norman managed to keep his own mouth in a controlled, stiff line. "Think I could use your bathroom to freshen up a bit?"

Our eyes met. It was so insane for me to feel this way. Since last night, I had fought the impulse to caress his tempting muscles. But the eyes were different. You had to look into the eyes to truly connect with a person. For the first time I really noticed the color of his eyes. They were hazel. They crinkled at me and I knew if I didn't step away at this very moment, I was in big trouble.

"Of course," I mumbled. "Use my bathroom. I'll get dressed while you're in there."

The toilet flushed and then the splashing of water as he washed his hands and face. I was tempted to tell him that he was welcome to use the shower if he liked, but what if Luke decided to visit me while he was there? What would I say to him? I had only one explanation for why Norman might be in my shower, and not one I was ready to share.

CHAPTER
<u>28</u>

I dressed in one of my own sundresses, not so fancy as Isadora Ferri's. This ensemble was mint green with white sandals. A color palette I loved. I sighed as I snapped on my other sandal. How was I going to pay for all the damage I had done to her wardrobe?

When he came out of the marble bathroom, Norman smiled his appreciation of my outfit, and we went upstairs on deck where Luke was having coffee. The other members of the team were already at the beach or out on the town. They were given another day off, as we still had to finish up with the police.

The two men were somber as we breakfasted on sausages and eggs, fresh tomatoes and sautéed potatoes. The entire meal was quiet and thoughtful. I was hungrier than I had expected, but then I had expended a tremendous amount of energy last night running and swimming, and climbing. My muscles ached, but the sporadic pain did nothing to offset my appetite. I took a double-dose of coffee, and it was when I was contemplating a third cup that Constantine arrived with his partner to ask us a few more questions. Freddie Spelnick refused to talk. When Luke was surprised that Freddie was in custody, I interrupted before Constantine could reveal the attack on me last night. I had to assure him that I was unhurt.

He was unhappy that the attack had happened under his very nose, but grateful for the foresight and speed of his bodyguard's actions.

"Don't know what I'd do without out you, buddy," Luke said.

"It's my job," Norman answered. "I heard a sound from Lucy's room. Her deck door was open. So it was easy to investigate. He wasn't hard to take down. He had no idea I was there."

Satisfied with Norman's answers and mine, Luke returned his attention to the policeman. He insisted upon backtracking to our account of last night's events.

"Why would Captain Spatz return to the yacht, do you think Signor Trevanian? It does not seem to me the best way to escape the law. A yacht does not start quickly once it is anchored, no?"

"No," Luke said.

"So why would he risk it? He could have taken his boat up the coast. A Zodiac has a very powerful engine. He would have lost me easily in my slower police boat."

I raised my head from swirling the dregs of my coffee. "Luke, didn't you say that Marco Ferri was the shipwright that built your yacht?"

"So?"

"So what if he had built in a secret hold, or several secret holds in which to smuggle the loot. You would never know. Not if the captain was in on it. They knew your habits, how you remained on shore most of the time and often at night, as did the crew. What could be easier than caching it right here—" I thumped the floor with a sandaled foot, "—on your boat."

Luke's eyes widened. "It's possible. What do you think Constantine? Do you have enough men to search this boat?"

Constantine whistled. It was a massive craft, the size of a small commercial cruise ship.

"We can try."

"And we'll help," Luke offered. "We'll get all of the yacht's crew and archaeology team to help. I'll call Emily right now."

Constantine beamed.

That afternoon the search team swept the entire yacht from bow to stern. We were exhausted and about to give up when my phone suddenly rang. My cellphone had been located inside the cave and returned to me this morning. It was Colleen.

"Lucy! It's about time you answered your phone. You've had me worried."

"Everything's fine, Colleen. Stop worrying, you'll upset junior."

"Well, I was wondering when you'd remember your poor pregnant sister." Poor indeed. I snickered. She was one of the most spoiled people I knew.

"So, is everything okay? I was right, wasn't I? Shaun isn't involved in anything shady with the museum?"

I did not hesitate to reassure her. "Yes. You were absolutely correct. Turned out to be a false alarm."

"So what's the problem? You sound a bit tired. The billionaire wearing you out?" She giggled.

I backed out of the hearing of my companions who were still searching the yacht and decided I should keep the details of this adventure to myself. No point in upsetting her.

"Lucy," she said. "What is it that you aren't telling me?"

"Nothing."

"I already know most of it. It's all over social media."

"What is?" I had visions of video being shot of me floundering in the sea while some maniac fired bullets.

"You forget. Nothing Trevanian does is a secret."

"What did you hear?"

"That his team was involved with some sort of a cold case involving a priceless artifact. Some religious art piece called the Black Madonna?"

"Well, we're still looking for it."

"Is that what has you so depressed? I heard that one of

the criminals killed himself over it by leaping off a sixty foot tower."

Oh my God, how social media exaggerated things! "Yes. There was a suicide. But I'm *not* depressed because of that."

She snorted. "So what is it? And don't lie to me. I'll know. Don't forget who you're talking to. I know you, and you *are* depressed."

I was not. I was merely somewhat tired, and frustrated, and lovesick. And sad. "It has nothing to do with the stolen icon. Or the suicide."

"Then what *does* it have to do with?"

"I can't talk about it right now." Honestly, I did want to confide in her. She was my sister after all. We told each other everything. But the men were around here somewhere, and neither of them must overhear. So I said nothing.

She wasn't deterred. "It's Trevanian, isn't it? Did he hurt you?" Her voice sounded grim. And disappointed. I knew she was rooting for team Trevanian because Shaun must have shared his misgivings with her. And she hated it when her husband was right. But he was *sooo* right. But not for the reasons he had thought. He had no way to know that it wasn't Luke who was making me sad.

"No, no. It's nothing like that."

"Lucy, if I didn't know you better I'd swear you were in love."

She didn't know the half of it. I glanced down at my shoes. How was I going to get out of this? The last thing I needed to confront was my feelings.

"Doesn't he love you back?"

Maybe. No. *Yes.* I was sure of it. Except that we weren't talking about the same person. The man I was in love with had secrets, darker secrets than even Luke Trevanian. They were buried deep in a secret hiding place, under a trapdoor, in a compartment that was right in your face, but you couldn't see, because of the obvious.

I suddenly looked up. A view of the gulf captured my eye. The sea sparkled, making me dazzlingly coherent. That was it. A secret compartment. A trapdoor. I realized there was one last place to look—

"Colleen, I have to go. I think I may have just located the hiding place of the Black Madonna. I have to go and see if I'm right."

"Well, don't forget to call me back!"

"I won't." I hung up on her.

Granted the deck was huge and it would be impossible to search every square inch of it for a hidden trap door, but I had a hunch as to where to start. I went over to the other side of the pool and stared at the rail where Tommy Buchanan had fallen overboard. There was a large iron spoke there with rope wrapped around it. The other members of the archaeology team and yacht crew were scattered all over the deck searching for likely hiding places.

I sought out Luke.

"Why is this here?" I asked, toeing the large iron spoke. "It's an odd place to have a mooring line, isn't it?"

Luke frowned. "Come to think of it, it is."

Norman and the two constables joined us, and we began to feel around the spoke. They pressed in various places. Finally in frustration Luke kicked his foot at it. He started to swear but we all heard a distinct click. Norman stepped on the planking around the spoke and a spring activated. The trap door shot up. As we gathered together to peer below, an audible gasp arose. Below us was a hold filled with ancient treasures. But the thing that caught my eye was the gold.

She was just as beautiful as I remembered when I saw her in the cave under the illumination of my cellphone light—the Black Madonna, her face and hands ebony black, and everything else solid gold.

***

The feeling of awe overpowered me as I stood in the church gazing up at the Black Madonna on the wall above the altar. She glowed with an ethereal light that wasn't just from the gold.

She was home. It was as though a weight had lifted from the world.

Luke was talking to Father Carmine who was thrilled to once more see the beautiful icon where it had hung for centuries before it was stolen. I still wondered where it had come from in the first place. No one seemed to know, and the old legend only said that pirates had stolen it and left it at Positano when the wrath of the sea threatened to capsize their ship and drown them.

"I am so glad *that* is over," I said to Norman who had come to join me. We were trying to keep things light between us.

He nodded. "Now that the theft is solved and the icon is where it belongs Luke can relax."

"Why do you care so much, Norman?" I asked.

"Why do you?"

I laughed. He had me there.

"Ready to finally start work in the underground dig?"

"I feel like the adventure should be over."

Norman's face turned momentarily grave. I knew what he was thinking. That the mystery of the Roman silver remained unsolved. While in the lab that infamous day, his wary eye had gathered data just as mine had. He too had noticed the distinct motif on the silverware. He mentioned it to me in passing, but neither of us breathed a word of our suspicions to Luke. We had no concrete proof that his soon to be ex-wife Arianna Chase was mixed up in anything unsavory. And yet the mystery wasn't finished. What was Captain Spatz doing in Arianna's office that day?

Luke came by and took my hand, while Norman turned his head to study the icon.

"Thank you, Lucy," he said.

"For what?" I rubbed my forehead, seriously bewildered.

"For saving my life."

I hesitated. "What do you mean?"

"I knew there was a reason I needed to bring you on this expedition."

It was true I had helped him solve the mystery of the Black Madonna and in doing so had cleared his name. Those criminal files could be opened now and nothing inside them could hurt him. "I hope having the Madonna returned brings you peace, Luke."

He squeezed my hand. The church was not an appropriate place to become amorous, but I could see in Luke's eyes a glint of mischief. I was wondering how I was going to tell him about Norman, or if I should tell him, or how I felt about him at all. I was so confused.

"Lucy. You still intend to stay, I hope? I know it's been a hell of a ride, and believe me none of it was planned. Besides, my yacht will be impounded until all of those artifacts have been removed and placed in the security of the government."

"Wouldn't miss it. But I'd better call my sister back and let her know the real story before all the rumors reach her through social media." I was glad that Shaun had nothing to do with—I stopped myself before I could finish the thought. An image of the Roman silverware flashed across my memory. Both Norman and I had agreed. It was decorated like the grape cluster in Shaun's silver for his Roman exhibit. Norman's quick eye had recognized the connection too.

"What is it, Lucy?" Luke stroked my hand.

"Nothing." I shook my head, at the same time flinging off his touch. "I'm imagining things."

His cellphone suddenly rang and he removed it from his pocket. He glanced swiftly at the Caller ID. He paused for a moment, before he said to no one in particular: "This can wait." He declined the call and wiggled his fingers. "Let's go outside."

The phone rang again and he turned it off.

"Are you sure it's not something important, Luke?"

"Not as important as this." He twined his fingers in mine and led me over the tiled floors and into the sunshine and warm breeze. We went to the balustrade and looked down on the beach and the aquamarine sea.

I sent a backwards nod at the church. "So, beautiful. I can't wait to start work on the frescos. Some of them are truly amazing."

"Wait till I take you to Pompeii. It's even *more* fantastic than the ruins under the church." He slid his hand down my side pausing at the curve of my hip. "They have secret rooms among the ruins, exclusively for men where all of the paintings and sculptures are erotic. I think the majority of the most risqué pieces have been removed and are stored at the Chamber of Secrets in the Museo Archeologico Nazionale. They have boxes of stone phalluses in every shape and size. Some even made into lamps. Want to go see that?"

I laughed. He was in such a good mood; I couldn't bear to be the one to end it. Besides Norman had made it perfectly clear that he and I would never happen. "When do we start?"

"How about right now?"

At that moment Norman came outside and stood in the doorway. He was quiet. I only knew he was there because of the shadow he cast across the courtyard. It mingled with the shade-bearing shrubberies planted in ceramic pots along the base of the balustrade.

He cleared his throat to announce his presence. I slowly turned. Luke looked at Norman. "What is it?"

"It's Arianna. She's been trying to reach you. She texted *me* to let *you* know."

Luke shrugged. "I turned off my phone. It's probably something to do with the divorce settlement."

I watched the two men as something silent passed between them. I was beginning to suspect that Arianna Chase had more than a few secrets.

"It has nothing to do with the divorce," Norman said.

"What then?"

"She says not to trust Spatz. He's got a sketchy past." Again that silent communication, a kind of unspoken understanding.

"A little late, I think. Hope you told her he's a non-issue?"

"I did. But there's more. It's not something you want to discuss in public. It concerns her current.... ah... project. I tried to get her to leave me the details—" He hesitated. "It seems the site of Pompeii has been shut down a few weeks for repairs. There was an accident in one of the structures; a loose wall came tumbling down. Someone was killed. They're conducting an entire site survey to make sure nothing else is loose and potentially dangerous to visitors."

Luke frowned. Norman flashed his phone in Luke's face.

Luke glanced at me. "Just Arianna over-reacting again. Hold on a second while I make a call." He ducked out of sight into an alcove of a building.

Norman and I avoided looking at each other. Luke's voice reached us where we stood. He sounded angry: "What are you still doing in Florence? I thought you were in Pompeii. I am not bailing you out this time. Bruno is expecting us at the ICOM meetings next week. You damn well better show up. I've gone to the trouble of finalizing the deal. We only need one more signature—*yours*."

"They sound like they're still married," I snickered.

Norman nodded. "Sometimes I think they may as well be."

My cellphone suddenly chimed. *Don't tell me it's Colleen again.* No. It was a text from my brother-in-law Shaun.

> ***Congrats, Lucy!***
> ***The director signed your requisition form***
> ***before she left for Italy.***
> ***You have the funds to purchase a 3-D printer!***

"Good news?" Norman asked, noticing the grin on my face.

"Great news," I said. "Arianna is letting me buy a digital 3-D printer."

I couldn't wait for Luke to get off the phone so that I

could thank him for using his influence. In fact, I wanted to grab the phone from him and thank Arianna personally.

Sometimes rocks need to hit me before I see the truth. Luke wasn't the only one who could influence my museum director. That infamous day which seemed eons ago now inched its way into my mind. I was carrying the requisition forms for Arianna to sign. I dropped them in a fluster when I saw the hunk of man meat, and smashed the crown of my head on the edge of the secretary's desk trying to pick them up. This time the memory did not make me blush.

How would Luke know that I wanted a 3-D printer? I never exactly told him.

I raised my head and looked at Norman. I turned my cellphone in his direction and he read the message from Shaun.

A slight smile appeared on his lips. "Are you happy, Lucy? You got what you wanted."

"Arianna must really like you," I said.

"Oh, she doesn't like me much. Just owes me a couple of favors."

"*You* did this. Didn't you?"

He shrugged. The smile grew slightly wider.

"Arianna would do that? For you? I'm not even your girlfriend."

"But we *are* friends."

Yeah, we were. Do hearts really flutter? Mine was.

His expression softened. His voice adopted its husky French drawl. A twinkle of amusement appeared in his eyes. "I'm glad you're getting your 3-D printer, Lucy. I'm even happier if it will help you to keep your job."

"Norman…. Thank—"

He placed two fingers to my lips to block the gratitude that was bursting to get out. "You're welcome."

At that moment Luke returned. "Sorry about the interruption, Lucy. What was I saying?"

I dragged my eyes away from Norman's, a smile still on my lips. "You were telling me about the Secret Chamber of exotic sex objects."

Now read on for a taste of the next exciting book
in the Fresco Nights saga.

POMPEII AT DUSK

CHAPTER

1

A Gorgon's head sat on my desk in the lab aboard the billionaire archaeologist's yacht. Luke claimed she was Medusa, one of three mythological sisters who had snakes for hair. It was quite a fascinating piece, a broken portion of fresco, almost perfect except for some discoloration on one cheek. Was this dried blood? Or was this just my imagination working overtime?

The piece was all the talk aboard the yacht. Where exactly had it come from? One thing was certain: it had not come from the excavation beneath the Church of Santa Maria Assunta where the team currently worked. Yes, Luke preferred his secrets. And, if he was going to keep his secrets then I had one, too. Contrary to what I had told him when he insisted I be his date, it took me *more* than fifteen minutes to change for a fancy dress ball. So sketching the Gorgon's head would have to wait.

I gave the precious fresco to Emily to test. She was our expert on the analysis of artifact residues. Luke wanted the stain identified. Why? I don't know, but he had his reasons. I carefully passed it from my cotton-gloved hands into hers.

"No problem, Lucy. I'll get the results back ASAP— Hey, have fun tonight."

I gave her a wistful smile, peeled off the gloves. "I wish."

"Well, if it helps. I don't think Luke really wants to go either."

I grinned, sent her a limp wave and went to the door.

Executive members of the International Council of Museums were meeting in Naples this evening and Luke Trevanian was the guest of honor. He was nervous about the event. Did that account for his distractedness? Why *was* he so anxious? I could think of no reason—except that Arianna Chase, his ex-wife was attending, too.

I left the lab, and walked the few minutes to my room. I checked the time on my smartphone. I should have quit earlier. Really, for someone like me (flat hair and colorless cheeks) it took time to primp for a fancy party.

Every time I entered my room aboard Luke's fancy yacht I felt like I was in sort of a fantasy world. He had given me a suite which included a master bedroom with a king-sized bed, a sitting room and a marble and glass bathroom with a standup shower and a spa-sized soaking tub. The decor was white, grey and black with red pillows (my contribution) arranged stylishly over a thick duvet on the mattress. Sheer, voluminous curtains draped the lozenge-shaped windows that allowed angling sunlight to stream across glossy cherry wood floors. Outside I had my own private deck.

Luke had his own cabin and we only shared a bed when the mood struck. It was a favorite axiom of his that everyone needed his or her own private space. He never tired of reiterating that it gave a person a sense of control. Not that I wanted to be in his bed all the time. It was true. Too much of a good thing could become bad. And while doing the horizontal tango with Luke was great, as far as he was concerned, sleep and sex were separate things.

That idea was new for me. *Me*, museum illustrator Lucy Racine, who before Luke Trevanian, had never dated anyone with such an obscene amount of money. So the eccentricity was odd. But after the fun this room was *mine*.

I wrapped a fluffy white towel around my head as I left the shower, and mopped myself down with another. I escaped the bathroom, steam following into the bedroom.

On the bed was my evening gown, a gorgeous shimmering black silk. Cut deep in a V at the neckline to a fitted waist, the fabric in back draped sexily low. On the floor below the bedside were matching black stilettos.

I looked nervously into the shiny mirror of the vanity. My skin was fresh and glamorously backlit by very clever lighting. My wet hair gleamed as I combed it out. I carefully applied my makeup. When my hair was almost dry, I styled it with the blow dryer into soft waves. Ordinarily I hated to fuss like this. I was a pretty casual person (like I said: flat hair and colorless cheeks). However, knowing that Arianna Chase was going to be at this shindig had me hyperventilating big time. I fussed my hair into cooperating before dropping the brush onto the vanity. I daubed on extra blush.

The silk dress slipped fluidly over my bare skin, and I went to the mirror to judge my transformation. Not bad. I had managed to convert myself from grubby artist to cocktail queen in forty minutes. On occasion I had dressed up for museum functions; I had never spent much on clothes. Luke had bought me this dress and now I realized because of the pricking under my arm that I had forgotten to remove the price tag.

"Careful, don't snag it," I muttered, twisting about. This dress cost more than three months of my rent.

Yeah, I still counted pennies. (Okay dollars. Pennies are worth zilch anymore.) Even though I am officially Luke Trevanian's girlfriend... Oh, God, how would Arianna feel about that? I mean being Luke's ex and all, and me being her employee, though I doubt she even knew it. Directors of museums generally had no idea who worked for them.

I flushed involuntarily. I had managed to zip up the dress without snagging the silk. Was I about to break into a sweat and ruin it? Why should I give a hoot what Arianna thought?

It was not like she could fire me. Wait a minute. She *could* fire me. Although on what grounds? That I was dating her ex? I glanced at my phone. I had ten minutes before I was supposed to meet Luke on the helipad and I was still wrestling with the tag in my armpit. We were taking a helicopter from his yacht—which was anchored offshore Positano—to the National Archaeological Museum in Naples.

I stepped over to the floor-length mirrors that covered both sliding doors of my luxurious closet to see if I could get a better view of the irritating tag. The movement of my leg in the sexy stiletto defined my calves nicely. My thoroughly moisturized thigh parted the dress where it slit, revealing a smooth, recently shaved leg.

A girl could get use to this. I sighed. Then I snapped myself out of my daydreaming. Oh crap, what was *with* this wretched tag? I dared not cut it. What if I cut my dress? That would be a fiasco. Not to mention three grand down the drain. Luke's three grand; he'd paid for it. But still money was money…. And I could never throw money down the drain, even if it was someone else's money. Or someone else's drain.

I gave up in frustration. Tearing the tag would be worse. I returned to the bathroom to find a pair of scissors. I was rattling the drawers and cabinetry underneath the marble countertop when I detected a presence behind me. I swung around and saw Luke's bodyguard standing in the open doorway.

"Hey, Lucy."

My heart gave a little flip. We stood and stared at each other. He was dressed in business attire. If it wasn't for the sexy French drawl I could have mistaken his silhouette for Luke.

"I knocked and no one answered," he apologized. "So I came in."

"I thought I locked the door."

"You did."

I smiled, decided not to bother asking how he'd gotten in, and turned back to the bathroom counter. It was his job to be able to pass through locked doors. "I'm sorry. I didn't hear you, Norman. I was looking for a pair of scissors."

His muscled arm came around one side of me, and he pulled a half-opened drawer out and poked a finger inside. "There they are."

"Thanks."

I took the small nail scissors, studied them for a split second, and then extended them to him. They looked incongruously miniscule in his big hand. "Will you please rescue me and cut this price tag off my dress? But please, *please* be careful."

"Sure," he said.

Norman took the scissors from me and I raised my arm. He was standing very close. I could smell his soap or shampoo or something. It was nice, subtle and very, very masculine. I got a grip on myself from the inside and forced my mind to ignore it. He gently slipped his hand underneath and caught the tag. His knuckles brushed my underarm. A thrill went down my side. I held my breath.

"There. Done. Anything else I can do for you?"

"No. Thanks. Is it time to go?"

"It is. Luke's waiting at the helipad."

***

Naples, compared to Positano, is a dump, despite being the third largest city in Italy. All of the ancient and beautiful architecture is there, but it has a neglected feel. Don't get me wrong; there's an air of rustic elegance about it, but it's one of faded splendor. There seems to be a pall of dust over the area, and a sense of lives having been lived in another time, a time of excitement and prosperity, a ghostly feel of centuries gone by which does not exist in upscale Positano, town of the rich and famous where we are currently based. It certainly does not measure up to the wealth and beauty of Rome. But while Rome is very much of the here and now, and exudes modern luxury and the success of a world capital, Naples is 'old world' and has a melancholy charm and magic all its own. Still, from the air and in the dusk it seemed mysterious and even a little dangerous, and that appealed to my sense of adventure. I'd even heard stories of how the city was a nexus for the black market, and that the mafia effectively ran it. So why was ICOM meeting here? All I could think was because it housed one of Italy's national treasures, the Museo Archeologico Nazionale, aka the National Archaeology Museum.

I felt safe enough as part of Luke Trevanian's entourage. The billionaire archaeologist surrounded us with opulence and personal protection. We regularly travelled from his luxury yacht via helicopter, boat or submarine. If we needed to leave the continent fast for any reason, there was always his Lear jet.

We touched down in a private courtyard behind the museum. We entered through a back door. The museum had grand domed ceilings with multiple arches into different connecting galleries. This place housed some of the most important pieces of art in Italy including valuable frescoes and mosaics from Pompeii. Luke drew my hand to his lips. Out of the corner of my eye I caught Norman watching. I felt a pang. Why did that bother me? It was his *job* to watch.

Luke kissed my hand. He was always nervous at these things. Odd, because his public persona was one of outright confidence, even arrogance. No one, he assured me, was aware of how much he hated the spotlight. He had only ever confided in *me*. "I hate how people's expectations put so much pressure on me," he complained. I found that hard to believe. What about Arianna? He had been married to Arianna Chase for ten years before the divorce, which by the way was far from finalized.

Our heels clicked down the marble hallway. A stout man with an entourage of his own came around the corner to greet us. It was the director of the archaeology museum. Several other guests accompanied him.

"So glad to see you," the director beamed. He was impeccably dressed in an exquisite black suit with crisp white shirt and black tie, which drew away from his lack of height. From the tip of his polished shoes to the top of his manicured head he looked the picture of wealth and breeding. Either they paid museum executives a lot of money or he had a night job on the side. I chuckled.

That remark never left my thoughts. I smiled graciously while Luke leaned forward and received the traditional Italian double kiss on the cheeks.

"*Ciao* Bruno," Luke said. "How are you? So nice to see you again." They yammered on in Italian, some words familiar to me, but most of the conversation unintelligible. I did get the feeling that they were catching up on old times. I fidgeted silently and twisted my hair, a long thick lock of which draped over my right shoulder. Then Luke suddenly remembered me. He drew his hand away from the director's arm where he had placed it in a gesture of affability, and laid it on mine. "Where are my manners? Bruno. Let me introduce my friend, Lucy Racine."

Why did I suddenly feel slighted? His *friend?* Is that all I was to him? "Lucy, meet the host of this magnificent palace, and a long-time acquaintance of mine, Signor Bruno D'Agostino." He spread out his hands, dropping mine, to take in the scene.

"*Buonasera, signorina.* Welcome to our fine establishment."

His eyes dropped to take in my gown. I think I met with his approval. Then he clapped a hand on Luke's shoulder and led him into the Atrium where the festivities were taking place. Luke had brought two bodyguards with him, and one now followed behind the dapper and very expensive tuxedo of his boss. Luke was a James Bond type, although his hair was never combed so neatly. That part of him was always rather beach-boyish. Even so, he looked striking no matter what he wore. In dress formal he was Hollywood handsome.

Feeling deflated, I remained standing in the corridor.

And then I noticed someone was still beside me. I turned to see it was Norman.

"Shall we?" he asked, his slight French accent suddenly appearing.

Was it just me? Or was the deep rumble of his voice irresistible? Ordinarily he spoke with the same Americanized intonations as the rest of us. Tonight the French lilt was a little more prominent than usual. In formal situations, Norman Depardieu reverted to his Francophone origins. Some sort of social defense mechanism? Certainly his powerful physique was more than enough to dissuade anyone from overtly slighting him. But the Frenchness gave him a sophistication, which made me believe that at one time he was something other than a bodyguard. Like Luke, Norman possessed dark secrets, but who was I to dig them up?

He was dressed more conservatively than was his habit tonight in a white shirt and dark jacket, and looked impeccably sexy. Curious how almost any man could look attractive in a suit. This was especially true of Norman.

He curved his arm for me to take. I looped mine into his and allowed him to escort me into the gathering.

The size of the Atrium and the volume of guests overwhelmed me. I had a sense of feeling impossibly small. It was the kind of sensation that could only be overcome with a good stiff drink. And I glanced swiftly around for a waiter or a bar.

Norman released my arm and encouraged me to mingle with the guests while he stood by the door with the other security.

It's strange. I have been to many events similar to this, though perhaps without a guest list quite so besieged by VIPs. Usually I was dateless. I might as well be dateless now. Luke had completely forgotten about me. I knew no one among the guests because I rarely travelled in his social or business circles. I was one of the lowly employees, a museum illustrator (albeit the head of my department at the ROM i.e. Royal Ontario Museum), and yet I felt like a

'Nobody' amongst these directors, curators, members of the boards of governors and multi-millionaire and billionaire donors. This particular event was meant for the movers and shakers in the museum world and I was neither. Besides, everyone was speaking Italian, French or German. I even heard a little Mandarin and some Arabic. And though I recognized the cadences of all of these languages, my vocabulary amounted to little more than *Bonjour*, *Grazie*, and *Dankeschön*. My Mandarin was nonexistent. And my Arabic nada. Although to be perfectly honest my French was mucho better than my attempts at any other language, thanks to having been educated in Canada where high school French was required.

I tried mingling. Most of the guests were acquainted with one another or else they were familiar through reputation, *or* they were simply famous from being a staple of the news media. I stepped up to a likely person who, similar to me, appeared to be at a bit of a loss. She smiled when I approached her and introduced herself as Amelia Krakow, an assistant curator from the Moscow Museum of Archaeology. I complimented her gown. She did the same for me and then the conversation turned to rare antiquities. We soon ran out of steam on the subject as I could sense her disinterest. If she was that bored why did she work in a museum at all?

She politely inquired about my job at the ROM. How *did* I manage to stave off the ennui if what I did was sketch objects all day? I frowned. What was this? Polite curiosity? More like mindless chitchat. I tried to explain how my daily routine involved other interesting tasks, including exhibit layouts. Her eyes darted sideways. Talk about a waste of effort. The whole ten minutes of our interaction, her gaze kept flitting beyond my head to see if someone better didn't come along.

Someone did. The pale eyes, which were focused beyond my shoulder suddenly brightened, and her mouth broke into a radiant smile. She excused herself—with me in mid sentence—and dashed off. I stood staring at an empty space with my mouth half open.

What a surprise.

A uniformed waiter approached me with a silver tray and offered up a glass of champagne. I glanced at the multiple flutes and accepted one. "*Grazie*," I mumbled.

As I took a sip, and then another, I realized it was quite a promising vintage, and sideswiped another glass before the waiter could slip away.

"Hullo," someone said to me. His English was heavily accented, but good.

This time I was prepared for the snub. I put on my nonchalant expression. To my surprise the newcomer was polite and civil. He was a man and it amazed me that I had caught his notice at all. Amidst the Armani, Versace, Dior and Vera Wang I hardly stood out. My gown was lovely, yes, but so were the gowns of all of these wealthy patrons of the arts. At least my dress was prettier than Amelia Krakow's. This thought arrived with belated venom. But what was the use in feeling slighted? That's what people did at these events. All I could do was refuse to play that game and turn on the charm.

"My name is Sulla Kharim. I work for the National Museum in Aleppo. Or at least I used to," he said by way of introduction.

He was a small man, not much taller than myself (granted I was wearing stilettoes). He had a slightly balding head and a short dark moustache and beard. He was olive-complexioned and wore a neat but definitely dated suit. His tie was too wide and his collar too large. It was obvious that he seldom dressed in formal attire.

"The National Museum in Aleppo?" I said. My heart skipped a beat. He was from the Middle East, from war-torn Syria. How had he managed to get out of the country in one piece to attend this event? It must seem strange to him to be surrounded by all the opulence of the western world. Then I remembered that at one time, not too long ago, Syria was a crossroads to Asia, Africa and Europe. It was one of the most thriving, heritage-rich countries in the world.

"Lucy Racine," I said, extending a hand and remembering to smile.

He gripped it firmly. Then dropped it. "I know."

He knew?

"You are good friends with Dr. Trevanian, the archaeologist, are you not?"

"Yes."

"I have been wanting to introduce myself, but there are always so many people monopolizing his attention."

Monopolizing? That was an interesting term to use, and very true.

I had tried more than once, myself, to intrude on his socializing without success. He would notice me when he noticed me and not before. That went for anyone else who desired his attention.

"He is a busy man. And very popular," I said as though that would excuse him.

"I understand he is interested in antiquities?"

"He is," I said. "But you will have to speak to him about that yourself. Is there something you wish to sell to him?"

"Actually, it is more…." He hesitated before he continued. "I have a proposition he might be interested in."

My internal alarm bells started ringing. Proposition? I knew quite well that antiquities in the Middle East were ripe for the picking. The Syrian government had its hands full trying to fight the rebel Islamic State. They had no time to worry about ancient monuments and art, and so smuggling of antiquities to purchase firearms was rampant. But here was a lone museum curator who needed our help. I looked around for Luke. He was the focus of several important people, and not one of them was Arianna Chase. Where *was* she anyways?

D'Agostino, the director of the Naples museum, seemed to be anxious. He was snapping at his assistants and asking questions. They were on the phone, and then *he* was on the phone, and I knew something was wrong. I told Sulla Kharim that I would mention his proposition to Luke at my earliest convenience and made to go to Luke's side. Kharim stopped me with a hand on my arm. Abruptly he removed it realizing how inappropriate it was to touch a woman who was not your wife, sister, or daughter. Or your mother. (In his culture it was considered rude, insulting) And even then…. "Please," he said. "I must meet with Dr. Trevanian. It is a matter of life or death."

I stared at him. He *had* to be joking. Nothing in the museum world was a matter of life or death. "Do you have a card?" I asked.

He withdrew a very plain business card from his breast pocket. It was white with a small burgundy-colored logo of the museum in one corner. "Please," he said. "I must see him in private. He *must* meet me tomorrow. Or it will be too late."

"Can you tell me what it's about?" I asked.

"I can tell only *him*."

"Where should he meet you?"

He indicated to me that I should return the business card. He flipped open a pen and scribbled an address on the back of it. It seemed to be a restaurant or coffee shop.

"I'll see that he gets this," I said as he extended it to me.

I shoved the card inside my pearl-beaded evening bag and hurried across the floor. The sense of tension in the room was gaining strength. Despite the fact I paused. What was really bothering the Syrian curator? And why was he so melodramatic? Evasive? I looked back to search for the strange little man. He had vanished.

"What's happened?" I asked Luke.

His companions stopped talking the moment I arrived. It was the perfect moment to interrupt. As he turned to me, the others speculated over the director's peculiar behavior and the lengthy delay. "I'm not sure," Luke said. "Bruno seems extremely agitated. Excuse me, Lucy. I'll go and find out."

Everyone here was a stranger to me. Although they

smiled appreciatively and politely, and gave me the requisite how dos and pleased to meet yous after I'd introduced myself, it was obvious they were only humoring me. There were things on their minds other than entertaining Luke Trevanian's current lover. All gossip as to what could possibly be distressing the director had ceased. I was an outsider. I was not privy to their conjectures.

I spun to face the exit and caught Norman's eye. He had remained in his original watchdog position. His face had become alert. He too detected an anomaly in the situation. According to the program the speeches should already have begun. The director should have introduced Arianna Chase from the Royal Ontario Museum. Her big news was to announce a multi-million dollar endowment made by Luke Trevanian to link the National Archaeology Museum in Naples with the Royal Ontario Museum in Toronto as sister institutions. The cash would enable the two to build a travelling exhibit and tell the comprehensive story of Pompeii. For the first time, the contents of the 'Secret Chamber' would be studied in full, and a selection of artifacts made available for foreign audiences.

Hanging around these people was useless. I still had no information. I sought out Luke in the sea of faces. He had disappeared along with the Italian director. I left the Atrium, went past Norman, into the corridor. The next thing I knew, he was beside me.

"Do you know what's going on, Norman?" I asked.

He shook his head.

I started down the corridor, my long gown swishing against my legs. I scowled. Why had Luke deserted me again? "Where's Arianna? She should be here by now."

"I think maybe that's the problem. She hasn't turned up. It's not like her to be late for an important event. Especially when she's the keynote speaker."

"You mean she hasn't arrived yet?"

"No one has seen her as far as I know."

I guess he *would* know. He was on familiar terms with

Luke's ex. Myself, she was a figurehead who wouldn't remember my name if you asked her. I turned a corner, and said to Norman, "You don't have to stay with me. I'll be okay. Just come and look for me when it's time to go home." It was meant to be a joke.

He laughed.

"Seriously. Why should you have to babysit me? I'm an adult woman. I'm okay on my own."

"Luke pays me to be with you," he said.

I darted him a sideways glance and kept walking. I had no idea where I was going. I felt agitated and helpless. I ended up at a gallery that made me stop in my tracks. It was the gallery of erotic art, the secret chamber that had been locked up out of the public view in the 19th century and then reopened in the mid 20th.

A large sign identified it:

THE CHAMBER OF SECRETS

There were dozens of stone penises, phallic wind chimes and oil lamps, and what I could only describe as naughty mosaics. The pièce de résistance was a stone statue of a satyr having sex with a female goat. These were only a tiny sampling of what was hidden in storage. Most of the erotic collection was considered too risqué for the public. But the promise of Luke's generous endowment had convinced the museum that this collection was what people wished to see, and furthermore it would help both museums out of their burning deficits.

I forced myself not to blush. I was a professional after all. I only wished that Norman had not accompanied me when I stumbled across this find.

"I should leave," I said, awkwardly. "Luke might be looking for me."

"Yeah, he might."

I felt stupid but it was a struggle to tear my eyes away from the goat. What a look of naked fondness in her carved eyes, while his—the satyr's—was that of lusty pleasure.

Norman chuckled. "What else could you expect from a satyr?"

I smiled. He had a way of putting me at ease.

"Better get back to the party." I sighed. "I hate these events. I always feel out of place. This is Luke's world and whenever I come to something like this it just shoves home to me that I'm a lame replacement for Arianna Chase."

He was silent for a moment. "He never compares you to her."

"But *I* do."

"You should stop it. She's the past. You're the present."

"I still don't know why he wants me around." I looked into Norman's face. He was a tall, muscular man, and the warmth in his expression contradicted the overt masculinity of his body. "I've asked him, you know. I've asked him why he wants me around. But he never really says."

"What does it matter? He wants you."

And *what do you want?* Why was it so much easier talking to Norman?

I was still nursing my second glass of champagne and found it was empty. Norman took the flute from me and shoved it into his pocket.

"Let's get out of this gallery," he said. Then he stopped. There was a set of silver in a display case that had caught his eye.

"What is it?" I asked.

He looked at me; then directed his stare back at the case.

I saw what had snagged his attention. The silver was arranged like a dinner place setting, as though any minute someone would sit down and pick up a spoon. On either side of the plates and silverware were oil lamps shaped like oversized phalluses. The wine goblet however was merely that—a goblet. This wasn't what had caught his eye. Because now my sight was also fixed on the display.

"Do you recognize anything about that dinner set?" he asked.

My head bobbed up and down. It was identical to the pattern on the smugglers loot that we had recently rescued from a cave in Positano.

And something else.

Should I elaborate on his observation? No. If my brother-in-law was involved in something shady I wanted to learn what it was first.

"That grape motif on the cutlery. I've seen it before."

Roman silver was a common find in archaeological sites. But I knew what he meant and I mustn't draw attention to it right now. I must feign ignorance.

So I giggled. I pointed to the phallus-shaped lamps. Did they make him uncomfortable too? Or did they trigger the giggle button?

I was never to know. He placed his hand on my lower back, just beneath the dripping folds of silk and nudged me back into the corridor. "Come on. Let's go. Luke will be missing you at the gala."

I thought not.

When we returned to the Atrium, Bruno D'Agostina had bad news. The chartered aircraft carrying Arianna Chase from Florence to Naples had crashed in the countryside with all four passengers aboard presumably killed.

If you enjoyed this book please leave a review at Amazon. It will help me greatly to spread the word. But the story doesn't end here! Parts two, three and four of the Fresco Nights saga will soon be released!

Fresco Nights
(Fresco Nights Saga Book One) – Deborah L. Cannon

Billionaire archaeologist Luke Trevanian and his sexy bodyguard Norman Depardieu seduce museum illustrator Lucy Racine into their shadowy world. Is it the end of her routine life? Yes! These are two mysterious men with dark pasts. She is attracted to both. They have the bodies of athletes, the charm of gentlemen and the alluring ways of con artists. Are they also a pair of crooks smuggling priceless artifacts? Lucy refuses to believe it until Luke whisks her off on his mega yacht to Italy's romantic Amalfi Coast. Their purpose is to dig up Italian frescos. Instead she digs up his past. That past involves a Black Madonna worth millions of dollars on the black market. Art thieves and Interpol are racing to get their hands on it. Will Luke's name be cleared of the theft? Can Lucy love a man with a shady past, whose ex-wife just happens to be her boss? Or is it the bodyguard she loves? Sometimes the heart doesn't know what it wants. In the heat of the night and the cold of murder, Lucy must decide what she wants.

Pompeii at Dusk
(Fresco Nights Saga Book Two) – Deborah L. Cannon

At a fancy museum gala in Naples, Lucy Racine and boyfriend billionaire archaeologist Luke Trevanian get bad news. The guest speaker has been killed in a plane crash on the cliffside of a small Italian village. The crash victim is not only Lucy's boss but also Luke's ex-wife Arianna Chase!

Luke insists that Arianna is still alive. New information suggests the plane was sabotaged because of a stolen Medusa. Arianna is not dead after all. She is the prisoner of a local smuggler. Now Luke is hell-bent on rescuing his ex. Is he still in love with her? Her suspicious behavior points Lucy to a smuggling racket that trades antiquities for guns. An underground network running from Syria to Pompeii leads straight to Luke's ex-wife. Confronted with the truth about Arianna's shadowy activities, Lucy turns to Norman. He is the only person she trusts, and the man she secretly loves. In this second installment of the Fresco Nights saga Lucy's life is about to change when she uncovers a terrorist plot with roots deep in the Middle East.

Midnight in Palmyra
(Fresco Nights Saga Book Three) – Deborah L. Cannon

Lucy Racine and her partners in crime, billionaire archaeologist Luke Trevanian and his bodyguard are recruited into a secret organization. What is ISORE? The International Save Our Ruins Effort. What is their mission? To save a woman curator and her two children from terrorists, and to intercept a convoy of artifacts from Syria bound for Europe's black market. The terrorists are relentless. They kill the woman curator. Now her children's lives are at stake. Lucy works in close quarters with Luke and Norman to plan the children's release. Can Lucy hide her desire for the bodyguard? He has sworn to protect her. He is devastated when she is kidnapped. Now Lucy's skills for survival are tested to the brink. The threat to her life exposes the heart-wrenching rivalry between her two heroes. But true confessions must wait until Lucy escapes the terrorists, and the team moves in to reclaim Palmyra's historical ruins and the lost children.

Baghdad before Dawn
(Fresco Nights Saga Book Four) – Deborah L. Cannon

An explosion in the tunnel of the Palmyra museum has collapsed on top of Lucy Racine's new love Norman Depardieu after he rescues a kidnapped Syrian girl doomed to be a terrorist's bride. To make matters worse, Lucy's pregnant sister learns of Lucy's new job saving antiquities from war zones. Horrified by the news, she arrives in Syria to bring Lucy home. Lucy must avoid her sister at all costs. There is hope that Norman survived the blast. A man meeting Norman's description is sighted among the militants in the desert. Why doesn't he return to the ISORE base? Lucy's love for the brave rescuer has her desperate to find him. But before the team can infiltrate the terrorist stronghold, Lucy is inside their camp. She faces a terrifying reality. Has Norman turned to the enemy side? Is he working for them? He doesn't recognize her. But one thing she does learn—all is not as it seems. Norman has a private agenda. It has to do with the Winged Bulls of Nineveh, which is in a stolen truck on its way to Baghdad. The greatest test of Lucy's strength comes in the thrilling fourth installment of the Fresco Nights series.

Acknowledgements

Thank you to author Barbara Kyle for her insights and her diligent editing of this book. Much appreciation also for the help and support of John. T. Cullen author and publisher at Clocktower Books, librarian Janice Williams and marketing consultant Catherine Starr. And as always, thank you to my husband for his support and the lovely cover.

About the Author

Deborah L. Cannon is a novelist and short story writer. She writes under three names: Deborah L. Cannon under which the Fresco Nights novels are written, Deborah Cannon under which are published The Raven Chronicles series and her Chinese epic fantasy *The Pirate Empress*, and Daphne Lynn Stewart who writes a series of Christmas romances for pet lovers. She is also a contributor to the *Chicken Soup for the Soul* franchise. She lives in Hamilton, Ontario with her archaeologist husband near the Royal Botanical gardens lakeside.

Made in the USA
Columbia, SC
02 September 2019